BARE, WHITE AND ROSY

'Come along, Natasha. Percy warned me you could be a bit of a brat about it sometimes, but I'm not having any nonsense. Lock the door and come over my knee.'

I simply melted, walking straight to the door and turning the big key he'd no doubt placed on the inside on purpose. He stayed as he was while I made my way back to him, now patient, his basset-hound face set in a placid smile, as if taking a young woman's knickers down and smacking her bare bottom was merely a pleasant and by no means unusual task. Maybe it was, for him, but however many times I get it I can never escape the feeling that spanking is the most inappropriate, undignified, indecent outrage that a man can inflict on woman. It also makes me wet.

'Down you go,' he said cheerfully as I got into spanking position across his lap. 'Bottom up, and we'll soon have you rosy.'

He sounded unutterably smug, and began to hum to himself as he went about the little routine of preparing my bottom, Wagner of all things, punctuated by painfully intimate comments.

'Skirt up. Ah, you wear a slip, how charming.'

My skirt was lifted, very carefully, and turned up over my back. My slip followed, showing off my stocking tops.

'What pretty stockings! Ah, that takes me back! And such lovely thighs, ever so slightly plump, the way a girl's flesh should be, so that it bulges around the stocking tops.'

Why not visit Penny's website at www.pennybirch.com

By the same author:

A TASTE OF AMBER
BAD PENNY
BARE BEHIND
BRAT
BUTTER WOULDN'T MELT
DIRTY LAUNDRY
FIT TO BE TIED
IN DISGRACE
IN FOR A PENNY
JODHPURS AND JEANS
NAUGHTY NAUGHTY
NURSE'S ORDERS
KNICKERS AND BOOTS
PEACH
PENNY IN HARNESS
PENNY PIECES
PETTING GIRLS
PLAYTHING
REGIME
TEMPER TANTRUMS
TICKLE TORTURE
TIGHT WHITE COTTON
UNIFORM DOLL
WHEN SHE WAS BAD
TIE AND TEASE
WHAT HAPPENS TO BAD GIRLS
BRUSH STROKES
SLIPPERY WHEN WET

THE INDECENCIES OF ISABELLE
THE INDIGNITIES OF ISABELLE
THE INDISCRETIONS OF ISABELLE
(Writing as Cruella)

BARE, WHITE AND ROSY

Penny Birch

This book is a work of fiction.
In real life, make sure you practise safe, sane and consensual sex.

Published by Nexus 2008

First published in Great Britain in 2008 by
Nexus
Virgin Books
Random House, 20 Vauxhall Bridge Road,
London SW1V 2SA

www.nexus-books.com
www.rbooks.co.uk

Addresses for companies within The Random House Group Limited can be found at: www.randomhouse.co.uk/offices.htm

The Random House Group Limited Reg. No. 954009

Distributed in the USA by Macmillan, 175 Fifth Avenue, New York, NY 10010, USA

A CIP catalogue record for this book is available from the British Library

ISBN 9780352345059

Penguin Random House is committed to a sustainable future for our business, our readers and our planet. This book is made from Forest Stewardship Council® certified paper.

Printed and bound in Great Britain by Clays Ltd, Elcograf S.p.A.

Typeset by TW Typesetting, Plymouth, Devon
2 4 6 8 10 9 7 5 3 1

Symbols key

 Corporal Punishment

 Female Domination

 Institution

 Medical

 Period Setting

 Restraint/Bondage

 Rubber/Leather

 Spanking

 Transvestism

 Underwear

 Uniforms

One

'You look as if you're trussed for the spit,' Percy remarked, grinning.

I made a face. He was right: with my head and chest sticking out over one end of the coffee table and my bottom over the other, I certainly looked as if I was ready to have something stuck up me, although probably not a spit. Not that I could stop him, whatever he wanted to do. My upper arms and thighs were lashed securely to the table legs, fixing me in a kneeling position, completely vulnerable, with just the minuscule red bikini I'd been sunbathing in to protect my modesty. With the high tide cutting off my little island and no human soul within maybe half a mile I was completely at his mercy.

'What are you going to do to me?' I asked.

He took a moment to ponder his options, lifting one podgy hand to pinch at the first of his three chins as his face set into a thoughtful frown.

'First,' he said, 'a little humiliation.'

I looked up as he stepped close, but all I could see was the swell of his more than ample paunch, which pressed against my face as he knelt. His hands slid beneath my chest, to take hold of my dangling breasts, one in each hand. I closed my eyes as he began to fondle me, his fat little fingers squeezing and stroking at my flesh, not with the intimacy of a lover but with the lewd, intrusive interest of a man intent on having a good grope of a girl who can do nothing to stop him. At last he took hold of the undersides of my bikini top and tugged, flopping my breasts out. Again his fingers found my flesh, pulling on my stiff nipples as if trying to milk me on to the living-room carpet and giving me a little jiggle before finally standing up again. His cock was now erect, making a small but prominent tent in the baggy green corduroy of his trousers.

'And your bottom, naturally,' he remarked.

He had stepped close again even as he spoke. I closed my eyes, even my newly stripped breasts unimportant as his fingers once again touched my flesh to pinch the waistband of my bikini bottoms. He was right behind me, ensuring that nothing whatsoever was left to his imagination as he began to peel them down, ever so slowly exposing me. Not that I was hiding much, not of my cheeks anyway, with more flesh out of the small red triangle of material than in, but cheeks don't matter. What matters is what's between, which was very slowly coming on show to his inquisitive, dirty gaze, first the pale-brown ring and puckered, pink central star of my anus, next the pouted, freshly shaven lips of my pussy, split to show the wet folds between, each and every detail bare for his inspection.

Already I could feel something akin to panic welling up inside me, making my muscles squeeze and my bumhole start to wink. He chuckled to see the state I was in and began to touch, exploring my bottom with that same intrusive, loitering intimacy he had applied to my breasts, squeezing my flesh, stroking my cheeks, smacking me just hard enough to make them jiggle, teasing me between them, tickling my anus and at last invading my pussy hole with one short, podgy finger. At that I broke, sobbing and gasping as he fingered me, tossing my head in a pathetic, futile effort to repress the overwhelming emotion of having my body so casually molested.

I knew he would fuck me, maybe worse, but that was his choice. He could do as he pleased, for all my squirming and wriggling, for all my protests. I heard his zip come down as he extracted his finger from my pussy and immediately imagined it being replaced by his cock. He shifted his position, pushing close, and I felt the hot, smooth tip of his erection press between my cheeks, pushing at my anus. A powerful shudder ran through me as I realised I was to be buggered, but I bit my lip, determined not to beg. Instead I forced myself to relax, readying myself for my own violation.

It never came. His cock slipped up between my cheeks, rubbing in my crease as his fat belly pressed against my cheeks and his balls squashed up against my pussy lips. Still I thought I'd get it, just as soon as he'd had his fun with my bottom slit, but he pulled away once again, to plant a heavy slap across my cheeks, leaving them stinging. I was going to be spanked and then sodomised, a thought that had me choking with outrage. It was unthinkable, impossible, that a fat, dirty old bastard like him could even dare to look at me sexually, never mind to touch me, to feel me up, to smack my cheeks, to stick his filthy little cock up my hole, but that was exactly what was going to happen. He'd begun to masturbate as he spanked me, tossing over my cheeks as he readied himself for my bumhole. My whole body was shaking, wracked with violent sobs as I thought how his cock would feel in my rectum. I wondered if he'd rub me off to make me come, to enjoy the feel of my anal ring tightening on his penis and bring my shame to a burning, helpless peak . . .

Something hot and wet splashed my cheeks and I realised he'd ejaculated over me.

'Percy! You said you'd put it in!'

'Sorry, my dear,' he puffed. 'I . . . I was overcome. It's been too long, and you're too beautiful. I couldn't hold back.'

'That's all very flattering, Percy, but how do you think I feel?' I demanded. 'You said you were going to bugger me and make me come on your cock, and now you've wasted it all over my bum. You're a selfish pig!'

'I'm sorry,' he repeated. 'Perhaps later? Or maybe . . .'

As he trailed off his hand had moved to my body once more, cupping my sex. I immediately realised what he was going to do, and it filled me with a sense of shame stronger even than when I'd had my breasts and bottom stripped. He was going to masturbate me, to bring me off as if I was just some little brat who couldn't be counted on to behave herself until she'd had an orgasm.

'Percy!' I protested.

He didn't even bother to answer, his middle finger now working between my sex lips with a practised thoroughness, not so much like a lover as like a vet performing some messy but necessary task on a cow or sheep. I felt fit to scream, my face burning with resentment and shame, both emotions made far worse because I knew full well that it was the right thing to do to me. Once I'd come I would feel far better, but that did nothing to dampen my fury as my body was manipulated. He'd begun to fondle my breasts again, slapping at them and pinching my nipples as he rubbed between my sex lips. A thumb was inserted up my pussy, his finger began to move faster and I gave in.

'Pig!' I gasped, and I was coming.

I was gasping and panting as he brought me off, wriggling my bottom on his hand and squirming in my bonds, still furious with him, still thoroughly ashamed of myself, but at the same time in a state of ecstasy. He didn't stop rubbing until the contractions of my muscles had died down, and as my pleasure faded so did my resentment, and the tension that had been building up for weeks.

'Pig,' I repeated. 'Thank you.'

'My pleasure,' he responded, and began to untie me.

I was stiff and sore, but a shower sorted that out. Once I was dry I slipped on a summer dress and a pair of sandals, not bothering with underwear. I seldom did, except to go into town, and not always then. The locals thought of me as a slut anyway, a wealthy, eccentric slut, but still a slut. They were too insular to appreciate my liberty, although quite happy to take advantage of it.

'How have you been?' Percy asked as I returned to the living room.

He had settled himself into a chair, once more the classic image of an elderly English gentleman and very far from the sadistic old pervert who had me over my own coffee table and amused himself with my body just minutes after arriving from the mainland.

'Much as usual,' I told him. 'I'm beginning to understand why they describe the island as two thousand alcoholics clinging to a rock. I might even join them.'

'What you need is a holiday.'

'I am on holiday, permanently, or in exile.'

Percy responded with a wry smile. I went to him, bending to kiss him and then put my arms around his shoulders, holding him to me until what was left of my tension had drained away. For weeks I'd been anticipating his visit, but until that moment I hadn't realised just how much I'd missed him and everything he stood for: intelligent and open conversation, easygoing friendship and, above all, guilt-free kinky sex. Plenty of people on the island wanted to fuck me, even to spank me, but not one of them could approach his combination of casual aplomb and sheer filthiness.

'Sorry I was cross,' I told him as I pulled away.

His response was to pat my bottom as I turned away, an intimate, almost proprietorial gesture and entirely appropriate from him to me. A younger man would have earned a slap in the face, but I gave him an encouraging wiggle before dancing quickly out of his reach. I sat down, feeling relaxed and pleasantly naughty. He spoke.

'You remember Hambling and Borse, don't you?'

'Yes, of course. Dad has an account with them.'

'In that case he is one of a dwindling band. They've been losing customers for years, mainly because they refuse to move with the times.'

'I remember their list, page after page of claret and hock. I used to recite the names of the German vineyards as if they were a litany.'

'As well you might, my dear. Ah, for a glass of Maximin Grünhauser Abtsberg, the Kabinett perhaps . . .'

I took the hint and went to the fridge, although the closest thing I could manage was a Piesporter. Percy made no complaint, smacking his lips as I pulled the cork.

'What about Hambling and Borse?' I asked.

'They're in difficulty, or about to be. Not that they're short of assets, what with the building in St James's, stock, agencies and so forth, but they've been losing money for years. They need a new manager, somebody dynamic but who appreciates tradition, qualities that appear to be mutually exclusive, or so old Gilbert Hambling says. So I suggested that you might like to take the job on.'

'Me? I don't know the first thing about management.'

'You don't need to. Everybody knows who you are, you're young, personable, you understand the trade and its tradition, but most importantly you have a knack with curmudgeonly old buggers like Gilbert Hambling and Otto Borse. Meanwhile, you're getting bored out of your skull here, aren't you?'

'Yes,' I admitted.

He was right. Having nothing to do and all day to do it in is not what it's cracked up to be. I was tempted, but there was still the reason I'd secluded myself on the island in the first place.

'What about the papers?'

Percy gave an airy flutter of his fingers.

'You are yesterday's news, my dear. At present they are in a foment because one so-called celebrity called another a rude name. I see no reason why they should even notice that you're back in London.'

'I'm not so sure, Percy. What about Pia Santi? I imagine the vicious little bitch would do anything to get back at me, and she'd certainly recognise me.'

'In the case of Miss Santi I took the precaution of ascertaining her whereabouts. She is in Los Angeles, and besides, in the unlikely event that life does become unbearable, you can retreat here whenever you wish. But really, I doubt that even Miss Santi would trouble to pursue you when there is no money to be made. She is nothing if not mercenary.'

'True,' I admitted, ignoring an instinctive touch of pique at how quickly the press had lost interest in me, 'Well, maybe it would be interesting, but I'd need a free hand and I absolutely refuse to do anything that involves paperwork.'

'You would need to discuss that sort of detail with Gilbert,' Percy said, 'but if you don't like their terms, you can always turn down their offer. It would be a shame, though, because if anybody can turn their fortunes around you can, and the wine trade would be duller without them. We face a creeping tide of base, grey commercialism, Natasha, which—'

'I know,' I interrupted before he could mount one of his favourite hobby-horses, along with the decline in educational standards, why young girls should be spanked on a regular basis and a wide variety of similar topics.

'You'll do it then?' he asked.

I didn't answer, but took a sip of my wine, staring out of the window to where puffy white clouds were rolling in from the west over the lip of the high wall surrounding my retreat. The tufts of grass growing between the stones were shivering in a light breeze and I could just make out the gentle, rhythmic splash of waves on the rocks beyond. For the last few days there had been a distinctly autumnal scent to the air. I'd never known anywhere so peaceful, or that provided me with such a deep sense of security, and yet I felt that if I spent the winter there I would go mad.

'I'll come to London,' I promised, 'at least to talk to them.'

'Good girl.'

He raised his glass to me, swirled, sniffed, and swallowed in a sequence so familiar to him that I'd known him to do the same with coffee and water, just as I occasionally did myself. I smiled to myself, already imagining the magnificent tastings I would organise in order to restore the reputation of Hambling and Borse. Clearly I would need a new wardrobe, smart designer clothes suitable for my executive role; also shoes, plenty of shoes. In fact, I would need to cultivate a new image: refined, efficient, cool yet definitely sexual, with a poise that few men would dare to aspire to . . .

A cough from Percy interrupted my daydream.

‘There is one other thing you should know, Natasha. I, ah, I may have been a trifle indiscreet when I was discussing things over dinner with old Gilbert Hambling. He had done me remarkably well, La Chapelle ’seventy-eight with the first grouse of the season and then a wonderful Eve’s pudding with a ’fifty-nine Bonnezeaux, which was quite superb. He’d used Bramleys and a variety called Charles Ross, with just the right amount of cinnamon, and . . . but where was I? Oh, yes, I’m rather afraid that I let slip about your penchant for being abused.’

Two

It was more than likely that my knickers would be coming down for a spanking, or repeated spankings. I'd run into Percy's wine-trade friends before, outwardly respectable old English gentlemen but in practice a bunch of lecherous old perverts. Neither Mr Hambling nor Mr Borse was likely to pass up the chance of getting me across his lap if he thought he might get away with it, and both belonged to a generation who regarded spanking their subordinates at work as an amusing way to pass the afternoon. I liked to think so, anyway, because the occasional well-smacked bottom would ensure that my job was never dull, while with any luck I could manipulate the situation to ensure that they both did as they were told. That was essential, because while I was reasonably confident of being able to turn their company around, it would be a great deal easier with their co-operation.

The knack was to exploit the American market, or so it seemed to me. While working as a wine writer prior to pulling off my *coup d'art*, I had always been struck by the curious American habit of wanting the best and only the best. It's ridiculous, of course, because enjoyment of wine is far too subjective for the concept to have meaning, but the fact remained that if the American market came to believe that a particular winery was 'the best' they would pay many times over the sensible price. Where the Americans led, the Far East would follow. All I needed to do was ensure that a couple of Hambling and Borse's agencies became identified as superlative and I would be home and dry, with a rosy bottom into the bargain. It was all rather appealing.

As I took the short flight from the island to Eastleigh Airport I was reading the Hambling and Borse price list Percy had given me. Their mainstay was claret, but the Bordeaux trade was too fluid for my scheme to work. Burgundy and the Rhône were better, and in both cases they held high quality but unfashionable agencies, which I was sure I'd be able to push forward. That was going to mean sucking up to the most influential of the American pundits, perhaps even sucking them literally, a thought that gave me a delicious thrill of sexual humiliation. All the really big names were whiter than white, but one, Earle Hayes, had a reputation as a bit of an old goat, and I've always loved the feeling of having no choice but to do something rude. To have my behaviour dictated by the needs of my job would be wonderful.

So wonderful in fact that had I not been squashed into a tiny seat next to a respectable middle-aged woman I've have been tempted to slip my hand down my knickers. To distract myself I began to read the various wine magazines Percy had given me and quickly realised that Americans weren't the only people I'd have to work on. The market had changed since I'd left England and, while their influence was still crucial in the US, the Far East had begun to look to one of their own. He was called Anton Yoshida, which presumably made him Japanese-French, and his articles were written with a high-handed, arrogant certainty that made him ideal for my purposes.

It seemed likely he would have the samc attitude to women as he did to wine, and I was smiling to myself as I imagined how I would allow him to bring me under his control, while all the while he was the one being manipulated. Outside my window the island was now invisible behind us, the English Channel stretching in every direction, a dull blue flecked with whitecaps. Several yachts were visible, seemingly too small even for dolls, and I let my mind drift into a daydream in which he took me boating and gave me a choice of succumbing to his demands or being thrown overboard to swim to shore. I'd beg and plead, but it would do me no good. First my top would come off, then my pants, as I was forced to strip out of my bikini before being put on my knees to suck him hard, casually fucked, spunked all over and then thrown overboard anyway.

I was still running through various permutations of my fantasy when the Isle of Wight came into view and we started to descend. The only person who knew I was arriving was Percy, who was completely trustworthy, but that didn't stop me feeling jittery and vulnerable as we came in to land, and I pushed my erotic thoughts aside. I was imagining banks of photographers at the airport, with the horrible Pia Santi at the forefront, but not even the customs officers paid me more than cursory attention, leaving me feeling relieved but also piqued. Waterloo was no different, and the cab driver talked to my tits, his bland, reddish face showing no recognition whatsoever. Percy was right. I was yesterday's news.

He'd offered to put me up at his flat in Maida Vale, but I needed a place of my own and had asked him to rent somewhere for me instead. I only knew the address, which was in Marylebone High Street, but I rang ahead and he was there to meet me, standing outside a tall red-brick block.

‘Here will do,’ I instructed, ‘by the gentleman in the tweeds. He’s my uncle.’

I got out as the cab stopped and gave Percy a long, lingering kiss full on the mouth, leaving the cabbie so taken aback he didn’t even ask for a tip. Percy took my bag, and spoke as we walked to the building’s entrance.

‘I take it that was as much for his benefit as for mine?’

‘I told him you were my uncle,’ I explained, earning myself a smack on the seat of my skirt just in time for the cabbie to see as he pulled away. ‘I hope you’ve found me somewhere nice?’

‘I like it,’ he told me, ‘although the stairs are a bit much, so I suggest the lift. May I say that you seem remarkably bumptious?’

‘I feel it. London’s so full of life after the island.’

I didn’t confess that my mood was partly nerves, but let him steer me to a tiny lift with a grille-work door. His hand strayed to my bottom as we ascended, kneading gently. Sex was just what I needed to calm me down, and it came naturally with him anyway. The lift came to halt at the top floor and I found myself on a tiny landing with a single door, a window looking out on to rooftops a storey below, and a short passage leading to the top of the stairs. Nobody was about, or likely to be. I pushed Percy back against the windowsill and got down on my knees.

‘Don’t you want to um . . . go inside?’ he queried as I nuzzled my face against the bulge in his trousers.

My answer was to unzip him and pull his cock and balls free from his underpants. He gave a soft tut and made himself comfortable, knowing me too well to think I’d stop. I began to lick and kiss at his balls, enjoying the bulbous, straining feeling and his male taste. He took me by my hair, not too hard, but firmly enough to let me know I was to be kept in place until he'd finished, just the way I like it. His cock was already beginning to stiffen and I took it in my mouth, closing my eyes as I let my mind drift back to my earlier fantasy.

Not that the situation I was in wasn't rude enough, on my knees in what was effectively a public corridor, sucking cock for a man more than twice my age, but the yacht fantasy had been going around in my head for too long to be ignored. I thought of how it would be, forced to strip and kneel in the nude, with the hot sun beating down on my back and bottom cheeks as my persecutor's penis stiffened in my mouth. The man wasn't even Anton Yoshida, but just a man, some complete bastard.

He'd be laughing as he watched me, enjoying his power as much as the feel of my lips on his cock, at least until his cock was hard and the pleasure too great to ignore. By then I'd have given in to my feelings, allowing my hand to slip between my thighs so that I could masturbate as I sucked him. He'd see, and give a final, derisive chuckle at my helpless arousal before closing his eyes in bliss, his cock now a solid rod in my mouth, just as Percy's was.

I took a moment to adjust myself, tugging my skirt up around my hips and slipping my panties down to leave my bottom bare. Percy had looked down as I came off his cock, and smiled as he saw what I was doing. I gave him my cheekiest grin in return, my eyes locked to his as I unbuttoned my blouse and pulled up my bra, spilling my naked breasts into my cupped hands, deliberately showing off to him. As I took his cock back in I was teasing myself, rubbing my fingers over my stiff nipples and feeling the weight of my breasts.

Stripping myself had filled my head with rude images: of how I'd look to anyone who came up the stairs, of being spanked for my dirty behaviour or taken unexpectedly from behind. But I quickly returned to my original fantasy. As soon as the man was hard he would pull me off his cock, turn me around and simply fuck me. I'd be on all fours, kneeling in the scuppers of the yacht, my naked bottom spread to him as he thrust into me. He'd do it hard and rather casually, using my body for his pleasure without thought for mine.

Percy had begun to push his cock into my mouth, squashing his balls and the turn of his paunch into my face. I was sure he'd have been saving up for me and would come soon. My hand went down between my thighs, to find my pussy wet and sensitive. I began to masturbate, revelling in the taste and feel of the cock in my mouth as I imagined another inside me from behind.

It would only take moments, a brief, contemptuous fucking before he spunked in me, deep up, only to whip out his cock and do it all over my bottom and back as well. By then I'd be rubbing my pussy openly, indifferent to the display I was making of myself and too far gone to find my humiliation anything but arousing. He wouldn't even let me finish, just laugh at me as he picked me up, lifting me with no more difficulty than if I'd been a doll. I'd scream in shock as I realised what he was going to do to me, kicking and hitting out in a pathetic attempt to resist him, begging for mercy and whining that he was being unfair. He'd only laugh all the louder, and in I'd go, tossed casually over the side, arms and legs and hair waving wildly, my horrified scream abruptly cut off as I hit the water.

At that thought I came, rubbing and sucking in a welter of humiliation and ecstasy as I imagined myself thrown overboard like a piece of refuse, worthless once

I'd been fucked. Three times I ran the scene over in my head, from the moment I was spunked up to hitting the cold water, each time driving me to a new, higher peak, and with the third Percy filled my mouth.

My flat was rather better than I'd expected. Percy has old-fashioned, masculine tastes, which generally involve a lot of dark colours and heavy furniture. He's also fairly unaware of his surroundings as long as he has a glass of something decent in his hand or a pretty girl to molest, so I had expected something respectable but basic. What he'd found was a converted attic space in a Victorian block, five storeys up and above most other buildings. Aside from a bathroom at one end, it was entirely open-plan, with three windows on either side, providing plenty of light and space. I'd got used to both while living on the island and would have felt claustrophobic otherwise, and although the constant buzz of the city was all around me it was no worse than my old flat in Primrose Hill.

I spent the first day relaxing and the next two shopping, while Percy did what work was necessary and provided dinner each evening. Networking was essential, but the London wine trade is small and more than a little incestuous so it was simply a matter of Percy letting his contacts know that I was back. The trade is also mercifully isolated from celebrity gossip, and for the first time I was grateful for the stuffy image I'd always railed against when I was a writer. Only on the third day did I make my way to the offices of Hambling and Borse in St James's.

The last time I'd been there was at a tasting, when my interest had been entirely in what they had to show, but my memories went back long before. I'd been a little girl, maybe no more than six, or seven at the most. Dad had taken me there for some reason, leaving me in a reception room with what had seemed an impossibly high ceiling. I'd spent a happy half-hour scribbling elaborate moustaches on to the faces of assorted *vignerons* and wine pundits in the magazines, only to discover that my most imaginative efforts had been as nothing compared to the reality of the man who eventually showed us out. Save for two pale eyes and a large red nose, his entire face had been concealed behind bushy ginger whiskers, an image that had stayed in my mind for over a decade before I was introduced to Otto Borse. Gilbert Hambling I had met only at tastings, and I remembered him only as a man with the face of a good-natured basset hound.

Nothing had changed: the tall grey-stone façade was as imposing as ever, the iron railings still thick with paint accumulated over a couple of centuries, the great black door different only in that I was now strong enough to open it. Gilbert Hambling still looked like a basset hound, and Otto Borse's moustache was if anything yet more luxurious, although now grey. Both greeted me effusively and I was shown into a private office at the rear, where a bottle of Champagne stood in an ice bucket, already half empty at shortly before ten in the morning.

'Bubbles?' Gilbert Hambling offered, indicating the Champagne.

'Please,' I responded and accepted a glass, wondering if the offer had been a deliberate test.

Neither man said anything, but to judge by Gilbert Hambling's grunt of approval I had made the right choice. It was good Champagne too, not from one of the big houses but a private estate.

'Patrice Beauroy, in Ambonnay,' Gilbert Hambling informed me. 'Fellow plays music to his vines, Bach generally. Daft as a brush, but it seems to work.'

‘He is the most conscientious of wine-makers,’ Otto Borse put in, ‘and in my view the best in Champagne.’

‘But unknown,’ I said.

‘Hardly that,’ Gilbert Hambling protested, ‘but with only seventeen hectares the supply is necessarily limited.’

‘Fifteen thousand bottles a year?’ I suggested.

‘Certainly not,’ he answered. ‘He restricts his yields to fifty hectolitres per hectare, so ten thousand bottles would be typical.’

I nodded, not wanting to argue the point. Percy had warned me that they were devoted to quality, and no doubt they would rather go down than stock some inferior brand merely because it could be handled in commercially viable quantities. As I’d suspected, the only answer was to get outrageous profit margins.

‘So,’ Otto Borse said, abruptly clapping his hands together, ‘Percy tells us that you are the person to restore our fortunes?’

‘I intend to do my best,’ I replied cautiously. ‘What is the situation, exactly?’

‘You can look over the details at leisure,’ Gilbert Hambling replied, ‘but these are the essentials. We’re not young men, Otto and I, and both of us feel that a quiet retirement is long overdue. Before we sell up, we need to get the company on a sound footing, otherwise the only people who’re going to be interested are the ones who’re after our assets, or so it seems.’

‘We would like,’ Otto Borse continued, ‘the firm to continue as it has done in the past, with an absolute commitment to quality, and to service. We realise that this may be a little much to ask, and that some degree of modernisation is inevitable, but there are dedicated young men out there, notably in the restaurant trade, and we would like to secure their interest.’

‘Will that also be part of my job?’

'Perhaps, if the opportunity presents itself. Percy says you want a free hand, although naturally there will be certain obvious restrictions.'

'Such as?'

'Not selling us down the river, basically,' Gilbert Hambling said with a laugh. 'Come, come, Otto, if Miss Linnet is to do her job properly we must not tie her hands.'

He finished with a knowing chuckle, which reminded me of what Percy had let slip and set me blushing. Neither seemed to notice, and we began to discuss the conditions of my employment, all of which I accepted. By the time I'd signed up we had finished the bottle of Champagne and I was feeling ever so slightly mellow. At last Otto Borse gave a purposeful clap of his hands and stood up.

'I have an appointment,' he declared, 'at the Aviators, who are one of our best clients.'

'A gentleman's club?' I asked.

'Indeed,' Gilbert Hambling supplied. 'We have several among our clients, although in the case of the Aviators Gilbert and I are members.'

It seemed entirely in keeping with the firm – crusty old gentlemen drinking hock, claret and port until it had begun to ooze from their ears – yet not enough to keep the company afloat. Perhaps it was the thought of so much pomp and gravitas, but for some reason I'd risen as Otto Borse left the room, giving Gilbert Hambling cause to chuckle.

'How deliciously well mannered of you,' he remarked. 'Percy was full of praise for you, you know, but I must say that if anything he seems to have understated the case.'

'Thank you.'

'Not at all. You are delightful, Natasha, and I expect that I will enjoy having you work for us immensely.'

He was grinning like the Cheshire Cat, again making me think of what Percy had told him.

'Immensely,' he repeated, 'especially as dear old Percy implied that the three of us share a certain penchant, and indeed that you are perhaps not averse to indulging said penchant with other gentlemen?'

It was obvious what was coming. He was going to suggest I have my bottom smacked. I'd known it was coming, but it wasn't easy to make the transition from business colleague to spanking toy. I found myself blushing hot at the thought of a trip across his knee, as if I were an inexperienced teenager about to have her private fantasies turned into humiliating and painful reality.

'I . . . I don't mind,' I managed.

'Splendid,' he said. 'Well then, if you would care to lock the door?'

'Lock the door?' I queried. 'Do you want to do it now?'

'No time like the present,' he responded. 'Come along, there's no cause to be coy, not with me. I've had many a little moppet wriggling over my lap across the years, I assure you.'

'I'm sure you have, but not me! Look, Mr Hambling, I . . . oh God . . .'

He had me badly flustered, far more so than had he gone about it the way most men would, perhaps taking me out to dinner first, or at least lunch. Yet there was something wonderfully authoritarian in the way he'd sprung it on me as a horrid surprise, and I do like the feeling that I have no choice. In fact, if he'd really known his stuff he could have just bundled me over and pinked me up without a word of warning, but what he did next was almost as good. Pushing his chair back from the desk, he made a lap, patting one leg as he spoke.

'Come along, Natasha. Percy warned me you could be a bit of a brat about it sometimes, but I'm not having any nonsense. Lock the door and come over my knee.'

I simply melted, walking straight to the door and turning the big key he'd no doubt placed on the inside on purpose. He stayed as he was while I made my way back to him, now patient, his basset-hound face set in a placid smile, as if taking a young woman's knickers down and smacking her bare bottom was merely a pleasant and by no means unusual task. Maybe it was, for him, but however many times I get it I can never escape the feeling that spanking is the most inappropriate, undignified, indecent outrage that a man can inflict on a woman. It also makes me wet.

'Down you go,' he said cheerfully as I got into spanking position across his lap. 'Bottom up, and we'll soon have you rosy.'

He sounded unutterably smug, and began to hum to himself as he went about the routine of preparing my bottom, Wagner of all things, punctuated by painfully intimate comments.

'Skirt up. Ah, you wear a slip, how charming.'

My skirt was lifted, very carefully, and turned up over my back. My slip followed, showing off my stocking tops.

'What pretty stockings! Ah, that takes me back! And such lovely thighs, ever so slightly plump, the way a girl's flesh should be, so that it bulges around the stocking tops.'

He was holding my slip up, the tail of my blouse too, with just the tuck of my bottom showing and maybe an inch of panty seat, then all of it as he finished his inspection of my stockings and thighs.

'What a perfect little peach!' he declared. 'Percy said you had a delectable bottom, but the half was not told unto me. And I see you're wearing silk. How delightful.'

He gave me a little pat on the seat of my panties. My face was already burning at the shame of my exposure and grew abruptly hotter as he pinched the waistband of my knickers between fingers and thumbs and lifted the material clear of my skin.

'And down come the knickers!' he declared, and peeled them slowly off my bum.

I must have had my panties pulled down hundreds of times, slowly, fast, even torn off, but perhaps never with such lascivious satisfaction. He gave a long, happy sigh as my cheeks came bare, and made very sure to strip me properly, inverting my panties around my thighs and giving a little tug to pull the material away from my pussy and leaving me showing behind.

'Beautiful,' he said. 'In perfect proportion to your waist, round and feminine, elegant yet cheeky, firm without being hard, and as smooth as cream.'

He'd begun to feel my bottom as he spoke, stroking and squeezing my cheeks with a casual intimacy that had me shaking uncontrollably.

'And between?' he queried, and I gasped as my bottom cheeks were spread wide to show off my bumhole and the rear view of my pussy to his probing gaze.

'Mr Hambling! You said a spanking!'

'And a spanking you shall have, my dear.'

With that he let go of my cheeks, took me firmly around my waist and brought his hand down across my bottom with a slap that echoed around the room. So did my squeal of shock and pain. He had huge hands and he spanked hard, putting his shoulders into the swing and holding me firmly in place as he applied smack after smack to my wildly bouncing bottom. My skin had been cold, and it had all happened too quickly to let me get fully turned on, so it hurt like anything, making me squeal and kick and wriggle across his lap, all of which he thoroughly enjoyed. At last I managed to get some words out between my gasps and yelps.

'Not so hard, Mr Hambling, please!'

He responded with a smug little chuckle and eased off. I slumped limply across his lap, too dizzy with reaction even to think of resisting as he began to feel me up between softer, gentler smacks. My bottom was aglow, bringing me slowly on heat, and he enjoyed himself with me, spanking me, groping me and increasingly teasing me with one thick finger tickling between my cheeks. I began to sob as his exploration grew more intimate, unable to stop myself – or to stop him. It felt too nice, for all the appalling shame as he began to tickle, making me giggle like a little girl and squirm my bottom about, which only encouraged him.

My sobs and giggles grew stronger as his teasing finger moved closer to my anus, only to turn to fresh squeals as another dozen hard smacks were applied to my blazing posterior. Again he stopped, this time to move my thighs gently but firmly apart, stretching my panties taut across his knee and opening my bottom. His finger went back between my cheeks, which began to squeeze together as he tickled in my slit, around my bumhole and on it, teasing the little bumps and crevices to set me squirming desperately in his grip. I was trying to stop him, or I was telling myself I was, not because I didn't like it but because at any moment I was going to break. Then I had, pushing my bottom up to let my cheeks spread fully open, offering him my bumhole to explore as much as he pleased, my pussy too.

'You delightful little tart!' he chuckled. 'Shall we see how wet you are?'

His finger moved down from my bumhole and, before I could protest, it had been eased in up my pussy, filling my hole and drawing an involuntary sigh from my lips. He knew he had me, and released his grip on my waist so that he could spank my bottom with one hand while still fingering me. I'd given in completely, my bottom thrust high to let him get as deep as possible and my thighs squirming on his.

'Little tart indeed!' he said as I began to rub myself on his leg.

I could get there, I knew I could, just by wriggling on his leg, so long as he kept his finger in and my bottom was being smacked. He'd treated me so well, firm and authoritative in order to get me over his knee where I belonged, rude and intrusive as he stripped me and felt me up, firm with my spanking and standing no nonsense when it came to getting access to my bumhole and pussy.

'I'm going to come,' I sobbed. 'Don't stop me, please . . . spank me . . . finger-fuck me . . .'

He set up a rhythm, easing one fat finger in and out of my slippery pussy as he smacked my cheeks one at a time. I let my mind drift, thinking of what he'd called me and how true it was. It was bad enough that I'd let a man more than twice my age pull down my panties and spank my bottom for kicks, but to let him tickle my bumhole, to let him stick a finger up my pussy, to rub my dirty little cunt on his leg until I came off . . .

It stopped.

'Somebody is coming,' he said quietly.

'Hey, no, I'm nearly there!'

'Sh! Natasha!'

I'd been right on the edge, so close I wouldn't have cared if half the population of London, with a few tourists for good measure, had watched me bring myself off. He had more self-control, easing me gently but firmly off his lap and under the desk a moment before there was a sharp rap on the door. I made to protest, but he was already on his feet and all I could do was curl up tight, struggling to pull up my panties in the tiny space as he asked the caller to wait a moment.

Fortunately the desk had a solid front, but I was blushing furiously as he coolly opened the door to his secretary and made an excuse about having been at the safe. She had brought copies of the relevant figures for me to peruse. It was a long way to the front desk, and she may or may not have wondered how I had managed to enter the room but was apparently gone. I found myself imagining her out at lunch with friends, giggling as she described how I'd given in to the boss on my first day.

By the time she went away I was no longer in need of an orgasm, but I still had a hot bottom, which I knew would keep me flustered for the rest of the day, or until I did manage to get myself off. The temptation to nip into the loo was considerable, but the moment was gone and I felt too embarrassed, so I applied myself to the figures instead. They proved soothing, in the sense that reading them almost put me to sleep, what with such fascinating pieces of information as that in the mid-'80s the original company had been transferred to an off-the-shelf parent called Monterprise Ltd, and that Gilbert and Otto paid £1 a year each for the rent of their upstairs flats.

Unfortunately as the shock of near-discovery died away and my boredom grew, my arousal came back. The warm glow of my bottom made it impossible to forget that I'd been spanked, which in turn kept me thinking of how I must have looked and how intrusive it had been, with inevitable consequences. Gilbert had gone out, so in the end I put the papers aside and went down to the cellar, knowing full well that if it was quiet I'd probably have my knickers down again before too long.

The bulk of their stock was in a bonded warehouse downriver at Silvertown, somewhere I intended to avoid unless it was absolutely essential to visit, but they had a policy of holding back a share of the better wines until full maturity, and these they kept in the cellar. Just reading the list had been a mouth-watering experience, but it didn't come close to the reality, which even succeeded in pushing the needs of my body into the background.

The cellar had a massive oak door, probably original. It opened with the largest key I had ever seen, revealing a flight of worn stone steps disappearing into absolute blackness, from which rose a dank, vinous waft familiar to me from a hundred visits to wineries across Europe. A light switch to one side produced a dim, golden glow and I started downwards, pulling the huge door closed behind me. The air was cool, so much so that I did up my suit jacket as I reached the bottom of the stairs.

A second door led off to one side, opening on to more or less the scene I'd been anticipating: a vaulted ceiling above a passageway with alcoves on either side, each stacked either with cases or with carefully arranged bins of bottles. Those nearest me were cases of Cissac and Pichon-Baron '89, which I gave an appreciative glance before moving on. Many of the bins were marked for keeping, and most of the others I recognised from the list, but I quickly realised that a lot of obviously mature stock wasn't being offered for sale at all.

Three alcoves were entirely given over to small bins of ancient port, never more than a dozen bottles of each but with three examples of the legendary '45 and others going back to the 1904. Beyond was a single bin of Lafaurie-Peyraguey '29, as golden as the darkest honey where the cellar lights reflected within the stack of bottles. Beyond came a set of Burgundies, wines from Clair-Daü and Marey-Monge dating back to '53s. I was entranced just to see such rarities, to drink in the musky, ancient smell and to stretch out my fingers and stroke the cool, hard glass.

There was Romanée-St-Vivant '64 from Marey-Monge, a wine I could remember tasting as a child. I used to come out of the nursery and demand a single drop from the tip of my father's finger before I'd go to bed, but on that occasion he'd refused to let me taste until he'd explained the significance of the wine and the story behind the vineyard. He'd then, very solemnly, poured out a tiny amount into a glass and allowed me to drink, filling me with gratitude and a pleasure that had never really gone away. The memory brought me close to tears, followed by a sudden burst of anger as I thought of the eight beautiful bottles that remained being swallowed by some cigar-puffing CEO, a prima donna or some overpaid nancy boy whose sole talent lay in being able to kick a ball around. For the first time I began to understand how Gilbert Hambling and Otto Borse felt.

I never did get my frig, and the rest of the day was rather dull, because, for all my determination not to get bogged down in paperwork, I clearly had to make myself familiar with the company. Percy had been right to say they were rich in assets but otherwise poor. Hopeless might have been a better description. Both Gilbert and Otto were paying themselves more than substantial salaries, with expenses to match, while their overheads were alarming, all of which made for outgoings their income couldn't hope to match. Despite accounts with most of the country's top hotels and restaurants, they simply didn't have the volume of trade necessary to make a profit. The private accounts were in worse condition, with an ever dwindling band of customers with impeccable taste but an average age of about sixty, my parents among them. To make matters worse they seemed to regard asking for payment with as much distaste as a dowager duchess might show to the suggestion that she drop her knickers to pee in the gutter.

I could imagine the response I would get to any of the obvious suggestions for saving money, and besides, it simply wouldn't be enough. What I needed were rich clients prepared to pay high prices – or, ideally, filthy rich clients prepared to pay extortionate prices. To that end I needed to work on Earle Hayes and Anton Yoshida, but the direct approach was almost certain to fail. Both undoubtedly had the attention of every hopeful marketing manager in the trade and received enough samples to drown in. It would be better to use reverse psychology and try and make them think I was deliberately hiding some superb product in order to prevent the price from rising beyond my own income.

By the time I left, my head was swimming with ideas and I felt exhausted. I made for Marylebone, thinking vaguely about food while wishing Percy had volunteered to stand me dinner for one more night. By the time I reached my block I had decided to order a takeaway and eat in the bath, perhaps exploring one of the eastern cuisines so common in London but unheard of on the island. My bum still felt pleasantly sensitive and I knew that I'd soon be masturbating over what had been done to me earlier.

There was a young woman standing outside the door, petite, smartly dressed and looking completely lost until she saw me, when her face split into a beaming smile.

'Tasha, hi!'

'Er . . . hi,' I managed, trying desperately to remember if she was an old schoolfriend, some forgotten one-night stand or a reporter.

'It's me, Lydia!' she laughed. 'You must remember me.'

'I'm sorry . . .,' I began, only for a subtle change in the light on her grinning face to bring back a flood of memories: of that same grin as she eased a candle up my pussy, as she sprayed my bottom metallic blue to humiliate me in front of her boyfriend, as she held me down across her mother's lap while I was spanked to tears with a hairbrush.

Then she'd been a wild teenager with red and green hair, piercings and a taste for leather microskirts with no knickers underneath. She'd also been a sadistic, controlling little bitch. Now she looked as if she'd just stepped out of the boardroom of a blue-chip company, with her designer suit and several hundred pounds' worth of hairdo. She also seemed genuinely friendly, although I wasn't about to take that at face value.

'You . . . you look different,' I said, the only words I could get out and in the circumstances a truly pathetic effort.

'You don't,' she said happily. 'You look exactly the same as the last time I saw you.'

I found myself blushing, unsure if what she'd said was a compliment or a subtle dig. As far as I could remember, the last time she'd seen me I'd been having my bottom smacked at a birthday party, although that had at least been my own choice.

'How are you anyway?' she carried on. 'I hear you've taken up an appointment as manager at Hambling and Borse?'

'Yes,' I admitted, slightly surprised because, although her parents were both in the trade, I was fairly sure she wasn't.

'I want to talk to you about that,' she said, taking my arm. 'Can I treat you to Thai? Is the Royal Elephant good?'

'I don't know. I've only been back in London a few days, but I was thinking of just having a takeaway.'

'Great. You go up and get a bottle on ice. I'll order.'

She didn't bother to wait for my answer, but gave me a last smile and disappeared in the direction of the restaurant. I was about to follow and turn down her offer, but my curiosity got the better of me. She'd said she wanted to talk about my job, and she was suspiciously friendly. I've allowed plenty of women to dominate me sexually, but with nearly all of them our relationship outside the bedroom has been as equals. Lydia had been different, always treating me as an inferior, which I'd found arousing but irritating. I decided to play along but to be extremely cautious.

The intercom system would enable me to let her in from my flat, so I went up and put one bottle of Gewürztraminer in the freezer and another in the fridge. It was annoying to have to postpone the leisurely bath I'd been planning in favour of a hurried wash, but I wanted to give the impression that I was a little in awe of her and so laid the table with my best glasses and some white linen napkins I'd bought in anticipation of entertaining various men. I'd only just finished when she buzzed to get in. She was already talking as she entered the flat.

'I adore Thai. I've got us Gai Phad Khing, Ped Aon Yod Pak, Nua Phad Nam Mun Hoi and jasmine rice. Let's eat.'

I had no idea what she was talking about, and suspected she was showing off, but to my surprise she began to dish up rather than expecting me to do it. The bottle from the freezer was already pleasantly cool and I poured out two glasses. She swirled her wine, sniffed and sipped, clearly appreciative but without the concentration Percy or Otto Borse would have shown for a single vineyard wine. Nor did she bother to comment, but took a swallow and a bite of food before starting to talk once more.

'Bottom line first. I'm with Orpheus Asset Management, who I don't suppose you've ever heard of? We're one of those companies that keeps the world moving on, and I am going to make you an offer you can't refuse.'

She'd put on a mock Italian accent for the last few words, and grinned at me before taking another swallow of wine.

'Hambling and Borse is a dinosaur,' she went on, 'yesterday's news, twentieth century.'

'Nineteenth, I'd have said. Eighteenth, even.'

'I like the way you think, Tasha. They're dead and buried, I'm sure you know that, and I have the solution. Orpheus want to make an offer and, believe me, it's a good one, but those two old farts in St James's won't even acknowledge us.'

'What are you planning to do?'

'Buy them out at a fair price and rationalise the company.'

'Which involves what, exactly?'

She hesitated, pretending to concentrate on her meal for a while, then pursed her lips in sudden decision.

'OK, I'll be open with you, because I know you think the way I do and will see that it's the best option. As we said, their set-up is outdated. Only global companies can afford to have a headquarters in St James's nowadays. For an outfit like Hambling and Borse it's a joke. So the premises go. We have offers from names that would make your eyes pop, and they want it badly, so we should get well over the market price, and even that's high. Then there's the name. When you're selling wine, there's nothing like a touch of snobbery to make the punters shell out. We sell the name to a supermarket, who set it up so it looks like they're in partnership with Hambling and Borse, which we estimate will give them at least a twenty per cent premium on their upper range wines.'

'And the stock?'

She shrugged.

'Whatever.'

There was no point in asking about the employees, who were obviously for the chop, or in telling her that her bit of blatant asset-stripping would give poor old Gilbert and Otto heart attacks. She obviously didn't care.

'They want me to make the company profitable and help pass it on to somebody who'll keep up with the same traditions,' I pointed out.

'You know as well as I do that's not going to happen.'

I made a face.

'They should be more than content with the Orpheus offer,' she insisted. 'Both of them will retire rich, while the name of Hambling and Borse will become one of the most prestigious brands on the market.'

'Associated with characterless bulk-production wines. You know how supermarkets work, Lydia, using their buying power to force producers to sell at little or no profit – which inevitably means poor quality, whatever it may say on the label.'

'I wasn't actually planning on drinking the stuff, Natasha.'

'I didn't imagine you would be, but don't you think it's a pity?'

'No. As long as somebody's still producing the good stuff and I can afford it, why should I care what the rabble is drinking? Don't tell me you disagree, because I know you and I know it's bullshit.'

'I didn't mean that. I meant, isn't it a pity to destroy Hambling and Borse?'

'It's business, Natasha.'

'Fair enough, but they're paying me to bail them out, not flog the company to an asset-stripper. Anyway, I don't have the authority.'

'Maybe not, but you can present one of our subsidiaries as a genuine buyer.'

'Why should I do that?'

'Because we'll pay you a percentage of what we make on the deal.'

I was taken aback for a moment as I realised that she was offering to bribe me, and blatantly at that. Not that it was all that shocking, given some of the things I'd known her to do, but I'd already let my surprise show and didn't answer immediately. She waited patiently as I finished my wine and opened the second bottle, not speaking until I'd refilled our glasses.

'Well? You know it makes sense, Tasha.'

'They'd be furious.'

'Who cares what a couple of drunken old buffers think? Anyway, they don't have to know you were in on the deal.'

'That's true.'

She was right: I could do it, and she would be the only one who knew the truth. I smiled and raised my glass, to which she returned a wicked grin.

'You haven't changed,' I told her.

'No,' she answered, either oblivious to irony or fully aware that she was an evil, scheming little bitch. 'Have you?'

Her voice had changed in tone, growing distinctly warmer, and she was looking at me over the rim of her glass. I ignored her, piqued at the memory of her behaviour, only to think again. Her casual assumption of superiority had always annoyed me, and yet . . .

'Before you came, I was going to eat my dinner in the bath,' I told her, smiling as I fed her the line.

'Why don't you?' she responded, as bold as ever.

Nothing further needed to be said. I stood up and made for the bathroom, taking my glass with me. It was rather a fine bath, a big old-fashioned tub with plenty of room. I poured in a generous measure of bath oil and turned the taps on full, filling the room with the scents of heat and jasmine. Lydia hadn't bothered to get up but was still seated at the table, watching me with a knowing, ever so slightly disdainful little smirk. I went to the bed, shook out my hair and began to undress – not a striptease, such as I would have given a man if he was watching me, but simply going nude without embarrassment. She had every right to see me naked, and I knew she would enjoy it without having to be rude.

'Your turn,' I told her as I came back to the table.

She refilled her glass and stood up, but as I came close she gave me a solid slap on my bottom.

'No,' she told me. 'You get in. I'll watch.'

Despite myself a little shiver ran through me, both at her tone and from the sudden, sharp sting where she'd smacked me. I crossed to the bathroom once more, sensing her eyes on my rear view and the red mark on my flesh. The bath was full, with bubbles already beginning to run over the side, so I hastily twisted the taps off, bending as I did so to let her see my pussy from behind – again not to be rude but to let her know that I didn't mind what she saw.

'In you get,' she told me.

She'd sat down on the loo, and watched as I climbed into the bath. The bubbles had come up so high that I was almost completely covered, just my boobs sticking out above the surface, looking big and pink and wet, feeling very vulnerable. Lydia watched, her smile now openly cruel.

'You're quite a big girl, aren't you?' she remarked. 'Hold them up.'

I obeyed, cupping my breasts in my hands and lifting them for her inspection, tingling with pleasure to be obeying her orders but not in the least ashamed. She was several inches shorter than me and pretty much flat-chested, but her waist was no slimmer, so it was impossible not to feel proud of myself as I showed off to her.

'Put some food on them,' she told me. She had collected our plates from the table, and handed me mine. 'You're going to eat your dinner off your tits.'

'Wouldn't you rather I ate it off yours?'

'Shut up and do as you're told.'

'Yes, Miss Lydia.'

'That's better. That's the Natasha I remember, you little slut. Now get on with it.'

She sat back, watching and sipping her wine as I scraped the contents of my plate on to my chest. It was hot, stinging my skin, and slippery, bringing that deliciously rude sensation that comes with being thoroughly mucky. I put as much as I could on top of my tits, piling a little mound of rice and bits of meat and vegetable on each globe, but most of it slid off, down my cleavage and into the bath. It looked disgusting but felt lovely, especially with the ginger and chilli in the sauces making my nipples tingle. I was tempted to smear it all over myself, but I'd been ordered to eat.

'You dirty pig,' Lydia said, giggling, her eyes now bright with cruelty. 'Go on, do it.'

I took my fork, carefully scraped up some of the mess and brought it to my mouth. Lydia's eyes were locked with mine as I ate, letting the sauce run down my chin. My nipples had gone stiff, one little pink bud peeping up through the mess, and as I took a second forkful I bumped it, giving myself a sharp little shock of pleasure and increasing my need to open my thighs to her. Her grin grew more evil still as I lifted my knees above the soap bubbles, well parted.

'Come on in,' I urged. 'Clothed if you like.'

She shook her head, but whether she wanted to play the stern mistress or was just being coy, or whatever her problem was, I no longer cared. Dropping my fork, I cupped my boobs, one plump, slippery globe in each hand, squeezing them and rubbing the mess over my skin before pulling them both up to lick my nipples and dirty my face. She picked up her own plate and began to eat, cool and poised while she watched me soil myself. Just that was enough to get me off, and I was going to masturbate for her when she abruptly stood up.

'Roll over,' she order. 'Stick your bum up.'

I obeyed without a second's thought, turning over in the bath to stick my bare bottom up above the bubbles, my knees open to make very sure she had access to my pussy and bumhole as well as my cheeks. She slapped me, once, twice and a third time, making me gasp with each stinging impact on my wet skin, then suddenly overturned her plate and brought it down on to my bottom with a soggy slap. I felt the food squash out over my cheeks and between, soiling my pussy and spattering my thighs.

She was laughing as she rubbed the mess into my bottom, and left the plate there, telling me to stay in place as she hastily began to undress. I watched from the corner of my eye, admiring her petite body and hoping she was going to make me be thoroughly rude with her before the evening was done. The plate slid slowly off my bottom as she stripped, leaving my filthy cheeks stuck high and open for her inspection, my bumhole still clean and pink between. Nude, she came back to me, slipped a hand between my thighs and rubbed me until I was panting and sticking myself up for more.

'Yes, like that,' I begged. 'Bring me off, Lydia, and spank me too.'

'Shut up, slut,' she retorted, and stopped rubbing.

Ignoring my groan of disappointment, she began to explore my bottom, stroking my cheeks and smearing the mess more evenly across them. Some of it had already slid between them, soiling my bottom hole, but she added more, squashing it into my slit and inserting something small but hard into my anus. I thought she was going to finger me and closed my eyes in expectation of the bliss of having my bum penetrated, but she simply left whatever she'd put in my hole and went back to fondling my cheeks. I tried to relax, telling myself there was no need to hurry, despite my already urgent need to come – but then whatever was up my bum started to burn. Lydia laughed as I began to wriggle, and planted a firm smack across my cheeks, spattering herself with sauce.

'It's a piece of ginger,' she told me. 'Hurts, does it?'

My response was a whimper, although the hot, loose sensation growing in my anus was more heat than pain. It made me want to stick my bottom up anyway, to be spanked and plugged and molested in any way she pleased.

'Right up,' she ordered. 'I want your pussy.'

I obeyed eagerly, lifting my bottom completely clear of the water and spreading my knees as wide as they would go. My hole felt open and ready, and I was expecting her fingers – only to have a handful of Thai food wadded up inside me. Lydia laughed, then gave a crow of delight and disgust as my hole closed to squeeze out the mess she'd just stuck up it. My bumhole was now burning and had begun to pulse on the ginger root, while my pussy was also beginning to sting and even my cheeks felt warm.

Lydia began to play with my bottom, spanking me and tickling my holes, pinching my cheeks and occasionally pushing a teasing knuckle between my sex lips. She'd sat down on the edge of the bath, her thighs wide, her hand between, rubbing herself as she molested me. I began to shake helplessly as she amused herself with my body. Twice she scooped up a handful of mess from my cheeks and fed it to me, giggling lewdly as I gobbled it up like a pig feeding from the hand. More bits of ginger were stuck in up my bumhole and pussy, until I felt loose and open, utterly out of control. Her slaps became hard, until I was gasping and wriggling in the pain of a full-blown spanking.

'Frig yourself off,' she demanded suddenly. 'Come on, slut, I want to see you get there.'

I didn't need to be told, but snatched back immediately, groping at my hot, eager pussy. She continued to spank me as I set my fingers to work, touching my burning bumhole to feel the pieces of ginger inside, plugging my cunt to leave myself agape in front of her, and starting to masturbate. I wanted her to see everything, to watch my fingers work in the slippery, fleshy folds of my sex, to see how excited she'd made me and how helpless I was under her command. I wanted her to punish me, spank my bare bottom until I howled, while I got off on my own humiliation. I wanted her to penetrate me, fill my bumhole and pussy with hot, slimy food, make me eat what had been up me while I came.

She gave me everything, save that last deliciously dirty detail, and that only because we came at the same time, with her calling me a slut over and over again as I brought myself off in front of her, naked and grovelling in the mess she'd made of me, soiled and spanked and penetrated for her amusement.

Three

I felt immensely smug the next morning, if perhaps not quite as smug as Lydia. After all, she knew she had me on a string, and that was that, while my own situation was anything but simple. I needed to think, and so instead of starting to engineer meetings as I'd intended, I took a long, hot bath – this time without Thai food.

My original scheme had involved a good deal of duplicity, but Lydia's visit had added a whole new dimension. For one thing I was going to have to be extremely careful about who knew what, including Percy. I would also need to decide exactly what to do before I started anything, and to think it all through very carefully in order to make sure there would be no mistakes and that as little as possible was left to chance.

By midday I had worked out as much as I could, and only then did I turn my attention to other things. The opening of the plan was still the same, and I quickly discovered that Anton Yoshida was in Paris, where he intended to comment on the vintage as the initial reports came in. Earle Hayes was harder to track down, so, not having been to France since the beginning of my self-imposed exile, despite living within sight of the Cap de la Hague, I decided to work on Anton first. That meant securing an invitation to an event he would be attending, which was going to be tricky. Fortunately, *Corkscrew* magazine were holding one of their lunchtime tastings on the Friday and there was sure to be somebody on the panel who could make the relevant introductions.

Percy was the man to secure me my place, and I spent the rest of the day at his flat. A single phone call took care of business, after which I told him what Lydia had done to me in the bath, but not the details of our business conversation. My description of having to stick my bottom out above the bubbles for spanking got him going, inevitably, and I spent a happy two hours being put through a punishment regime that culminated with him coming all over my hot cheeks.

The *Corkscrew* tasting was intended to back up an article they were doing on the top wineries of the Napa Valley. I knew that would mean a series of big whites and strong, heavy reds, which I don't really care for, so I resolved to spit and stay sober. They'd moved to new premises, the top two floors of a squat office block in Putney. The tasting room was large and open, looking out over the Thames, and they had lined the wines up on two sides, each decanter placed just so on the white tablecloth with glasses beside it and a place number large enough for even the most bibulous old hack to see.

There was no shortage of bibulous old hacks, five in all, of assorted shapes and sizes, along with three smart young women, two of whom were from the magazine. I knew most of them more or less well, and had soon been introduced to the others. We were already running late, but it wasn't until I spoke to Percy's old friend John Thurston that I found out why.

'Oh, we're waiting for Earle Hayes. He's always rather late. Likes to imagine himself as the grand old man, I suspect. Here he is now.'

As he was speaking there had been a shift in the attention of those around me. I turned as well, to see the man himself standing in the doorway. I'd seen him a few times before, but more often in photographs, and he was taller than I'd have expected, although his heavy, serious face and shock of pale-grey hair were unmistakable. The two girls from the magazine were already fussing around him like those fish that accompany sharks, and most of the others had also moved towards him. I decided to wait my turn and continued talking to John, who was not one to be impressed by celebrity.

'Extraordinary the way perfectly sensible people hang on to his every word,' he remarked. 'Still, I suppose today's tasting is his speciality, and apparently he's keen to increase his influence on the UK market, so there may well be money in sucking up to him. You're with old Gilbert and Otto Borse, Percy tells me, so I suppose you really ought to be doing the same?'

'I'm managing them so, yes, I suppose I should. There's another man I want to contact too, Anton Yoshida. Do you know anything about him?'

'A little. He's a new boy, but extraordinarily influential in the Far East. His father's some kind of bigwig in Japanese industry, I believe, which no doubt explains how he got his contacts. Yes, I can see you'd want to meet him, but I'm afraid I'm not even on nodding terms with the fellow. Let's try little Jacqueline.'

He signalled to one of the magazine girls, who came across. After a conversation in rapid French she trotted away again, returning with the information that Anton Yoshida was expected to be at the launch of a new brand of prestige Cognac that was being held at an appropriate hotel in the Place de Bourges. I thanked her and she left with a smile. Both men were now in my sights.

'Good luck,' John remarked, 'although from what I hear he's not easy to influence.'

'I have my means,' I assured him. 'Speaking of which, any good reviews you might see your way to providing will be appreciated.'

He raised his eyebrows fractionally. They were bushy and ginger, like his hair, while his body was big and slightly gangling with a pronounced paunch. He knew me well, and his reaction sent a sharp thrill through me at the thought of having to give myself to him. Not that he was on the day's menu, because I was after bigger fish.

'Shall we begin?' I suggested.

The tasting was of the sort that had always put the most strain on my professional objectivity. Just about all the wines were good of their type, so it was mainly a question of separating the merely vast from the colossal, especially with the reds. Not one of them had less than thirteen degrees of alcohol, so that, despite my most determined efforts to spit, my head was spinning and my mouth tasted hot long before I'd reached the end of the table. The last wine was an absolute monster, fifteen degrees of alcohol and so dark it was almost black. I was holding it up to the light to admire the colour and earnestly wishing for a glass of cold Champagne when one of the magazine girls appeared by my side.

'Natasha? May I introduce you to Mr Hayes? Mr Hayes, Miss Linnet.'

Earle Hayes extended a hand, his normally stern face twisted into a beaming smile.

'Delighted to meet you, Miss Linnet,' he said, his accent strongly West Coast but with a curiously English inflection that might have been put on. 'What do you make of the Bear's Den?'

'The name certainly suits it,' I replied as the magazine girl gave a polite bob and moved away.

He laughed, then peered deeply into his own glass as if expecting a small grizzly to emerge. I was more than a little surprised that he'd sought me out, but was not about to pass up the opportunity of ingratiating myself with him. It was also interesting, and amusing, to note that while the rest of us were tasting the wines blind, he obviously knew which was which.

'Seriously, though,' I went on, 'I think it's exceptional. The colour and concentration are extraordinary, the fruit, oak and tannin are in harmony, the flavours pronounced. It's a Cabernet Sauvignon, isn't it?'

'Cabernet, obviously,' he agreed. 'I'd say forty-four, maybe a forty-five.'

Having read his column a few times I knew what he was talking about: the mark he intended to give it by his system, with minus fifty meaning undrinkable and fifty representing perfection, as if there could be such a thing. I didn't intend to argue, but I knew what his score would do to the price and made a mental note to try and get hold of a few cases. His tasting sheet showed the scores he'd given the other wines, and as I pretended to concentrate on the contents of my glass I was desperately trying to memorise them so that I could be in agreement with him over lunch while seeming keen to get my opinion in first.

I was the only one. With the exception of John Thurston, everybody else waited until Earle Hayes had made his pronouncement and hastened to support whatever he'd said. I'd never seen such a bunch of sycophants, and would have said so, had I not been working to my own agenda. John merely watched and allowed himself the occasional quiet grin at some particularly unctuous comment.

Lunch was accompanied by a series of wines, all of them poured with a generous hand. I did my best to hold back, but with John sitting next to me and determined to top up my glass at every opportunity it wasn't easy. He was doing his best to charm me too, and I knew I'd be receiving an invitation to join him afterwards, and what he had in mind for me. Normally I'd have gone for it, but I needed to concentrate on Hayes, who was at the far corner of the table. Hayes was also very much the centre of attention, and I was trying to decide how to play the situation, but he made straight for me as soon as lunch was over.

'Miss Linnet, I was wondering if I might have a word? If you'd excuse us, Mr Thurston.'

He was quite forceful, which I liked, and John had the grace to move on, leaving me with a clear run, far more easily achieved than I'd have anticipated.

'I understand you're managing Hambling and Borse?' Hayes asked, again providing me with exactly the lead I needed.

'Yes,' I admitted. 'In fact, I was hoping you would taste some of our wines – privately, that is.'

'I would be delighted, in fact . . .'

He would have gone on, but the editor had turned up and was pointedly hovering within hearing, so Hayes broke off to speak to him. I waited, but the man seemed to have an endless supply of platitudes and other people were constantly drifting in and out of the conversation. I finally decided to play the helpless, swooning female, leaning heavily on his arm with the clear implication that I was drunk and needed support. He quickly steadied me and I managed an embarrassed smile at the others before I spoke.

'I'm sorry. I think I need a little fresh air. Would you be very kind and give me a hand, Mr Hayes?'

He and the others shared amused and condescending smiles, but he went for it, taking me by the elbow and steering me gently to where a tall glass door opened on to a balcony overlooking the Thames.

'I'm not really drunk,' I told him, 'but I'd rather like to talk to you alone. The thing is—'

I broke off, again because people were coming towards us, then went on hastily.

'Did you come by car? Would you mind giving me a lift?'

'Where to?'

'Anywhere, really.'

He smiled, and for the first time there was a bit of a twinkle in his eye. Again he took my arm, this time in a distinctly proprietorial fashion, and began to move towards the door. We made our excuses as we left, and I caught more than one muttered remark. I had hoped to manage things rather more subtly, and my face was flushed with embarrassment as we left the *Corkscrew* offices, but it was too late to start afresh. Not that it mattered if half the wine trade knew I'd been seduced, not the way they deferred to him.

I was going to get it too, just the way I'd planned: obligatory sex on his terms, at least at first. His car was in the yard at the rear of the office block, in the space reserved for the MD of *Corkscrew*. It was some big American thing, black and shiny and new. He held the door open for me and I climbed in, relaxed back into the big leather seat and closed my eyes to let the warm, dizzy sensation of all the alcohol I'd drunk wash over me.

Hayes was chuckling as he got into the car, and his hand moved ever so briefly to my knee, a purposeful touch that he could have excused, if I'd protested, by saying that he needed to get at the gear shift. It was rather a gentlemanly thing to do, and gave me a last chance to back out, but I simply smiled, feeling like a fine little slut. He chuckled again, as he started the car.

'You know, it's been years since I took a drive alone with a pretty girl. Kind of takes me back.'

'I bet it does,' I answered him, teasing. 'I know what you Americans are like. I've seen the films.'

'What films would those be?'

'The ones where some guy drives a girl out to somewhere lonely and makes her suck his cock or walk home. I hope that's what you're going to do with me?'

He nearly hit the gatepost, but managed to recover in time, blowing his breath out in surprise as he turned on to the road.

'Pretty forward, aren't you?' he said.

For a moment I thought I'd made a mistake, and he would turn out to be one of those awful men who like to think women are prudish innocents who need to be tricked out of their knickers. Then he spoke again.

'Just the way I like it.'

I gave a low purr and wriggled down into my seat, causing him to mutter something under his breath and speed up. He'd turned south, up the hill, making me wonder if the scene of my seduction would be Wimbledon Common. Even two years ago that had been a bad idea.

'There are too many cameras around here,' I told him. 'Turn down the A3.'

He did as he was told, driving well above the speed limit as we got on to the dual carriageway. I kept myself warm by stroking my nipples through the fabric of my blouse, until they were making little hard bumps in the material. Just to let him have me wasn't enough: he seemed quite experienced, and I needed to stand out from the crowd. That meant I had to be good, and do whatever he wanted, an appealing thought that heightened my arousal as I teased myself. He kept glancing at me and shaking his head, as if in disbelief at how open I was being, which encouraged me all the more.

Soon I'd eased my skirt up, just to the level of my stocking tops, so that he could see that I was in suspenders and watch me stroke my thighs. So could various lorry drivers, but the traffic was light and we passed them quickly, so that even if they did look they'd get only the briefest of glimpses. That added to my excitement, making me want to give more, first an inch of two of bare thigh, and then as my caution gave way completely, the front of my panties. I was in white silk, bulging gently over my pussy mound and pulled up a little between my lips. Just the thing to get the boys going.

'I've got to have you,' Hayes grunted, finally breaking his silence. 'I've got to have you now.'

'We'll get arrested,' I said with a laugh. 'Come on, a bit further, and we'll soon have your cock out. Are you big?'

'Big enough.'

'I'll suck you, then, and maybe let you fuck me over the back seat if you're a good boy. If you had a little skinny one I'd let you put it up my bum.'

'Jesus!'

Again I laughed. He had a reputation for never using bad language, but plainly there were limits. I shut up and stopped playing with myself, partly because I was scared he would crash and partly because we'd reached the edge of London and I was trying to remember how to get to any of the dogging lay-bys or quiet car parks I'd visited in the past. We were in my old friend Monty Hartle's part of the world, and he'd introduced me to more than a few, including one that couldn't be more than ten minutes' drive away.

It actually took me twenty to find it: the entrance to a long-abandoned chalk quarry on a lane leading only to a handful of big gin-belt houses. There was just enough space to get properly off the road, into a quiet green space thick with the scent of buddleia bushes growing out from the sides of the quarry, perfect for rude open-air sex. I didn't waste any time, but responded to his need to kiss me as I drew down his fly and pulled out his cock and balls. His mouth tasted of wine, making me more eager still as I tugged at his rapidly growing shaft and fumbled the buttons of my blouse open to let him get at my breasts.

He took the hint, helping with the last button before tugging up my bra to spill them out, warm and bare in the autumn sunlight. I let him feel me, enjoying his boyish eagerness to touch, and the feel of his thumbs on my nipples as he rubbed them to hardness. He was even stiffer, his cock having come up to full erection as soon as he got his hands on my boobs. I wanted to see, and pulled back, taking a breast in each hand to show off for him while I in turn admired what he had for me.

I love the way a man's cock and balls look sticking out of a smart suit, and he hadn't lied about his size. He was big, and pink, and smooth, a really beautiful cock, and eminently suckable, but he was staring at my chest as if I was presenting him with the Holy Grail. I laughed and gave them a playful bounce, making his eyes pop.

'You're kind of big,' he breathed, 'not too big, but big, and real.'

'You can fuck them if you like.'

'Oh, sweet Jesus!'

'In a bit.'

He was mine, utterly in thrall to my boobs, and, while I knew I'd have to give him whatever he wanted, that was no reason not to get my own. Laying myself across the seats, I went down on him, first licking and kissing his bulging balls before taking him in my mouth. The position left my boobs dangling and he quickly took advantage, slipping a hand under my chest to fondle me as I sucked. I was not going to be happy if he wasted it in my mouth, and I was careful, sucking gently and teasing him by licking under his foreskin with the very tip of my tongue. His breathing grew deeper and his fondling rougher as he grew more excited, but when he began to thrust up into my mouth I stopped, giggling as I released his erection. He tried to push me back down, but I wagged a finger at him.

'Don't be in such a hurry, Earle. You want to fuck my tits, don't you?'

'Dead right I do,' he answered, puffing. His accent had completely lost the English veneer.

'We need more room,' I pointed out, pulling the door open.

I'd planned to get in the back, but the day was too beautiful, and being fully exposed would make the sex even more fun. Not that we were likely to get caught, but it's nice to imagine myself being watched. There was some piece of ancient, rusting machinery among the buddleias, and I sat down on it, cupping my breasts to offer my cleavage as a cock slide. He didn't waste any time but squatted down in front of me, pressing his cock down to let me squash him between them, his shaft hot and hard against the softness of my flesh.

His suit trousers were rubbing on my nipples as he fucked my cleavage, making me ever more eager to touch myself, but I knew it would be better still if I forced myself to wait. I'd wanted to feel I was being used anyway, and it was nice to be titty-fucked before I was allowed to come. It would even be nice if he came up my cleavage and in my face, leaving me to rub off in front of him with his mess all over me, and I was beginning to think that was going to happen when he suddenly stopped.

'Lie back.'

It was a brusque order, urgent and demanding. I would have obeyed, but I didn't get the chance. He grabbed my ankles, making me squeak as I was tipped upside-down. I had to snatch at a buddleia branch to stop myself falling off the machine, and I was anything but comfortable. He didn't care, pushing my skirt up around my hips and hauling my panties down my thighs even as I struggled to keep my balance. I squeaked again as my legs were pushed higher, with his hand twisted in my pulled-down panties, leaving my bottom stuck out and my pussy vulnerable to his cock, which went up with one shove, making a wet, squashy noise as I was filled.

I was clinging on for dear life as I was fucked, not daring to let go of the branch, my body jerking like a demented puppet and my boobs bouncing wildly. His eyes were locked on them with a feverish intensity and he seemed indifferent to the rest of my body, save that my pussy made a convenient place to stick his cock. It was just what I wanted, dirty and rough, and I'd have brought myself off in front of him if I'd been able to get at my pussy. I couldn't, or I'd be head-down in a clump of nettles and I wasn't at all sure he'd stop. All I could do was cling on, gasping as he thrust into me, praying he'd finish quickly and wishing he'd keep going forever, all at the same time.

He finished quickly, jerking his cock free at the last instant to empty himself over my thighs and belly, soiling my rucked-up skirt and even splashing my breasts. When he let go of my panties I very nearly fell off, but managed to pull myself back up, spreading my thighs to my hand without bothering to get comfortable. My pussy was soaking and the hair of my mound matted with his come. My skirt, bra and blouse were dirty, and my boobs spotted with white. I'd been well and truly spunked over, used and spunked over as if I were no more than a fuck toy, and it felt absolutely wonderful.

I cried out loud as I came, showing off to him with one hand clutching at my cunt while I smeared his mess over my boobs. He was staring, his cock hanging from his fly, slowly deflating as he gazed in astonishment at what he'd made me do. When I'd finally come down from my high he didn't seem to know quite what to say, so I went first.

'Thanks, that was good, very good.'

'I'm glad you enjoyed it,' he managed. 'You are one very amorous young lady.'

'So I'm told. My bag's in the car, please, or do you have a hankie I could borrow?'

'Why, certainly,' he responded. 'I have tissues in the car too.'

He was every bit the gentleman once again, passing me his handkerchief and then going to fetch some tissues and my bag, his cock still out and slippery with my juice. The last time I'd been in that quarry had been with Monty Hartle, who'd come in my face and hair, then expected me to suck his cock clean before he'd help me tidy up. Hayes was very different, infinitely more considerate, although he'd been very nearly as rude with me.

'Would you like a drink?' he offered as I began to adjust my make-up.

'An orange juice would be perfect, followed by a coffee.'

'Sure. I suppose there's a bar around here someplace.'

We found a pub, once the haunt of coach passengers on their way to Portsmouth, now largely given over to retired stockbrokers and women in tweed. I chose a table by the window and watched with amusement as Earle Hayes took in his surroundings with open relish.

'I just adore England,' he told me as he put our drinks down, 'which brings me back to what I wanted to speak to you about. Can we talk business?'

I nodded, wondering what he wanted and whether I dared lay my cards on the table by asking for favourable reviews of Hambling and Borse wines in return.

'Like I'm sure you know,' he began, 'I'm well set up back home, but over here I've not had an easy time. You Brits like tradition. You like names that go back a hundred years or more, like Hambling and Borse. I've been thinking of buying a British company for some time now, and I know you need to sell, so if the price is right . . .'

He trailed off, spreading his hands.

My plan was not going to script. Earle Hayes was a writer and an opinion-maker, not a merchant, and it had never crossed my mind for an instant that he'd be a potential buyer. Like Lydia, he seemed to be mainly after the name and presumably the premises, and like Lydia's his offer would be utterly unacceptable to Gilbert and Otto. In fact it was a moot point which suggestion would send them into the more extreme state of apoplexy, selling out to an asset-stripper or to an American.

His offer was fair, for a failing company with good assets, but the better Hambling and Borse were doing, the more he'd be expected to pay. Therefore he was hardly likely to praise any of their wines, at least until he had control. Until then his best choice was to ignore them, as he explained to me quite candidly while we drove back towards London. I kept my own council, letting him talk and trying to reappraise the situation.

It was growing increasingly complicated, but there was no reason to deviate from my plan. If I couldn't have the good opinion of Earle Hayes, then I would have to seek out Anton Yoshida all the more urgently. The two were rivals, and so it seemed likely that if one chose to comment on a particular wine the other would do so too, or at least be asked for his opinion. Both liked to present an image of omniscience, so neither could easily admit that he had not tasted something the other had praised. Better still, if I could get some favourable comments on the Hambling and Borse wines from Yoshida, then Hayes would have little choice but to praise them as well, or it would look highly peculiar when he took on the agencies, as he hoped to do.

I needed to get to Paris, and to choose a wine with which to impress Yoshida, ideally by serving it while he was in the process of bedding me. The Patrice Beauroy Champagne was ideal, the traditional drink of seduction and a wine of impeccable quality. I chose a hotel behind Les Invalides, convenient but sufficiently discreet for my purposes, then sent a case ahead, along with a cheque large enough to ensure good service and no arguments about corkage.

There was no difficulty in securing an invitation to the Cognac tasting; for all Hambling and Borse's woes, they were still much sought after as clients. It was all rather peculiar, with a lavish dinner and some sort of theatrical entertainment laid on, all in aid of promoting Kavanagh's new *Cordon Noir*, which was to sell at over a £1,000 a bottle and appeared to be aimed exclusively at the gullible. I could think of worse places to be, and no doubt there would be other, more interesting events – I knew I'd been lucky with Earle Hayes, and it might take a while to get my hooks into Anton Yoshida.

I had another good reason for going to Paris. Both Lydia and Earle Hayes were keen for me to make a decision, and I could only make excuses for so long. They were also both keen to get me into bed, or the bath, or spread out on some piece of rusting machinery – which would have been fine if the after-sex conversation hadn't focused entirely on why I should accept their offer as soon as possible.

On the Saturday it was Earle Hayes and a cock between my tits before being rolled up and fucked on the bed. On the Sunday it was Lydia, who not only tied my hands behind my back and spanked me with a shoe but threatened to withhold my climax unless I agreed to her terms. On the Monday I left for France, early.

Four

I was in Paris in time to take a leisurely lunch beside the Seine, and with three days to go before the tasting I was able to have a thoroughly good time, shopping, sight-seeing and road-testing the concierge at my hotel. He was one of those Frenchmen with a rude, happy-go-lucky attitude to sex, an exhibitionist streak and the morals of a polecat. Sucking his cock under the reception desk as he gave two elderly American tourists directions to the Eiffel Tower was especially good fun, even when he told them, in French, that it was in his tart's mouth. The male half of the couple may even have understood.

On the Thursday morning I went shopping again, only with far more purpose. If Yoshida's column was anything to go by, his tastes focused on brand and image. I was determined that he would see me as his ideal, and made a careful selection of designer clothes, right down to my knickers, exclusively French and every article a top name. On the island I'd seldom worn anything more elaborate than a sundress or jeans and a jumper, so the prices came as a bit of a shock, but I put it all on expenses anyway, as well as the two hours I spent bringing my hair, nails and skin to perfection.

By the time I was finished and ready to go, the local slobs on the island wouldn't have recognised me. In fact, looking in the mirror I barely recognised myself. My hair had been put up in an elaborate confection of curls that altered the line of my face, making me seem haughty yet slightly vulnerable, an image enhanced by both my clothes and my make-up. I'd chosen a pair of elegant black heels that lifted me by more than three inches as well, and it was only as I was making my way towards the Place de Bourges that it occurred to me that if Anton Yoshida was part Japanese he might very well be shorter than me.

I needn't have worried. On arrival I was escorted into a huge, ornate room which had been carefully laid out in order to separate the guests into three distinct classes, according to their idea of status. The lower part was reserved for the rabble, reporters and so forth, with good but plain settings. A single step led up to the next level, to which I was steered, where everything from the furniture to the flowers was just that little bit grander. The upper part was not only another two steps higher but cordoned off by a thick crimson rope, while the appointments were so extravagant as to seem almost pastiche. This area also had its own door, in which was standing an elderly gentleman who looked like a reincarnation of François Mitterrand, and next to him Anton Yoshida.

He was taller than his companion, six foot at least, and very slender, with slick jet-black hair. Both the way he held himself and his expression suggested nonchalance and charm, but also a conviction of his own superiority. He looked younger than I had expected, too, which complicated my already mixed feelings about a possible encounter. I prefer older men, and while they need to be confident they should also be properly appreciative. They should also be unashamedly dirty, and I had a nasty suspicion Anton Yoshida might turn out to be a prude – and, worse, unaware that he was a prude. On the other hand, there was no denying his good looks, so the fact that he wasn't my type at all meant that being obliged to give myself to him would be an exceptionally strong experience.

Not that I could even introduce myself, for the time being. Three extremely large men in monkey suits were spaced out along the crimson rope, trying to be unobtrusive and failing miserably, and the guests were being steered very firmly into their correct areas. He was at least alone. A wife or girlfriend would have made my task infinitely harder, if potentially more satisfying. I could only hope that we'd be allowed to mingle later, but for the moment there was nothing for it but to make polite conversation with my fellow second-class citizens and wait for the evening to get started.

It was the most peculiar wine event I had ever attended. The food was good if not wonderful, but it was accompanied by a selection of wines from Southern and Allied, the multinational food company who'd just bought out Kavanagh, and there wasn't one that I'd even have used to cook with. They also had jugglers, fire-eaters and some girls in diminutive green outfits who I think were supposed to be fairies. I enjoyed watching them, and tried to gauge Anton Yoshida's reaction to the occasional flash of bottle-green panties, but his manner was distinctly formal and gave nothing away.

He was very much the star guest, seated to the right of the man he'd been talking to earlier, evidently the CEO of Kavanagh. They were in the company of various corporate bigwigs, actors, sports personalities and the owner of the hotel, who looked as if he'd have been more at home running guns in the Middle East. They were presumably the sort of people Kavanagh wanted to impress, and I realised that if my plan worked they would be the sort of people I was forced to associate with. Suddenly the lazy boredom of the island seemed highly appealing, but I'd made my bed and was determined to lie in it, regardless of company.

Other than having the Kavanagh logo on every available surface there was no reference to Cognac at all during the meal, and it was only after we'd been served coffee that the fairies ran from the room to return each bearing a huge silver platter on which rested a single bottle of the *Cordon Noir*. They'd spent a fortune on presentation, and the word 'bottle' hardly does justice to what was really a decanter of cut and smoked glass decorated with black ribbons edged with gold, black and gold wax seals and the name in gold leaf.

The appearance of the Cognac was greeted with a round of applause, in which I joined somewhat self-consciously. Each table had a personal fairy, who began to pour out samples of the rich brown liquid as the Mitterand lookalike got to his feet. He began to speak, but my attention had been distracted, and not by the Cognac. Our table fairy was far more interesting, petite and dark, with a black bob and mischievous upturned nose. Each time she poured a Cognac she kept her legs perfectly straight and bent from the waist, making her tiny green skirt rise to show off a perfectly round little bottom encased in skin-tight green panties. I was sure that if she was game she would be far more fun to take to bed than Anton Yoshida, and it was with considerable difficulty that I forced my mind back to the task in hand.

My Cognac had been poured into a large balloon glass, and I spent a while warming it in my hand and trying to ignore our fairy, who was now on the far side of the table, so that each time she bent I was given a fine view of two little round boobs nestled in her green velvet bodice. Possibly they were trying to create a deliberate association in our minds between the Cognac and sex, because the Cognac certainly didn't have much going for it otherwise. It was good, but nothing more, and had I been served it blind I'd have put it down as an XO from one of the more commercial houses.

A thousand pounds a bottle was a ridiculous price, but I seemed to be in the minority in thinking so. Most of those around me were going into raptures, and to judge by the way Anton Yoshida was nodding, and passing what were evidently enthusiastic remarks to his neighbours, he evidently thought the same. Again and again I pushed my nose into the glass, trying to catch the supposedly wonderful nuances of flavour being discussed all around me. I was wishing Percy was there, or John, just to let me know that my palate hadn't died on me, but try as I might I could detect nothing more than a delicate fruit tinged with caramel. During my wilder years I had faked old brandies, and my efforts had been considerably better.

We were given ten minutes to consider the virtues of the *Cordon Noir* before the dinner came to an end. The large men in monkey suits began to roll back the rope and I realised that I finally had my chance. Unfortunately everybody else in the room seemed to have the same idea, and both the lower and middle sections were moving *en masse* towards the top table. I was much too far away to make an elegant approach to Yoshida, and was forced to join the crowd waiting to catch his eye.

My patience lasted all of two minutes before I decided to try some networking instead, with the aim of meeting him as an equal at some more conventional tasting. I was also keen to try my hand with our table fairy, who at least might prove a fun companion while

I was in Paris, and at best a playmate. She and her fellows were now serving Champagne, yet another brand from a Southern and Allied subsidiary, which made her easy to corner.

'*Champagne Raoul Leclerc?*' she offered, extending her tray as she gave the prettiest little curtsy.

'*Merci, jolie fée,*' I said, taking a glass and a risk that if she'd didn't respond well she probably wouldn't be much fun anyway. '*Allons papoter?*'

She looked slightly concerned, her eyes darting towards where the *maître* was hovering by the door.

'I will if you like,' she answered, in perfectly good English but with a strong Irish accent.

'Sorry, I assumed you were French,' I said, laughing.

'I knew you were English because I heard you talking,' she told me, 'but look, I'm not really supposed to mix with the guests. I'm Rhiannon.'

'Natasha. They're so stuffy here. Quickly then, would you like to meet up?'

'Sure.'

I hesitated, not wanting to rush in and destroy any chances I might have, but I could smell the scent of her skin and the perfume she was wearing, while her little round boobs were quivering ever so slightly in her bodice and her small heart-shaped face looked irresistibly kissable. Going around Paris with her but without the option of sex was going to be torture, so the only sensible option was to make my move and pray she didn't slap my face.

'I don't mean just for company. I'd like to take you to bed.'

Her face went crimson and she looked at the floor, mumbling a single word.

'Maybe.'

I snatched a pair of business cards from my pocket and scribbled the address of my hotel on one of them.

She took them without another word, hastily wrote her mobile number on the back of the second and gave it back to me, blushing so prettily that I couldn't resist kissing her, just a peck, but full on her green-painted lips. A shiver, a shy smile and she'd hurried away, leaving me flushed and hot from the top of my head to the tips of my toes. I wasn't sure if I was on a promise or not, but her sweet, shy reaction had got to me in a way I'd seldom experienced. The Champagne was pretty ordinary but it was badly needed and I gulped it down. When I lowered my glass I found Anton Yoshida looking directly at me.

My response was instantaneous: I smiled, raised my glass as if offering him a toast and winked. He barely reacted, one corner of his mouth flicking up for an instant, but I knew he'd seen me kiss Rhiannon and that I had him. Very few men indeed can resist the thought of a bisexual girl and the chance of a threesome. I had him, and my best bet was now to play it cool.

I was feeling deliciously smug as I began to mingle with the crowd. It had been entirely accidental, but with one cheeky kiss I had managed to turn around what had seemed to be an impossible situation. Anton Yoshida could no longer keep his eyes off me, save the occasional glance at Rhiannon, but I made very sure not to return his attention. There were plenty of interesting people to talk to anyway, business cards to collect and chocolates to nibble, while they were clearly determined that the Champagne would not run out.

My intention was to wait until the crowd had begun to melt away and then make my move, just in case he didn't have the guts or simply intended to eye me up. I was beginning to grow impatient when he excused himself to those around him and left the room. At first

I thought it had all gone wrong, but he returned by the other door just a couple of minutes later, thus avoiding the cluster of people by the top table who were still waiting to talk to him.

'Good evening. Miss Linnet, I believe?'

He'd evidently already asked about me. His tone was formal yet slightly wry, his accent Received Pronunciation with just a trace of the exotic.

'Natasha, please,' I responded.

'You seem to have enjoyed this evening?'

'It's had its moments, as I suspect you saw. This Champagne, on the other hand, is execrable, but I have a far better one in my hotel room, already chilled.'

His eyebrows rose a fraction. It's remarkable how many men are still surprised if a girl doesn't play coy.

'I did,' he admitted, and made an attempt to play me at my own game. 'So the question would seem to be: shall we go to bed together, or shall we attempt to add your pretty little waitress to make a threesome?'

I glanced around, half hoping to find Rhiannon but concerned that even if she was willing to play with me the suggestion of a threesome might be going too far. Even if she did go for it, which seemed unlikely, the two of us would be more or less obliged to attend to Anton, whereas it would be more fun to have her to myself. So I was only mildly disappointed to find that there was no sign of her. Nor were there any other fairies about, the tables being cleared by men and women in plain white.

'Too late,' I said. 'What a pity. Never mind, I'll tell you what I'd like to have done with her, while I play with your cock.'

He wasn't as startled as Earle Hayes had been, but his hand had begun to shake, making the surface of the Champagne in his glass tremble. I gave him a knowing smile, then spoke quickly, as the hotel owner was approaching.

'Shall I wait?'

'No. I must be discreet. We go to your hotel. A car will collect us from the back. Ten minutes.'

I nodded and managed a bright smile for the hotel owner, whose eyes flicked to my chest and hips before he responded, possibly considering adding white slavery to his gun-running operation. He made a few polite remarks before turning his attention to Anton and I was able to excuse myself.

My first thought was to look for Rhiannon, but she was nowhere to be found. That was probably just as well, as I was far hornier for her than for Anton, and I was drunk enough to have gone with her and stood him up if she'd wanted me. Evidently she didn't, and it was impossible not to feel disappointment even as I made my way to the rear of the hotel. As promised, a car was waiting for me, large, black and with Anton Yoshida in the back. I lowered myself in, smiling, and gave the chauffeur directions. He never even turned his head, but nodded as we set off.

I was keen enough, despite missing out on Rhiannon, and immediately allowed my hand to glide over Anton's leg to his crotch. He put his hand on my wrist, controlling but gentle, and let me feel for a while. His cock made a soft, appealing bulge within his trousers, which began to swell as I kneaded gently. I wanted him out and in my mouth, and the presence of the chauffeur only made the idea more exciting, but when I tried to pull down his zip my hand was removed.

'Patience, little one,' he urged.

He put his arm around me as he spoke, and held me there as we drove. I quickly let my hand slip to his cock again, stroking and squeezing through his trousers to get him erect. I imagined how it would be if he made me suck him off, and the chauffeur as well, or if they took turns with me over the bonnet, or made me a spit roast, taking turns in my mouth and up my pussy. He was obviously too prissy for anything so rude, but I soon had him nicely erect and it did no harm to think about the possible consequences.

At my hotel he gave the chauffeur a generous tip and pulled me quickly through the door. My dirty-minded concierge, Jean-Marc, was at the desk and gave me a grin and a wink as we passed. I returned the wink, hoping to make it clear that if things didn't go too well and Anton left he was welcome to come up.

My room was warm and illuminated dim gold by street lights and the reflections of Les Invalides, a pleasantly sexy atmosphere. The moment the door was closed I pulled him close, scrabbling for his fly as our mouths met, but he drew away after only a moment.

'Ever so impatient,' he remarked, plainly amused. 'That's not how to do it, little one. Come, you said you had some Champagne?'

I nodded, flustered. It would have been just as easy to have a drink after a quick fucking as before, because I was fairly sure that's what I was going to get. He sat down, very much at ease and clearly expecting me to serve him. I went to the fridge and extracted one of the bottles of Patrice Beauroy I had put in to chill, along with two glasses. He watched as I popped the cork and poured, apparently enjoying making me work, but raised his glass in salute as he took it.

'*Santé.*'

'Cheers. It's good, isn't it?'

'Yes. Now, why don't you get that pretty mouth around my prick while I drink it?'

He didn't need to push me. I got straight down, more than keen to be on my knees giving a blow job to a man sipping his drink, which has to be one of the most deliciously submissive positions a girl can be in.

'Would you like my breasts bare?' I offered, my own words provoking a sharp thrill.

'Why not?' he responded.

I met his gaze as my hands went to the top button of my blouse. He returned a small, cool smile, watching as I exposed myself. There was no question of who was in charge any more, not with me on my knees with my boobs out while he sat calm and composed in a chair, but that was just fine. I was trembling as my buttons came loose, one after another until my blouse was undone far enough to allow me to pull it open and show off my cleavage and the lacy black cups of my expensive new bra. His smile grew a trifle broader at the sight, and broader still as I tugged my cups up to spill out my naked breasts for his inspection.

'You are well shaped,' he remarked. 'You have good skin too. They are rather large and heavy, perhaps, but that is the way with so many of you English girls. Make your nipples come stiff.'

Cupping a breast in each hand, I began to rub my nipples with my thumbs, still holding his gaze as they quickly popped out, only to close my eyes as the pleasure grew too strong. He gave a soft chuckle, a sound that held more than a little contempt, then spoke again.

'Come to me, little one.'

I let go of my boobs, keen to show him how obedient I was, and looked up to him as I crawled across the floor. He set his knees apart, showing off the bulge in his suit trousers.

'Now you may have what you need,' he said, and eased his fly down. 'Take out my prick, my balls also.'

I didn't need telling, but tried to be slow and sensuous as I slipped one hand into his briefs. He felt hot and silky, his shaft still half stiff from my earlier fondling, his balls satisfyingly large and heavy. I took it all out as I'd been ordered, slipped his cock straight into my mouth and sucked eagerly.

'Slowly, little one,' he urged. 'Do you need to be taught how to do it? Maybe you do. First lick my balls while you bring me erect in your hand.'

'Yes, sir,' I answered as I let his shaft slip from my mouth.

'I prefer "Mr Yoshida",' he told me. 'Now then. You will use your mouth on me for a while and I will come in your mouth. Then, after a rest, we will play a little game. Have you ever been tied? I mean properly secured, so that you are absolutely helpless.'

I nodded, now with my tongue out as I licked his balls and tugged gently on his rapidly growing cock. He was still drinking his Champagne and began to stroke my hair, watching my face and the sway of my breasts as I worked on him. What he'd said about needing to be taught had got to me, no doubt on purpose, and I gave of my best, licking and sucking his balls, running my tongue up and down his shaft to tickle the underside of his foreskin, kissing his helmet and sucking it quickly in between my lips.

That finally broke his resolve. He gave a soft moan, wound his hand into my hair and pulled my head down on to his erection. I did my best to suck properly and not to gag, but he seemed determined to fuck my throat. His suave persona had vanished. He'd dropped his Champagne, spilling the glass down his front and into my hair, freeing his second hand, which he twisted into my hair, painfully hard. Still I struggled to play the willing little fuck slut, and not bite or throw up in his lap. He was oblivious, calling me a bitch, a slut and worse, first in English, then in French, but as he changed his grip to hold me firmly by the ears he broke completely, swearing in Japanese and thrusting his cock as deep as it would go down my aching throat.

I was choking, and about to twist his balls for him, when his body suddenly froze, every muscle rigid as he gave a last cry and spunked down my throat. Only by a frantic, painful swallow did I prevent the lot coming back out by way of my nose, and when he finally let go I was left gasping and retching, with tears running from my eyes. A slimy mixture of spunk and spittle ran down my chin to fall in wet gouts on to my boobs and down my blouse, but I was dizzy from the lack of air and too far gone to mind about soiling my clothes. He certainly didn't care, lying back with a long, satisfied sigh, but then he'd only got his shirt and trousers a little wet, while my hair was dripping with Champagne and my face and breasts soiled.

'Very good,' he said after a while. 'You do it well, in fact. I am sorry if it was maybe a little painful, but a woman must learn to accept a man as he is and not how she might wish him to be, is that not so?'

I made a vague gesture, not wanting to argue. My own glass was where I'd put it down when I was ordered on to my knees. I retrieved it and swallowed the contents gratefully, then poured myself another. His glass had survived being dropped and he held it out for more, which I provided.

'I need to clean up a little,' I told him.

'Stay as you are,' he instructed. 'I enjoy seeing what sex does to a woman. You had gone to such trouble to make yourself perfect, and now look at you. Your hair is a state, your clothes dishevelled and dirty, your fat English breasts shiny with sweat and my come.'

I managed a weak smile, wondering whether he knew more about me than he'd admitted, including my taste in sex, or was simply a complete bastard. Either way he had me where he wanted me, because I had little choice but to do as I was told if I wanted to impress him, and that knowledge alone would have been enough to make me horny, without being made to crawl and strip and suck and swallow.

'Do you want me nude?' I offered.

'No,' he responded. 'I like you as you are. I'll even let you keep your panties, but show me the front.'

I knelt up, opening my legs and tugging my skirt up until I was sure the bulge of my pussy would be showing to him. My panties matched my bra, black and lacy and very expensive, hopefully to his taste. He nodded, saying nothing but inspecting what I was showing, once more calm and reserved. I'd began to tremble again, and I knew I was wet for him, so wet that even if the black silk hid the stain he could hardly fail to smell me.

'You have taste,' he finally remarked. 'Black silk is appropriate for a young business woman, I suppose, although personally I prefer plain white, which evokes simplicity and innocence.'

I nodded, all too familiar with the Japanese taste in girls' underwear, white cotton worn taut over full bottom cheeks and a shaved pussy, an image pinched from the British. With luck that wasn't the only home-grown kink he'd taken on board.

'Do you like to spank?' I asked.

'No,' he told me. 'I like to tie girls up. If I choose to beat you it will be with a strap or cane. But not you, I think. You are too knowing, too in control of your feelings. I have something rather different in mind for you.'

He sounded genuinely evil, alarmingly so, which must have shown on my face because he laughed before going on.

'Don't look so scared, little one. I do not intend to hurt you. Your concierge knows I am with you, does he not? Yes, he does, so relax and let me take you somewhere you have never been before. Get on the bed.'

I hesitated, but only for a moment. He was a little frightening, but I was safe enough.

'My safe word is "red",' I told him. 'You'll honour that, won't you?'

'Naturally,' he assured me. 'Merely say it and I shall stop, immediately. Roll over on to your front and put your arms behind your back.'

As he spoke he took several coils of rope from his pocket. They were quite thin but looked soft, and each was a different colour, red, black and white. Again I hesitated, but did as I was told, my bare boobs squashing out against the bed cover as I got into position. He took hold of my arms, first securing my wrists before making a criss-cross of red rope up to my elbows, pulling my arms back and forcing my chest out. With my elbows tied off, he worked the rope back down to my wrists and fixed them securely in the small of my back with a double loop around my waist.

I began to shake, very conscious of my helplessness, making my boobs and belly quiver as he moved me this way and that. He took no notice, concentrating on his ropework. After satisfying himself that my arms were immobile he paused to push up my skirt, leaving it high up on my hips so that my knickers were fully exposed. I let him manipulate me, my emotions growing stronger by the moment as he removed my bra and opened my blouse to get at my breasts. He took the black rope, looped it around my chest and tied it at the front.

My breasts were already thrust high, and he wound each with rope in turn, tightening it just enough to make them bulge and redden, leaving two long tails of black rope lying down my front. I'd begun to kick a little, not voluntarily, but overcome by my helplessness, and he had to take a tight grip on my ankles before he could lash them together. Now unable even to walk, I could only lie shivering on the bed as the rope was led up one leg and tied off in a loop around my knee. He rolled me fully on to my back and pushed my legs up, spreading my bottom and pussy within my panties and making me vulnerable to his cock.

The white rope was pulled around behind my back, tied into the red and taken around to my other knee, looped off and led back to my ankles. He'd spread my knees, leaving my breasts pushing out between them and my bottom straining against the seat of my panties, while it was all I could do to wriggle my fingers and toes or shake my head.

Taking hold of my body, he drew me down the bed until my bottom was sticking out over the end. I realised I was almost certainly going to be fucked, or sodomised if it amused him. All he needed to do was turn down my panties and I'd be bare, while I was so wet that the juice had begun to trickle down between my bum cheeks. His cock had begun to stiffen again too, simply from tying me up, but he hadn't finished. Apparently satisfied, he stood back to admire his handiwork, only to delve into his other pocket and extract two more coils of rope, both purple.

He tied them to the rope holding my ankles together and led them out to the bedposts, leaving me able to wriggle my body but with barely an inch of pull in any direction for my feet. I could see why, because I could squirm my bottom and make my tits jiggle as he dealt with me, but there was no escape. Only when he had tied off the final knot did he allow himself a smile. He'd left his cock out from start to finish, occasionally stroking it, but he now took it in hand, rolling his foreskin back and forth as he looked down on me.

I'd assumed he'd torment me in some way, perhaps carry out his threat of taking a strap to my bottom, or rubbing something on to my nipples and sex to make them sting. Instead he seemed content to have me in bondage, only reaching out occasionally and then to run his fingers over the knots and sections of taut rope as frequently as my skin. It was certainly turning him on, because, although he'd come less than an hour before, his cock was quickly hard. But his casual attention to my body left me boiling with frustration.

'Do it,' I told him. 'Fuck me, or anything you like . . . please.'

His mouth twitched briefly, a tiny movement but rich with cruelty and delight. Again he began to touch me, running a knuckle over the taut skin of one tightly bound breast, briefly catching my nipple and pulling it up, only to begin to stroke the knot between them. He was leaning over me as he did it, and I could feel his cock, now fully hard and nudging the tuck of my bottom and the seat of my panties.

'Pull them down, fuck me,' I demanded.

He nodded, his hand moved to my spread sex and he pulled the gusset of my knickers to one side, baring my pussy to his erection. I sighed as it went in, sliding deep up me with one easy push, and I'd got what I wanted. He took hold of my breasts, squeezing them as he fucked me, moving his cock in and out with long, slow motions that quickly had me wriggling against him for more.

I knew he was getting off on my inability to control my reaction to what he'd done to me. The more I squirmed on his cock and begged to be fucked harder, the more he'd enjoy it, but I couldn't stop myself. With my hands free I'd have been masturbating, always a girl's last choice for freedom of expression if she's not getting what she needs. I had no way to touch myself, and my frustration was soon greater than my pleasure, setting me wriggling in my bonds and pleading for more.

Then I got it, sudden, hard and unexpected. One moment he'd been easing himself in and out and enjoying my boobs, far more casual than any man with his cock in a girl has a right to be. The next he had gone berserk, swearing in mingled French and Japanese, his hands locked like claws on my aching breasts and his cock jamming in and out of my hole so hard and deep that he had me screaming with the first thrust.

He'd come so recently that I knew I'd be fucked sore, and I was as out of control as before. Now I was over the brink, lost to pleasure as he rammed himself home inside me harder and harder, his thrusts rising to a furious crescendo that brought me as close to orgasm as I can get from just the friction of cock and cunt. Then he stopped. I lay gasping, my body shaking, expecting him to take a moment to get his breath back and then begin again. Instead he slid his cock from my pussy and climbed on to the bed.

'Suck me clean,' he ordered, pushing himself at my mouth.

I realised that he'd done it inside me after all, and gaped, taking him in to suck my juices from his cock and swallow them down. He spent a while in my mouth, still hard, and as he slid himself slowly in and out between my lips his hand went to my sex. I pushed back, wriggling my eager, spread cunt on his hand as he began to knead me through my panties, until I was on the brink of orgasm. He stopped, eased his cock from my mouth and climbed from the bed to look down at my helpless, sweaty body with the expression of amused contempt I was coming to both love and hate.

'That should do. I think,' he said.

'No,' I answered, 'not quite. I haven't come.'

His smile grew crueller and he reached out to tweak one straining nipple, making me jerk in my bonds.

'Do it,' I sighed. 'Make me come.'

He shook his head.

'Please?'

'I think not.'

'Please, Anton? Just rub me a little. I was nearly there!'

'I know,' he told me.

'Then make me come. Please make me come, Anton. You can't be that cruel!'

'Can't I? I rather think I can be as cruel as I please.'

I began to sob, no longer able to speak for my frustration, and at that he suddenly began to tug on his cock again. He hadn't come at all, but he was going to now, over my bound body as I lay racked with sobs and begging for release. I knew that, but I still couldn't stop myself.

'No, not that, you pig! Anton, please, just rub me off! You can spunk on my pussy and rub it in. Think how humiliated I'd be. Or in my face . . . yes, do it in my face while you rub me off. Please, Anton, please . . . I'm begging you! I'm begging you to spunk in my face, you inconsiderate bastard! Oh, for fuck's sake, Anton!'

He'd done it, all over my feet. I collapsed, limp and exhausted, and defeated too. Yet surely he would now take mercy on me?

'I have seldom met such a slut,' he remarked as he milked the last drop of sperm from his cock.

I nodded. He wiped his cock on my skirt.

'That was most amusing,' he said, 'but thirsty work.'

He poured himself another glass of Champagne, swallowed half of it, spent a moment examining the label with a critical eye and returned to the bed, where he stood over me. I looked up from hazy eyes, sure that whatever I said he would merely make it an excuse to torment me. It was better to stay silent and hope he'd grow bored with the game. He'd untie me and I could finish myself off in front of him as a final degradation.

'Champagne?' he offered.

I nodded, opening my mouth. He raised the bottle, holding it over me, and tipped with care, pouring the cool liquid into my mouth. He also splashed my face, then moved lower and poured it over my breasts. My skin was hot and taut from the binding and the Champagne felt wonderful, but it was trickling down my cleavage and around my chest, wetting the bed.

'We have to sleep in this!' I protested, but I was pushing my hips out again.

He merely shrugged and continued to spoil me, wetting my jacket and blouse, my bare tummy, my skirt and the front of my panties, a sensation so lovely it had me writhing again.

'Please, yes, with the bottle, go on, rub me off with the bottle. Oh, thank you . . . thank you so much!'

As I pleaded he pulled my panties aside and rubbed the cold, hard glass between my pussy lips. I almost came at the first touch, only to have the bottle neck moved lower, pressing to my hole, and in. He tipped it up and I groaned as I felt my cunt fill with cold Champagne. It was going to be lovely, perfect, a climax to beat all climaxes, just as soon as he put the bottle back on my clit.

'Now, do it!' I begged. 'Just do it, you pig!'

He gave the bottle a shake and I gasped as I felt my pussy swell in the sudden gush of bubbles. My muscles were burning and twitching, my hole contracting on the bottle neck and my bumhole squeezing, my whole body on a plateau of ecstasy just short of orgasm. I moaned as the bottle eased free. He let go of my panties, which snapped back just in time to receive what had been put up me, a single heavy gush that made the silk bulge and burst out around my bottom cheeks.

'Now!' I screamed and the bottle neck pressed between my lips.

'No.'

I didn't answer. I couldn't. He had to do it, but he had stepped away, and merely emptied the last inch of Champagne over my naked belly and the ropes binding my feet.

'No,' he repeated, and began to put his cock away.

I watched, shaking violently, sure he would come back to me. He didn't, but tidied himself up, taking his time as I came slowly back from the edge of ecstasy. Finally I spoke.

'You are going to make me come, aren't you?'

'No.'

'Come on, Anton, it's only fair. You've come twice! Look, I mean it. Red! Red, red, red, red!'

'I've stopped, haven't I?'

'That's not what I mean, and you know it! Come on, don't be a pig!'

He laughed.

'Oh all right, just untie me then.'

'I think not.'

'What?'

'I think I'll leave you as you are.'

'OK, the game's over, Anton.'

'Not at all,' he said as he moved towards the door. 'You like to be punished, I suspect? This is your punishment.'

'No, Anton!' I squealed, beginning to panic. 'Not really punished. Hey, don't go!'

'You deserve to be punished,' he informed me, and laughed as he opened the door. 'I am always amused when people try to manipulate me, especially when it is a pretty girl. *Ciao*.'

'What do you mean, manipulate you?' I demanded. 'You've got it all wrong!'

'I rather doubt that. I know exactly who you are, Natasha, because when you played your little gambit with the waitress I took the precaution of finding out. You're manager for that old fool Gilbert Hambling and his cabbage-eating partner, aren't you?'

'Yes, but . . . but this is starting to hurt, Anton.'

'Oh, it will be quite painful. Let us hope that teaches you a lesson.'

'OK, OK, I've been taught my lesson. Not let me go!'

'No. Good-night.'

'Anton! I'll scream. I'll call the police!'

'I doubt that. You are a respectable business woman. It would never do for the police to find you like this. However, if you are going to I suggest doing it quickly. Think how much more embarrassing it would be if they found you with those pretty panties sodden with piddle and bulging out around a pound or two of turd.'

'You bastard! Look, at least loosen the knots on my wrists so I have a chance, please? I'm begging you, Anton.'

He paused, making a doubtful face, then spoke again.

'Oh, very well, as you have provided me with such an amusing evening. I shall give you a chance.'

My bag was on a table by the door and he picked it up. Rummaging inside, he produced first my mobile, then the card on which Rhiannon had written her number.

'No, Anton!' I squeaked. 'Don't call Rhiannon!'

'I do not intend to,' he informed me. 'I intend to place the phone by your head. With a little effort and the use of your rather pert little nose you should be able to call her if you wish. Alternatively, I could send the concierge up on my way out, which was my original plan. Take your pick.'

'Neither! For goodness sake, Anton, please just untie me. I'll do anything for you, anything. I'll be your slut, to be used when you like, any way you like—'

He cut me off with a brusque laugh, then spoke again as he laid my mobile beside my head.

'Really, once you were free? I doubt it. I advise against playing games with me, Natasha, because you will always find me one move ahead. Now goodnight ... oh, and incidentally, the Champagne, it was excellent. But I have signed a contract with Southern and Allied to talk up their prestige cuvée, with a nice fat bonus when the price rises above that of Cristal.'

He returned to the door, gave me one last flutter of his fingers and left. I was cursing and sobbing, but a little voice in the back of my head was telling me that he was only playing with me. Obviously he had realised that I'd been trying to manipulate him, and what I'd been put through was a very real punishment, but he would come back. He had to.

I lay still, trying hard to control both my body and my emotions. My muscles ached and I was sticky with Champagne and spunk and my own juices, but it was harder to get over the turmoil in my head. He'd well and truly messed my mind up, and it wasn't over. I could ring Rhiannon and beg for help, or yell for Jean-Marc. Maybe Jean-Marc was about to come up anyway, if Anton had tipped him off, but then Anton himself had to be coming back. Soon I was sobbing, despite all my efforts at self-control, and I kept remembering what Anton had said about me wetting and soiling myself. I'd drunk a lot and my bladder was already beginning to ache. If I let go I'd pee all over the floor, while my panties were so taut over my bum that if I messed myself most of it would come out at the sides. I could not be found in that state, I simply could not.

The choice was Jean-Marc or Rhiannon. I didn't mind Jean-Marc seeing me the way I was, and no doubt he'd expect some dirty reward for releasing me, but I could cope with that. Possibly he'd even take advantage of me first, but he would untie me in the end. Unfortunately I was on the third floor and if Anton hadn't told Jean-Marc about me I'd have to scream the hotel down to attract attention. The door wasn't locked, so it was more than likely that I'd have an audience of several dozen assorted tourists and businessmen admiring my soiled, helpless body before I was set free.

To be rescued by Rhiannon would be more embarrassing than Jean-Marc. I'd had sex with him, and, while I was sure she'd been tempted, she had turned me down. On the other hand she was a woman and wasn't going to fuck me or violate my bottom before she untied me. Also, she would be able to come up to my room without drawing the attention of half Paris. She was the best choice.

I twisted my head around to press my nose to my mobile phone.

Five

My rescue was hideously embarrassing, but it could have been worse. By good luck, Rhiannon was drinking in a bar just a few streets away. She came immediately and, while she was shocked by the state I was in, I managed to blame the more perverted details on Anton, which was pretty much the truth. We were still trying to clean up the mess when he came back, having intended to leave me for two hours, probably long enough for me to wet myself. I had the satisfaction of surprising him, because he hadn't thought I'd dare call Rhiannon, and also of telling him to fuck off in no uncertain terms. Unfortunately I was too exhausted and stressed to take advantage of her curiosity about my behaviour.

I spent the whole of the following day either plotting revenge or masturbating myself sore over what had happened. Even as I came I would be cursing Anton, but I couldn't stop myself, and after my eighth orgasm I realised that I was obsessed with him and that it would take weeks or even months to move on. That happens to me sometimes, but I've come to understand that it doesn't mean I genuinely love the person involved, or even like them. I was definitely not going to give Anton the satisfaction of knowing what he'd done, let alone call him to take advantage of the fact. He'd had more than enough from me.

He'd also made it abundantly clear that he was not willing to help me promote the Hambling and Borse wines. To judge by what he'd said, he only praised the famous names and those who paid him, which was infuriating. If I'd known the bastard was corrupt I'd have offered him a bribe in the first place and saved myself a great deal of trouble. I did wonder if it would be possible to expose him as a fraud, but with no proof it would be his word against mine and I could see who'd come off worse. It would do me no good, and I had now lost my two best chances of bringing my wines up to astronomical prices.

I wasn't at all sure what to do next, and it was only my native obstinacy that prevented me from abandoning the whole thing and staying in Paris for a go at seducing Rhiannon. She was obviously intrigued but too shy simply to be taken to bed, so it would need time. Unfortunately I couldn't even close my eyes without seeing Anton Yoshida's smug grin, and besides, a lot of people were going to be disappointed in me if I backed out, including Percy. So I contented myself with buying Rhiannon an enormous bunch of flowers and headed back to London.

Another reason for leaving was that the vintage looked like being a disaster. The wet summer had left most of the French vineyards badly affected by mildew, with Bordeaux the worst hit region. How Anton was going to cope with that I had no idea, but I was certainly not going to follow him around the country from one group of depressed *vignerons* to the next. The prices of older wines were likely to rise, and it was just possible I'd be able to bring our 2005 clarets to the attention of the public without the help of either Earle Hayes or Anton Yoshida.

Lastly, there was the message Gilbert Hambling had sent, asking for a report on my progress. In the circumstances there wasn't a great deal I could say, as all I'd really managed to do was get heartily abused. I assured him I'd be in London on Monday, and as I sat on the Eurostar I was trying to work out how to put the best spin on events. By the following morning I'd decided that the best I could do was show that I hadn't been wasting my time and propose a tasting aimed at investors hoping to capitalise on the probable price rises for recent good vintages.

I dressed in another of my smart new skirt suits, only fractionally less fine than the one Anton Yoshida had put in urgent need of a trip to the dry cleaners. Just knowing how smart I looked helped to keep me feeling efficient and in control, and my mood was positively bullish as I got out of the cab in St James's and clip-clopped my way across to the building. Gilbert was alone in his office, seated behind the enormous desk. His jowls lifted into a smile as he saw me.

'Ah, Natasha, there you are,' he greeted me. 'Do take a seat. Coffee? No? Well then, how are you doing? I confess that I had expected you to spend a little more time in the office.'

'There's not really much I can do here,' I told him. 'I need to get out and meet people. So far I've had two offers for the company, both quite generous but unsuitable.'

'Ah ha! And who were these from?'

'You'd probably prefer not to know.'

'Not at all.'

'If you insist. One from a company called Orpheus Asset Management, and the other from Earle Hayes.'

'Hum . . . I see what you mean. Still, good work.'

'A good start at least, I like to think,' I lied. 'I also need to arrange a tasting.'

'The Hambling and Borse tasting is in November, at the Aviators Club.'

'Then we can have two, although the Aviators would be an excellent venue.'

'Two?'

'Yes. The one I'm planning is rather different, you see. The thing is, the Bordeaux vintage looks as if it's going to fail.'

'So I hear.'

'In which case we're in an excellent position to benefit from our stocks of older wines, particularly the '05s and '06s, which are sure to appeal to investors and . . .'

'Investors? Natasha, we at Hambling and Borse do not sell wine as an investment. We sell it to drink.'

'Yes, of course, normally, and I agree with the principle, but in the circumstances—'

'I'm sorry, my dear, but that is out of the question.'

I drew my breath in, trying to be calm, but it was beginning to feel as if everything I did blew up in my face.

'We need to increase our income,' I said carefully, 'also to raise our profile among those who're prepared to pay high prices.'

'I am fully aware of that, Natasha,' he responded, 'and yet we have commitments to our regular customers.'

'Who are buying at well below market prices in some instances. At the very least we need to raise our Bordeaux prices by fifty per cent, and a hundred or more for some of the reserved stock.'

'We couldn't possibly!'

'If we don't we're going to end up being pulled into little pieces by Orpheus Asset Mangement or somebody similar. You know what they want to do, don't you? They want to buy the Hambling and Borse name and sell it to a supermarket to be used for their premium brands.'

'Good God!'

'Exactly, so we need to act. Let me show ten or a dozen different Bordeaux and a few of our agencies from other regions, that's all.'

'But our regular customers . . .'

'We'll bring in cheaper wines to fill the gap.'

'What? Absolutely not! It would ruin our reputation.'

'You won't have a reputation to ruin if you don't get your act together, you obstinate old goat!'

I'd tried to stop myself even as the words came out of my mouth, but I'd said them and Gilbert was going slowly purple.

'Sorry,' I managed, my temper draining away on the instant, 'but I'm only trying to help.'

'By calling me an old goat?' he demanded. 'I think you should mind your language, young lady, or those knickers of yours may have to come down again.'

'Sorry,' I repeated. 'That was rude of me, but I'm serious.'

'So am I, I assure you.'

'No, look . . . I . . .'

He certainly sounded serious, and I stopped in confusion, genuinely outraged by the thought of a proper spanking, but with my nipples instantly stiff and my pussy tight. I took a deep breath, forcing myself to think clearly before I began again.

'I was rude, and you would be right to spank me, but we really do need to resolve this. At least let me use my contacts to try and bring in some new clients for a tasting, and auction some of our surplus Bordeaux afterwards? Please, and I promise I won't mention investment.'

He paused to consider, frowning. All I'd really done was rephrase my suggestion, and I was fairly sure he knew that I'd still be inviting potential investors.

Suddenly I felt immense sympathy for him, as an ageing man struggling to preserve values almost everybody else had rejected, in terms of both business practice and the right to smack naughty girls' bottoms when he felt it necessary. At last he replied.

'Very well, so long as you assure me you will do nothing to bring the name of the company into disrepute.'

'Thank you,' I said, and meant it.

'Perhaps you'd care for a drink at the Aviators and we can arrange matters? I've been meaning to introduce you to some of the boys anyway.'

'Yes, thank you. Should I give my expenses to Melanie, or would you like to look them over?'

'I'm sure they're fine, but I'll pass them along to her if you like.'

I dug the invoice and the envelope with my receipts in it out of my bag and passed them across. He gave them a casual glance, then did a double-take, his eyes widening slowly as he took in my figures. I managed a weak smile.

'I don't mean to be critical, Natasha,' he said, 'but this does seem rather a lot. Two thousand five hundred Euros for a skirt suit? One hundred and ninety Euros for a set of underwear?'

'I don't mind bearing a proportion of it,' I assured him hastily, 'especially the clothes, but believe me it was money well spent.'

'On underwear?'

I shrugged, blushing. He shook his head and continued to scan the list, only for the expression on his face to change abruptly, from irritation to pleasure.

'Of course, yes, the classic situation,' he said, 'although while I appreciate that you like to have something to receive your punishments for, you needn't go quite so far for the sake of verisimilitude. Nevertheless, you do have excellent timing.'

I wasn't at all sure what he was talking about, except that he was obviously going to use my profligacy as another excuse to punish me. He put the papers down on his desk and rubbed his hands together, now beaming with delight. My initial puzzlement had begun to give way and I bit my lip, feeling distinctly embarrassed and more than a little sorry for myself. I'd come in feeling brisk and businesslike, and now it looked as if I'd be having my knickers taken down for another spanking, because that was undoubtedly what he thought I was angling for. It was not what I'd been expecting, not at that moment, and I felt awkward and slightly ridiculous. I wondered if I could back down gracefully.

'Maybe another . . .,' I began, only to stop.

He had reached into his drawer and pulled something out, a magazine, which he tossed casually on to the desk. I thought it would be a copy of *Corkscrew* or something like that, and it took me a moment to realise what the plump gentleman in a dinner jacket and an orange waistcoat on the cover was doing. Rather than addressing a tasting or showing off his cellar, he was attending to a pretty girl in school uniform, with her gymslip already turned up as he pulled down her knickers. It was abundantly obvious what he intended to do with her, as the magazine was *Kane* and he was holding one.

'Oh,' I said as my stomach began to churn. 'Look, Gilbert . . . Mr Hambling, I thought maybe another spanking, some time, maybe, but the cane really hurts!'

'Is that not the idea?' he asked. 'And indeed, is that not what you deserve?'

'No! Well . . . perhaps, but I really . . .'

I trailed off, feeling thoroughly sorry for myself and on the edge of telling him it just wasn't going to happen. Yet ever since he'd spanked me I'd wanted it again, and I knew that to turn him down would ruin the sense of his authority over me, which was what had made it special. He nodded, perhaps aware of my conflicting emotions and certainly enjoying my discomfort. I also knew I'd be OK once my bum was warm.

'Oh, all right,' I said miserably, 'but you're to spank me first, and not to use the cane until I'm quite pink.'

I was pouting furiously as I went to the desk, where I leant forward, resting my arms on its surface with my bottom pushed out behind. He watched, one corner of his big, loose mouth twitching with amusement, admiring the shape of my body but making no move to take my punishment any further. It was I who spoke first.

'Well? Aren't you going to spank me?'

'Yes,' he told me, 'but not yet. No, no, don't get up, I prefer you in that position.'

He'd set me blushing again, hotter than before, but I did as I was told, bending over with my bum up in spanking position. He pushed the copy of *Kane* under my nose.

'The fellow on the cover is a member of the Aviators,' he informed me. 'One of the idle rich who need not be concerned with concealing his peccadilloes. He particularly wants to meet you, as do one or two others, so if you are willing I'll call ahead and engage a private room?'

The implication was clear. If I went over to the Aviators I would be lunching in private with a group of lecherous old bastards who not only knew that I received corporal punishment but almost certainly fancied a turn at dishing it out. At the very least I'd be spanked in front of them, maybe passed around from lap to lap, then caned. I found myself nodding.

'Splendid!' he declared. 'A moment, if you please.'

He made a call, and meanwhile I remained in position. I was imagining the coming exposure of my bottom and my beating, now with rising excitement but still a great deal of embarrassment. He made me feel small and vulnerable, wonderful sensations in their place and ones I'd rarely experienced in recent years. When he put the phone down he extended his hand and I took it, allowing him to lead me from the room like a puppy on her master's lead.

At the door he let go, and we left the building like any other pair of business associates making their way to lunch. There were plenty of people about, and it felt strange to think of them going about their daily routines, all unaware than one among them was being taken to have her bare bottom smacked in front of a bunch of dirty old men.

The thought was enough to keep me warm all the way to the club. Not that it was very far, only in King Street, where it was housed in a great square grey-stone building four storeys high that projected an air of gravitas and maturity. The doorman was in full livery, an old boy with a military air whose disapproving scowl vanished as he saw Gilbert. I was given a rather different look, as if to say that while I was allowed in with my chaperone I had better behave myself.

I returned a cheeky smile, determined not to let the atmosphere of masculine dignity oppress me, and deliberately clicked my heels on the polished wooden floor as we crossed to a desk where another commissionaire stood. He too was polite to Gilbert but gave me a look that suggested he knew exactly what I was up to, setting me blushing despite myself.

Stairs ascended beside the desk and I hurried up them, keen to escape the knowing glances from behind. All I succeeded in doing was making my boobs bounce and giving the man a prime view of my bottom wiggling beneath my skirt, and I was sure I heard a chuckle as I passed out of his sight. I had to wait for Gilbert on the landing, but took his arm as we continued upstairs, which made me feel protected though still a woman in a man's environment, and a slut at that.

We climbed to the fourth floor, where a landing ran round the stairwell, with doors on every side. Gilbert selected one of them and admitted me to a room looking out over the mews at the rear of the building. The walls were panelled in oak and hung with the portraits of various long-dead imperialists; the carpet was deep and bore a dignified pattern of brown and old gold. The furniture consisted of a single table under the window and a ring of chairs, on each of which sat a man. Some were short, some tall, some fat, some thin, but every one of them was over fifty and dressed in a fashion that suggested old money. A school cane lay on the table.

I'd been expecting to be taken in and left alone to dwell on what was about to happen to me, while Gilbert assembled the troops, so I was more than a little taken aback to find them ready and waiting. One notably fat gentleman with a huge gingery-white moustache even had a clothes-brush in his hand, its purpose all too obvious. That could only mean that Gilbert had been sufficiently confident of my acquiescence to inform his friends in advance. Maybe the commissionaire downstairs was in the know, too.

He was – because at this point he came in behind us. I stood gaping at my reception committee with my face burning and no doubt the colour of a beetroot. Otto Borse was there, looking smug, but I didn't recognise anybody else. I didn't need to. Their self-satisfied, somewhat predatory expressions revealed confidence and hunger – enough of both for me to be sure they wouldn't feel we needed to be introduced before my panties were pulled down in front of them. Gilbert, always the gentleman, did the honours anyway, naming each of them as I stood there blushing and fidgeting in the middle of the carpet. Only one name sank in properly, that of the man with the ridiculous moustache and the clothes-brush: the Right Honourable Vernon Flyght, chairman of the club committee and therefore, by order of precedence, the first one to spank me. The clothes-brush was a huge old-fashioned thing with a handle and I found myself biting my lip and whining in protest.

'Not first, please! That will really sting, and you promised to warm me up!'

The Right Honourable Vernon Flyght gave a cluck of amusement.

'It is intended to warm you up, my dear,' he assured me, 'but don't fret. You're not the first little filly I've had across my knee by a very long way and I know just how to handle you. So does everybody else in this room.'

'Everybody else? I thought I was going to get a warm-up spanking and then the cane?'

'So you shall, my dear, but surely you can see that it would be unfair to deprive any one of us of the pleasure of your bottom?'

'But there are fourteen of you!'

'Fifteen. Stubbs will want his turn, naturally.'

I turned round to see the commissionaire standing with his back to the door, grinning at me. My mouth opened to protest, closed again, opened again and finally closed as I realised that I probably looked like a goldfish trying to gulp in air. Gilbert finally broke the silence.

'Now come along, Natasha, pop your knickers down and bottom up for the boys, eh?'

I nodded weakly and reached up under my skirt to tug my expensive silk panties down over my hips and bottom. That was as far as I intended them to go, so that I could at least walk over to Vernon Flyght with a little dignity instead of shuffling along with my knickers around my knees. Unfortunately they fell down, all the way to my ankles and as I stepped forward one of my heels caught in the fabric. I tripped and staggered forward to sprawl across his lap, and it was only because he was such a fat bastard that he and the chair didn't go over backwards. I was left at an angle across his lap, bum high and knees apart, with my ankles trapped in the tangle of my panties.

It couldn't have been a much more humiliating position, and they all had a good laugh at my expense, while Vernon gripped me round the waist to prevent me getting into a less undignified pose. My face was burning hotter than before. He didn't give me a chance to ready myself for my exposure, but simply lifted the tails of my jacket and blouse, then tugged my skirt up to lay my bottom bare for all to see. I'm not in the least bit overweight, but for some reason my bottom always feels huge when I'm over some man's knee and stripped behind – a fat, pink, wobbling ball of girl-flesh, thoroughly rude and in this case made ruder still because he'd got my knees cocked apart and my pussy and bumhole were already on show.

I wasn't ready at all but, as I twisted round to beg him to let me at least get into position properly, I saw the clothes-brush raised over my bum, which he was admiring as if he'd been fasting for a week and I was a piece of sirloin steak.

'No, please!' I squeaked. 'You said you'd warm me up!'

'So I shall,' he assured me, and brought the brush down across my cheeks.

It wasn't hard at all, barely even a smack. He simply pressed the wood to the turn of my cheeks and began to wobble them, pulling my flesh this way and that to make my already open pussy spread and my bumhole stretch. There was more laughter at the sight and I immediately began to sob with humiliation at the view I was giving them, which I could picture all too clearly in my head: the full spread of my naked cheeks, my thighs open, my fancy knickers in a tangle around my ankles, my freshly shaved pussy pink and bare and already moist, the pale brown ring of my bumhole on blatant display and winking to show off the wet red centre.

'Pig!' I managed, but only earned myself a smack of the brush that made me gasp.

I thought my spanking had begun, but he hadn't finished playing with me. Turning the brush over, he began to use it on me as if I'd still had my skirt in place and he'd been removing some fluff. The bristles were quite stiff, and they tickled and stung at the same time, getting me giggling helplessly and wriggling my feet in my panties. They all thought that was hilarious, clapping and encouraging him, although one or two were telling him to get on with spanking me so that they could take their own turns.

'There is no hurry, gentlemen,' he assured them. 'I believe we have her for as long as we please. Is that not so, Gilbert?'

'Absolutely,' Gilbert assured him. 'Take as long as you like. I certainly intend to.'

'What about me?' I demanded. 'I can only take so much, you know!'

'Rest assured that you are in the hands of experts,' Gilbert responded.

I shook my head, far from convinced. Vernon had put the clothes-brush down on my back and had begun to feel me up instead, cocking his knee up to lift my bottom for his inspection and leaning forward to peer between my cheeks. I hung my head, breathing deeply, and surrendered to him as he fondled me, taking his time to enjoy the feel of my cheeks and to inspect my anus and cunt. Even when he put a finger in, all I could manage was a whimper of protest that sounded like pleasure. At that he gave a knowing little chuckle and slid a second finger in beside the first, opening me wide and finally bringing my resentment to the boil.

'I only volunteered for a spanking,' I pointed out. 'And the cane. You're taking liberties.'

'You wanted to be warm, didn't you?' he asked reasonably, and his thumb found my clit.

My sarcastic answer turned into a gasp as he began to masturbate me, rubbing right on my bump, with his fingers pushing in and out of my open hole. I struggled to drive the pleasure out of my head, but I couldn't do it and gave in, slumped spread on his knee, panting out my ecstasy in front of them all. Soon I was wriggling my bottom and rubbing against him, and at that he picked up the clothes-brush with his free hand and began to spank.

It stung like mad, but I was already too high to resist, merely wriggling a bit harder for a moment before pushing my bottom up for more. I was going to come, but it had all been so sudden that my body had left my mind behind, so that I was painfully aware of just how unspeakably lewd I looked even as my pussy hole began to contract on his fingers. He was spanking hard too, making my cheeks dance and setting my feet kicking in my panties in a final, pained flurry before the climax hit me. I screamed, in ecstasy but no less with an overwhelming sense of embarrassment that left me snivelling and limp when he finally stopped.

'Up we get,' he said gently, giving my bottom a gentle pat.

I couldn't do it immediately – my reaction had just been too strong – and when I did I was shaking and unsteady. He was grinning, both amused and aroused, which was no surprise. The air was thick with the scent of my pussy, while I was a dishevelled mess, my skirt still up but my tails hanging down so that just the turn of my now red bottom cheeks was peeping out beneath, my pussy showing at the front and my panties in a puddle around my feet. He'd broken my resistance, leaving me confused and a little dizzy but compliant. When the man next to him patted his lap I went straight over, sticking my bottom up for spanking without a second thought. He began immediately, talking as he slapped my cheeks, striking upwards to make them spread and quiver.

'Quite the little tart, isn't she, Gilbert? You said she was willing, but I'd have expected at least some resistance.'

'Percy Ottershaw trained her,' Gilbert answered. 'He's something of an expert.'

'So it seems,' another man put in. 'He's certainly done an excellent job with this one.'

A fourth man was more critical. 'She's obedient, yes, but I prefer them to put up a bit of a fight myself.'

'Old Percy spanked that out of her years ago, apparently,' Gilbert put in.

'That's a shame. I love to break them in.'

'There's something in that, of course, but there's a lot to be said for a knowing tart.'

'I agree with Clive. It's best when they put up a fight.'

'Especially if they try to keep their knickers up. This one just dropped them to order.'

Light laughter greeted this final remark. All the while I was being spanked, my bottom bouncing to hard, rhythmic smacks that were bringing the heat to my cheeks with a vengeance. Every word made my sense of humiliation more bitter, until I began to sob and shake, at which the spanking stopped.

'Is she all right, d'you think?' the man who was holding me asked.

I nodded, unable to take the chance to escape. He stopped anyway, releasing me and sending me on my way with a final pat to my now hot bottom. My knickers were in the way and I stepped out of them as I went to the next man, climbing obediently across his knees with my bottom well lifted to allow him to readjust my clothes to get me fully bare. I waited as my skirt was tucked into its own waistband and the tails of both my jacket and blouse wedged underneath, then I settled into spanking position. But he wasn't finished.

'Aren't we forgetting something, gentlemen?' he remarked, and his finger moved to my blouse.

I pouted resentfully as my buttons were opened and my bra flipped up to leave my boobs dangling for all to see. I know my bottom has to be bare for punishment – that's inevitable – but there always seems to be some bastard who wants to strip my tits as well, and because they're big they jiggle and bounce while I'm smacked, which is hideously embarrassing. He had a good feel too, stroking and squeezing my boobs even as he began to spank me. My nipples were stiff and sensitive after my orgasm, and he began to pull at them as if he was trying to milk me, adding to my shame and confusion.

'A delight,' he said after a moment. 'I don't suppose you'd care for a job as a maid, my dear? Topless, naturally, but the salary would reflect your extra duties.'

'No,' I retorted, with very real indignation, but he simply laughed and began to spank me harder.

The next man was worse, cold and harsh, spanking me hard and full across my cheeks as if he was really punishing a naughty girl rather than enjoying a willingly offered bottom. I wondered if that was what he was used to, and whether the position I was in had previously been occupied by his wife or even daughters. He certainly did it well, leaving me rubbing my cheeks and shifting from foot to foot when I was finally allowed up from his lap.

There was no respite. I was taken down by the next man, the one who'd been on the cover of *Kane*, who was another groper; then the next, who spread my thighs so that every single one of them had a prime view of my open cunt. I no longer cared, dizzy and shaking as I was passed from lap to lap, my bottom smacked and stroked, pinched and fondled, my boobs molested and even slapped, my pussy fingered and my bumhole tickled and teased. By the time I got to the commissionaire I was so juicy that I was slippery between my thighs and my stocking tops were wet.

He was much rougher, bundling me over his knee and spanking so hard that he got me kicking again, and squealing too. By the time he'd finished I was gasping for breath and so weak-legged I could barely stand. But there was no mercy. Gilbert looked me in the eye and pointed to the table on which the cane had been laid.

'Bend over,' he instructed. 'Feet apart, back well in.'

I knew the drill and adopted a position that not only left me completely vulnerable to the cane but flaunted every detail of my rear view. My legs were shaking terribly, and I had to rest my upper body on the table, even though it meant my tits were squashed out on the cold, hard wood. The cane was directly under my nose.

Behind me the men were enjoying the view, those on either side adjusting their chairs to make sure they could see right between my legs. It's a rare man who can beat a girl without also wanting to rob her of every last scrap of modesty by looking at what he's made her show.

'Perhaps you would care to do the honours, Stubbs?' the Right Honourable Vernon Flyght suggested. 'Unless you prefer to insist on your privilege as her owner, Gilbert?'

'No, no, not at all,' Gilbert assured him. 'With the cane it's often better to watch than to wield. Besides, I can do it whenever I wish.'

'Owner?' I queried, but they ignored me.

The commissionaire came forward and picked up the cane. It was an ordinary school cane, long and brown and wicked, with a crook handle, and capable, as I knew from bitter experience, of inflicting a great deal of pain. My bottom cheeks tightened as he got behind me, and again as the thin, hard rod was tapped on my flesh.

'Six of the best,' Gilbert instructed, 'but good and hard.'

'Yes, sir,' Stubbs responded, and lifted the cane.

My cheeks squeezed tight again as I looked back. His face was stern, purposeful, with just a hint of malice; after the way he'd spanked me I knew better than to expect any mercy. He was a sadistic bastard too, holding the cane high above my bottom until I'd begun to sob in frustration and only then bringing it down. I heard the swish and the crack of wood on my bare flesh, felt the impact, then the sting, so painful it had me gasping again and jumping up and down on my toes to set my bottom jiggling.

Several of the men laughed at what admittedly must have been a ridiculous sight, and I forced myself to get back in position. The cut across my bottom was already burning and I knew I'd be badly welted, so badly that it would be two or three weeks before I could go to a spa or show my bum without making it obvious what had been done to me. I imagined the humiliation of having my caned bottom inspected by giggling girls or having some disapproving matron realise that I'd been punished.

I stuck my bottom out, half eager, half scared. Stubbs lashed the cane down again, drawing a second line of fire across my cheeks and once more setting me gasping and dancing on my toes. It hurt enough to make me wonder what the hell I was doing offering myself to the evil old bastard, but I soon had my bottom stuck out again. The third cut was harder still, leaving me sobbing and shaking my head, with tears starting in my eyes. Still I pushed my bottom high as soon as I could, trembling with fear even as I offered myself.

'By God, I'd like to fuck her,' one of them growled, distracting me at exactly the wrong moment so that the fourth stroke caught me off guard.

That broke me. It was just so unfair, to be beaten in front of them with my bottom flaunted naked, every detail of my wet, ready cunt open for their inspection, and not one of them with so much as his tie undone. I wondered if Stubbs would fuck me, sticking his cock up my hole from behind, not to pleasure me, not even for his own enjoyment, but to give the ring of dirty old bastards watching us something to toss over later. I burst into tears, imaging how it would feel to be fucked for their amusement, with Stubbs's cock up me and his paunch slapping against my caned and spanked bottom as he thrust into me.

Still I held my pose, and they were too high on my pain and exposure to worry about my tears. Again Stubbs brought the cane down across my bottom and again I jerked and squealed, kicking and jiggling my bum. I was going to get it, I had to, my cunt filled with cock by the man who'd beaten me, by the man who'd earned the right to use me as he pleased. Maybe he'd even put it up my bum. Maybe they'd all have me, turn and turn about in all three orifices until I was dribbling spunk and sore.

I thrust my bottom out as high as I could, deliberately showing off as Stubbs measured up for the sixth and final stroke. It came down across the fattest part of my cheeks, biting into my flesh and sending a jolt to my pussy not so very far from orgasm. I was done, well and truly beaten, my bottom on fire, my pussy agape, my bumhole pulsing lewdly between my reddened cheeks. They could do as they liked: fuck me, bugger me, make me suck their dirty old cocks one by one and spunk in my face.

'There we are, my dear,' Gilbert remarked, 'all done, unless . . .'

He left the question unfinished, but there was no mistaking his meaning. I nodded urgently as I got to my feet, still ashamed of myself but needing it too badly to back down. One of the men gave a dirty little chuckle.

'Into the cupboard with her then,' Vernon announced.

Vernon's words left my puzzled. Surely I wasn't going to be tied up and left again? Stubbs had put down the cane and crossed the room to slide back a panel I hadn't realised was any different from the others. It closed off a sort of janitor's cupboard, full of junk and cleaning utensils, but with a single chair positioned so that a man could sit in comfort with a clear space in front of him, a clear space just large enough for a girl to kneel while she gave a blowjob. They'd even put down a piece of carpet.

'I'm not the first, am I?' I asked.

'By no means,' Vernon assured me, 'although you will be the first to go in there without financial inducement.'

I managed a wry smile, reflecting what a slut I was to go willingly when other girls had had to be paid. There was a mirror among the portraits and I turned my back to it, trembling harder than ever as I inspected my bottom. He'd caned me beautifully, laying six neatly spaced double welts across my bottom flesh, which was flushed an even pink from my spankings. Now I was going to suck cock for the men who'd beaten me – maybe more, maybe all fifteen of them.

'Come along, in you go,' one of them said, and reached out to apply a firm pat to my bottom.

Again I smiled, struggling to show how in control I was, and as I walked to the cupboard I deliberately wiggled my hips to taunt them. I was deceiving myself. They were in control, because they'd beaten me so well that I wanted to be used in any way they pleased. I was obviously expected to do it kneeling too, but that felt right, and I got down on the little square of thick carpet without demur.

Vernon made a polite gesture to Gilbert, who joined me in the cupboard and slid the door shut. There was no window but a small ventilator set high in the wall, through which dirty grey light filtered down, illuminating the pale shape of his cock and balls as he flopped them out of his trousers. Evidently there was to be no preamble. I would be treated just like the girls they paid, expected to do as I was told without making a fuss.

I took him in, his cock already half stiff from spanking me and watching me beaten. Through the haze of my arousal I was aware that not only was I sucking cock for a man who'd just punished me, but also that he was my boss. That was something I'd never done before, because I'd never really had a boss, and it was nice. I wondered how many girls ended up on their knees with their boss's cock in their mouths, and how many got spanked first. Not many, I imagined, not nowadays, but it was just the fantasy I needed.

He was rapidly growing hard, and he had a nice cock, quite big and pale with a fat, kissable head and big balls that just cried out to be licked. I obliged myself, masturbating while I flicked my tongue over the taut, wrinkly skin of his scrotum and rubbed my face against him. There was a long queue waiting for my attention, but I was not going to rush. I wanted to savour all fifteen cocks and to masturbate while I did it, making myself come.

My hand was between my thighs before he was even fully erect, rubbing in my wet slit as I revelled in the delicious shame of being made to go bare-bottom over men's laps, being spanked, then made to suck off the very same men. I imagined having no choice, surrendering first my bottom and then my mouth to some bastard because he'd sack me if I didn't give in. He'd fuck me too, over his desk with my hot red bottom cheeks parted to show off my bumhole and the mouth of my cunt as his erection slid in and out. I'd be given to his friends and clients, used to sweeten business deals and brighten up dull afternoons in the office. He'd make me wear tarty underwear or none at all, have me sit with my skirt pulled up while I took dictation, make me wear a plug in my bumhole to keep me ready for buggering, force me to bend over in front of his friends and show it off, make me suck on it while they took turns to fuck me up my arse . . .

Gilbert came in my mouth, a great gush of spunk that I struggled to swallow, my cheeks bulging as he held himself in deep to make sure I couldn't pull back before he'd finished. It left me gasping, with a trail of spunk and saliva running down my chin, which I hastily licked up as he tilted my chin and looked down at me. I was still rubbing, right on the edge of orgasm, but he didn't seem to realise, contenting himself with a gentle kiss on the tip of my nose before sitting back to put his cock away.

I slowed down, eager to come with a cock in my mouth. Gilbert left and Vernon replaced him, treating me with the same casual disdain, cock flopped out and into my mouth with barely a word of greeting. Like Gilbert he was half stiff, but I was now urgent, sliding my mouth up and down to get him erect as I rubbed myself and once more returned to my fantasy. Now I was bent over my boss's desk, my skirt and tails turned up to show off my bare bottom, the base of my butt plug sticking out obscenely from between my cheeks. There'd be six of them, clients, laughing at me as my boss eased the thick plug in and out of my gaping bumhole, and louder as it was extracted and put in my mouth.

That was just too rude not to come over, but I held the image in my head as I gobbled eagerly on Vernon's now rigid cock: myself in my smart little secretary's suit, my bottom stripped and spread, my anus agape and about to be plugged with my boss's cock, six men laughing at my unbearable humiliation as my mouth gaped to take in a plug drawn straight from my rectum, the taste thick in my senses as I began to suck. Vernon whipped his cock free just as my pussy began to go into contraction and jerked furiously at his shaft as I shut my eyes to focus properly on the awful degradation I was wishing for. My orgasm was long and hard, every sensation magnified: the feel of my fingers on my pussy, my burning clit, the heat of my smacked and welted bottom, a wet, stickiness on my skin. I'd come, and so had the Right Honourable Vernon Flyght, all over my face.

Most of it was over one eye, which I didn't dare open, but at least he had the decency to offer me a handkerchief to mop up with. By the time I'd finished he'd gone, to be promptly replaced by Otto Borse. I'd come twice and my pussy had begun to get sore but I was still high and took him in willingly enough. He was even bigger than Gilbert, with a thick, meaty foreskin and great hairy balls that tickled my nose as I tried to get him right in. He was nice about it, stroking my hair as I sucked, and firm only when it came to holding me in place to make sure I swallowed.

He was my third. I couldn't even remember the name of the fourth, but he was very controlling, holding me by my hair and making me purse my lips so that he could fuck the bud of my mouth. Like Gilbert and Otto he made me swallow, and so did most of the others, with just a couple doing it in my face or insisting I hold my mouth open to be spunked in. I took it all like a good little slut, meek and obedient, while my excitement gradually rose once more. When one of them told me he was going to masturbate over my smacked bottom I climbed up on the chair without hesitation, kneeling for him and helping him toss until he spattered my cheeks with spunk.

I'd been ready for fucking from the start, but blowjobs seemed to be the order of the day, and it was only Stubbs who really took advantage. By then my fingers were back between my legs and I was masturbating as he came in. His cock was flaccid and tasted oily, and he sat on the very edge of the chair so that he could grope my tits while I got him erect. That made me feel dirty and eager. I couldn't help but remember that he was the one who'd actually applied the cane to my bottom, and I could happily have got off on that, but he wanted more.

'Dirty little tart, aren't you?' he grunted, squeezing my tits.

My mouth was full of cock but I nodded.

'You'll do anything, won't you, now we've got you feeling good and dirty?'

Again I nodded, wondering what he had in mind for me.

'I bet you'd even lick my arse?'

This time I hesitated, in very real disgust, but he was right. I did feel dirty, deliciously dirty. Pulling back from his cock, I answered him.

'You filthy bastard. Go on then, make me.'

His response was a nasty, dry snigger, full of contempt as much as lust. I rocked back on my heels, scarcely able to accept what I'd just volunteered for but unable to resist. He stood up and as he unfastened his trousers I was trying to make excuses, telling myself that I was only doing it because I'd been told to be a good girl, that if I refused he'd force me, that I was just being kind to an old man who might never have the chance to enjoy a woman like me again – anything rather than admit that I actually wanted to push my tongue in between his buttocks and lick.

I could only see him faintly as he pushed his trousers and underpants down around his ankles before flopping back into the chair. He lifted one leg free of his trousers and underpants, then hesitated, reached out to a nearby shelf, and passed something to me.

'Stick that up yourself, why don't you?'

My hand closed on something round, smooth and hard, which I could just make out as the handle of a brush, the sort that goes with a pan. To have to stick it up my hole while I licked was a gloriously dirty thought and I didn't hesitate, reaching back to ease it in up my sloppy pussy. Being penetrated felt good, and I was only sorry there wasn't another one to go in up my bum at the same time. I used my finger instead, squatting down to push the brush against the floor as I tickled the little wet hole between my cheeks.

'Get licking,' he ordered as he pulled his legs up to spread his buttocks.

'You have to make me,' I told him, my voice hoarse.

'Awkward bitch!' he answered, and reached out.

He grabbed my hair and I squeaked as I was hauled in. I fought back, struggling to stop it happening, because I was determined that if I did it he would really have to make me. His slit was matted with hair, clammy and pungent with a male smell strong enough to make me gag as I was pulled closer. I was close to panic, but still wriggling my penetrated cunt on the brush handle, needing what was going to be done to me, but only under his control.

I got it, my face pulled hard between his buttocks and rubbed from side to side to make his slit open. His coarse anal hair was rubbing on my nose and lips and his smell almost overwhelming, but I kept my mouth firmly shut, wanting him to talk to me.

'Lick!' he ordered. 'Lick my fucking arse, you stuck-up little bitch.'

That was better. My tongue poked out to find the large, blubbery star of his anal ring, and to lick. He gave a groan of satisfaction and began to wank, his balls slapping in my face as I flicked my tongue over the crevices and bumps of his anus, struggling with the acrid taste and the bits of hair in my mouth but unable to stop myself, and not only because he had his hand twisted tight into my hair.

It was the final, unspeakable degradation, to end up licking the commissionaire's anus after everything else I'd been put through, and my hands went straight back between my thighs to frig and to tease my bumhole open. I no longer needed fantasy, because what I was getting was dirty enough: my tits swinging, naked and sweaty; my bottom stuck out, red with spanking and welted from the cane; my anus a wet brown star with my finger pushed well in; the brush sticking out from my cunt; my fingers busy between my sex lips; and, best of all, my tongue up some dirty old bastard's arsehole as he masturbated. He wasn't just any dirty old bastard, either: he'd spanked me and caned me, made me suck his cock and lick his balls, pulled my face between his buttocks and called me a stuck-up little bitch because I wouldn't lick his arsehole.

Now I was doing it, urgently, my tongue well up as I rubbed frantically at my cunt. I was going to come again, my hole already in contraction on the brush handle, my own anus pulsing hard on my intruding finger. I heard him grunt and felt his spunk splash in my hair as his arsehole tightened on my tongue, and that pushed me over the edge. My tongue pushed in, as deep as I could get it. My whole body had gone tight as my orgasm engulfed me, while splash after splash of spunk landed in my face and hair. Then my head was jerked violently up and his cock jammed into my mouth for him to finish off by spunking down my throat.

I nearly fainted, and was left gagging on the floor, panting for breath and still clutching my cunt. The brush had fallen out when I came, and its bristles dug into my tender bottom as I rolled over on to my back, utterly exhausted. So was he, gasping in air as he lay back in the chair, and for one awful moment I thought he was going to die on me. He didn't but was still breathless when I finally managed to climb to my feet.

Cleaning up was urgent, to say the least, but fortunately, now that they'd had me, Gilbert and his friends were behaving like gentlemen once again. Only Stubbs was ungrateful, checking that the landing was clear and grudgingly showing me to a bathroom, where he watched with his back to the door as I stripped and washed. I didn't complain; I'm used to men who can't understand that, just because I can be utterly filthy, it doesn't mean I don't deserve as much respect as any other woman, if not more.

By the time I had finished and returned to the room only Gilbert and Otto remained. It was gone one o'clock and they were keen to get their noses in the trough, pointing out that not only did the Aviators have an excellent menu but most of the wines were their own. I was so full of spunk I felt sick, and I was sure my belly had begun to bulge. The last thing I wanted was lunch, so I contented myself with a few glasses of Schoenenberg Riesling while Gilbert and Otto gorged themselves on grouse in a port sauce.

They were well pleased with themselves, talking expansively and explaining the background of their little club. Most of them had been at school together, it seemed, that or university, and so had built up an intimacy long before. That created an enduring bond of trust and meant they could hire girls for their dirty games with the minimum of risk – or, in my case, find themselves a genuine slut to play with. By no means all the members of the Aviators were in the spanking club, so they had to be discreet, but with well-paid girls and well-bribed commissionaires they had managed to avoid the attentions of both the less tolerant members and the press for nearly ten years.

I took it all in, happy to listen and to sip my wine because an idea had begun to form in my head. By the time they were munching their way through portions of spotted dick and custard served with a '67 Coutet I had my solution.

Six

It was simple and effective, or at least it would have been had I not decided that certain personal issues needed to be resolved at the same time. I was back in my office, checking my calls. One of those ‘personal issues’ had phoned that morning, Lydia, and she rang again as soon as I’d lowered myself – rather carefully – into my chair. She wanted a decision, and told me that Orpheus Asset Management would have to reconsider their offer if I didn’t accept it within twenty-four hours, a line so old and cheesy I couldn’t help but laugh at her. At that she changed her tactics, threatening me with a spanking and inviting me to dinner almost in the same breath. I accepted but pretended to be busy until the following Saturday, just to keep her warm. As I put the phone down I was smiling to myself, sure that I had her nicely hooked.

The other call that morning had been from Earle Hayes, asking me to meet him for a drink. He was no longer part of my scheme, so I ignored it, too sore behind to be tempted by rough sex. Also, while I hate showing my smacked bottom to men who’re not into it, because they never understand. Not only that, but somebody, probably Stubbs, had pinched my knickers, leaving me bare under my skirt and feeling extremely vulnerable. As the sick feeling in my stomach and the ache of my jaw subsided I began to feel increasingly randy.

In order to distract myself and pass the time I began to search the net for reports on the vintage, which turned out to be less pessimistic than I'd expected. The dry autumn was helping, although to make anything worthwhile they'd have to leave the picking later than just about any year in living memory.

I left at five and took a cab to Marylebone High Street, intending to throw a simple dinner together, put my feet up with a bottle of wine and tease myself to a badly needed climax over what had been done to me. They also had been quite rough, so that beneath my excitement I badly needed a cuddle, making me wonder if I shouldn't go to Percy instead. He'd also cook for me, so I could skip the throwing-together-some-dinner bit and go straight to the wine. I called him and he said he would come over immediately.

With a little effort I could shower and towel myself down in time for him to find me naked, lying face down on my bed so as to spare my tender bottom. The position was sure to arouse both his sympathy and his lust. I thought I'd have enough time, only to find Earle Hayes standing on the pavement outside my flat with an enormous bunch of roses. He'd already seen me, and there was nothing for it but to smile and search for an excuse to put him off without offending him. After all, even if I almost certainly didn't need him any more he was far too influential for me to risk an open snub, and they were beautiful roses. I also preferred him not to know about Percy, because it might cause complications if I did need to allow myself to be seduced a second time.

'Hello, I, er . . ., I wasn't expecting you,' I stammered, accepting the roses as he held them out to me. 'Thank you.'

'Pleasure's all mine. I thought I'd scared you off.'

He leant forward to kiss me and I let him, reacting a little despite myself.

'I don't scare easily,' I told him, 'but—'

'Glad to hear it,' he interrupted, 'because I have a proposition for you.'

'That's sweet, Earle, but I'm afraid my . . . my uncle is taking me to dinner tonight. I can't let him down.'

'Oh, that's not a problem. What I was going to say was, how do you fancy a little trip to Bordeaux, all expenses paid of course?'

I hesitated. It was a generous offer, especially from him. Even if the locals were likely to be a bit fed up the wines would be brilliant and the opportunity for making contacts incomparable. If my scheme didn't come off for any reason, that might be invaluable, and after the mess I'd made of my first plan I didn't want to take any chances. It was also sure to mean getting my tits fucked and several nights of rough sex without the kinky bits, but I could cope with that. On the other hand I had a lot to do in London and I didn't want to tell him yet that his bid for Hambling and Borse was unacceptable.

'Well?' he asked, grinning and evidently assuming I was overwhelmed by his largesse.

'Perhaps,' I responded cautiously. 'I need to think about it. When would we be going?'

'Next weekend, just the three days.'

'Oh.' I realised it was practical, as long as I cut Lydia off, but blushed at the thought of him seeing the welts on my bottom and having to explain myself. 'Um . . . I'd need to rearrange my schedule.'

'You're coming then? Good.'

He'd decided for me, playing the dominant male, and I let it pass. After all, I could always change my mind, and the important thing was to get rid of him before Percy turned up. The street was full of cabs, any one of which might contain him, and I really did not want to have to introduce him as my uncle.

'Yes, OK, thank you,' I answered quickly, 'but one condition, no talking shop.'

'We'll be attending several tastings, and—'

'No, I mean about Hambling and Borse.'

'Sure.'

'Thank you. Anyway, I must hurry.'

'Hang on, you don't know where to meet up or anything.'

'I'll call you.'

'I'll write it down for you, won't take a second. Do you have an address book or something?'

He'd already produced a pen, and I began to burrow in my bag for something to write on, simultaneously holding the roses under one arm. Inevitably I dropped them, just as a deep red cab pulled up beside us and disgorged Percy on to the pavement. He bowled over to us, as round and red and fat as ever. I struggled over what to say, determined not to introduce the word uncle into the conversation, but Earle Hayes did it for me, greeting Percy with a beaming smile and an extended hand.

'Mr Ottershaw, isn't it? Why, I had no idea you were little Natasha's uncle.'

I caught the flicker of surprise on Percy's face, briefly followed by annoyance before he recovered himself.

'Mr Hayes, good afternoon, 'he said, accepting the other's offered hand. 'Natasha, my niece . . . yes, yes.'

'Wonderful girl.'

'Not altogether,' Percy said with a laugh. 'In fact, I still have to spank her occasionally.'

I dropped the roses again, and my handbag, spilling the contents all over the pavement, my face blazing crimson. Earle Hayes was completely taken aback and managed a sort of strangled gurgle that might have been a laugh, but Percy continued as if he'd merely remarked on the weather.

'Yes, and I recommend you do the same, should you feel it necessary. I read your article on the use of new oak for Chablis, by the way. I'm glad to see you don't advocate . . .'

They began to discuss the article, leaving me scrabbling about on the pavement with my face red and my chest flushed. Only by keeping my knees tightly together could I be sure I wasn't giving the entire street a flash of pussy, which made it more awkward still, although after a moment both men bent down to help me, Percy giving me a friendly pat on my head as he reached to retrieve an errant lipstick. The colour of his nose, redder even than usual, indicated that he'd had a drink or two already. Otherwise, I was sure, even he wouldn't have dared say anything so outrageous. But he had, filling me with an overwhelming embarrassment made worse because it was all my fault, especially as I should have known they'd have met each other.

Even after I'd got everything together they carried on talking for a while, while I stood there blushing and fidgeting. Only when they'd exhausted the topic of whether or not Chablis should be aged in oak did Earle Hayes go away, kissing me on the cheek and shaking Percy's hand. As he climbed into a cab, Percy's expression changed from beaming to enquiring.

'Your uncle?'

'Yes, well . . . but . . .,' I stammered, 'you . . . you didn't have to say you spanked me!'

He merely laughed, stepping up behind me as I struggled to get my key into the lock. I was painfully aware of the target my bottom presented beneath my skirt, and sure he'd smack me where everybody could see, but he waited until we were indoors before placing one podgy hand under my cheeks to steer me upstairs.

'No knickers?' he remarked.

'No,' I admitted.

'So how did you come to lose them? Or have you taken to going bare?'

'Somebody pinched them, one of those old bastards at the Aviators Club. I suppose you know them too?'

'One or two, although I'm not a member myself. You imply that somebody other than Gilbert and Otto has been at you?'

'Yes, their friends at the club, fifteen of them in all.'

'What was it, a little striptease? A spanking?'

'A spanking. They passed me around, and gave me the cane, and . . . and made me suck them off, all of them, in a broom cupboard.'

'You must tell me about it, everything.'

I didn't answer, thick with humiliation at my own words as much as at what he'd done to me in the street. My face was still burning, my resentment very real, but there was nothing I could do to fight down my arousal. Percy knew exactly the state I was in, chuckling merrily to himself as he followed me up the stairs and into my flat. I didn't wait to be asked, but tugged up my skirt the instant the door was safely shut, showing off my smacked and welted bottom.

'A neatly delivered caning,' he remarked, peering close to inspect my hurt flesh. 'Gilbert?'

'The commissionaire, a man called Stubbs.'

'A good man with a cane, this Stubbs. Hmm . . . I had meant to spank you for your impertinence just now, but there are other ways to punish a girl, and for now I suspect that a little cream would do you good.'

'Yes, please.'

He went into the bathroom and I busied myself putting the roses in water, returning to the living room to find him seated at the table, on which was a box of tissues and my moisturising cream. My skirt was still up, and I simply put the vase down on the table, shrugged off my jacket and laid myself down across his lap, my bare bottom lifted for his attention. He begun to rub the cream into my cheeks, making gentle circular motions on my hot skin. I relaxed, yielding to his caresses without thought for my dignity, something I can only really do with Percy. Any other man, and I remain very much aware of what I'm showing, of the humiliation of my surrender to intimate, loitering touches; of my exposure, my punishment, my penetration, however much it turns me on.

As his fingers began to move down between my cheeks I simply spread my knees a little way apart, offering him what I knew he wanted. Sure enough, one creamy finger was soon tickling my anus to make the little fleshy ring open and squeeze. I closed my eyes in bliss as a short, fat finger was inserted gently but firmly into my rectum, thinking of how I must look, bare-bottom over a dirty old man's lap, my cheeks marked with welts and glossy with cream, my pussy flaunted, his finger stuck well in up my anus. To most women my age it would have been unthinkable, incomprehensible, a grotesque molestation so inappropriate that they wouldn't even be able to accept that it was possible without coercion, never mind enjoyable. To me, that was part of the pleasure, as was the feel of Percy's cock stiffening against my side and the knowledge of where it would be going.

'You're going to bugger me, aren't you?'

'Eventually.'

'Good.'

He gave the soft, dirty chuckle I'd grown to know

so well. I pushed my bottom up against his hand and gave him an encouraging wiggle, for which I got a gentle smack on each cheek.

'Have patience,' he told me. 'Now, you were saying that Gilbert and his fiends put you in a broom cupboard and made you perform fellatio on them. All of them?'

'All fifteen. I ended up with so much spunk in my tummy I felt sick.'

'Dirty girl.'

'Stubbs the commissionaire was the worst. He was the one who gave me the cane . . . and he made me lick and suck his balls . . . and his bottom. He made me lick his arse, Percy . . . he forced me to lick his arse.'

'A likely story.'

'He did!'

'Oh, I'm quite sure you licked his anus, but I know you too well to believe that he forced you. Now how about Earle Hayes? John Thurston told me you'd gone off with him after the *Corkscrew* tasting, so I suspect he's had your knickers down too, hasn't he?'

'Yes, but . . . but he hasn't spanked me. He just likes rough sex, and to fuck my titties.'

'And very fuckable they are too, but how can any man who gets his hands on you not spank you? I wouldn't have thought it humanly possible to resist your behind.'

Even as he spoke he'd begun to do it, spanking me gently with one hand as he nuzzled the other between my cheeks, his finger as far up my now sloppy hole as it would go.

'Not everybody's a pervert like you,' I told him, 'and . . . and it wasn't fair to tell him you spank me, especially when he thinks you're my uncle!'

He laughed, but also began to spank harder, making my welts twinge with pain.

'Ow! Percy!'

'Up you get, then.'

He didn't bother to extract his finger from my bumhole but helped me to my feet with it still stuck well in, and positioned me on his lap with my penetrated bottom stuck out over his leg as if I was trying to go to the loo outdoors. My pussy was against his leg, wet and sensitive, tempting me to rub myself off while he fingered my bum.

'Hands on your head,' he instructed, apparently reading my mind.

I obeyed, bum and boobs thrust out back and front as he continued to handle me, now tweaking open the buttons of my blouse until he could tug it wide across my breasts. Two quick motions and the cups of my bra had been flipped up, spilling out my boobs, which he began to caress. I wanted to get his cock out, but he was in no hurry, exploring my body until I was wriggling with pleasure and moaning too. Only then did he leave my breasts alone, to quickly tug down his fly and free the small pink spike of his erection into one hand.

'Pop yourself on,' he ordered. 'Up your bum.'

He didn't need to tell me. Even as he eased his finger from my hole I was twisting around and reaching down, to stick my bum out into his lap and guide his erection to my gaping anus. I was nicely ready and he slid up without difficulty until the full length of his cock was wedged up inside my rectum and my empty cunt was pressed to his oversized balls. His hand went to my mouth, offering me the finger he'd used to open my bottom for buggering. I opened up obediently, sucking away like a good little slut as I wriggled against him.

'Good girl,' he told me. 'You may come if you wish.'

I nodded urgently, eager to play, although I knew he only wanted me to reach orgasm so that he could feel my bumhole in contraction on his cock. That knowledge just made it all the nicer and, as he pulled his finger from my mouth to cup my breasts, I was already squirming against him. I could feel the soreness of my bottom from my beating, his podgy fingers groping my boobs, the stiff little rod of his cock in my rectum, his leathery scrotum against my cunt. My hands went to the back of my head, for the sheer pleasure of being an obedient little tart. I didn't need them, anyway; I could easily get myself there on the pleasure of being buggered . . . molested and buggered . . . stripped and molested and buggered . . . stripped and spanked and molested and buggered.

With that thought I came, wriggling my bottom urgently against his great fat balls as I squirmed and bounced in his lap, revelling in the feel of his hands on my breasts and his cock up my bottom hole, thinking of all the things he'd done to me, including embarrassing me in front of Earle Hayes. It was too much for him and he also came, jamming himself deep as my pulsing bumhole sucked up his spunk. At the thought of him coming in my rectum I hit another peak, the last before I let myself go slowly limp in his arms.

He was puffing with effort, but managed to find his voice as I lifted myself carefully off his cock.

'Bend over the table, Natasha.'

I glanced back, curious, but obeyed, aware that my position showed everything, including the spunk bubbling out of my still open bumhole and down over my cunt. Not that it mattered, not in front of Percy, but I was hoping he hadn't decided to beat me again.

He had something else in mind, less painful but even ruder. He extracted a rose from the vase, carefully removed the thorns and inserted the stem up my bottom. A second followed, and a third, before he was satisfied.

'That,' he informed me, 'is for telling Earle Hayes that I am your uncle. You will remain as you are until dinner is ready.'

I made a face, imagining what Earle Hayes would have thought if he could have seen me with three of his roses stuck up my bottom, and how I'd look. Generally Percy let me do as I pleased, but occasionally he liked to remind me that when it came to men he was in charge.

At least, he was in charge when it came to sex, some of the time anyway. When it really comes down to it I admit to no master, and to no mistress either. That was something Lydia obviously didn't accept, because she called me the next morning before I'd even finished my coffee, demanding a meeting. I was only half awake and told her to call again at a more civilised hour, but she wouldn't give in and I ended up agreeing to meet her for tea at Fortnum's, knowing the restaurant didn't open until noon. The previous afternoon she'd seemed happy enough to wait until the weekend, so she was presumably under pressure from her boss to force a decision.

I went into the office first, where I was made to drop my panties for Gilbert and Otto to inspect my bottom, which inevitably left me feeling vulnerable and rude. With a couple of hours to spare I made another inspection of the cellar, checking what was actually there against what was on the stock lists. So far as I could judge, whoever had put everything on to the computer had simply ignored all the smaller bins, regardless of their worth or how rare they were. There were also one or two curious misspellings and the entries conformed to the labels rather than the official classification, all of which suggested that the work had been done by somebody with more business sense than knowledge of wine, so definitely not Gilbert or Otto.

A carefully phrased question to the secretary revealed that she'd hired temps to do the donkey work, a fact I was pondering as I walked up to Fortnum's. Lydia hadn't known about the opening hours and was waiting in the food hall, studying a display of pumpkins and wearing a slightly cross expression. She got straight down to business.

'Tasha. Good. You're going to make a decision today, and you're going to make the right decision.'

I didn't answer, but followed as she clip-clopped across to the lift, where a uniformed commissionaire who looked very like the wicked Stubbs ushered us politely in. As we ascended Lydia continued to talk, waving bits of paper at me as she did so. The restaurant had just opened, and I ordered afternoon tea as Lydia waited impatiently with her documents spread out on the table.

'This is the deal,' she told me the moment I was ready to listen. 'You get your bosses' signature on this agreement and you get two per cent of what's left after the debts have been paid off.'

'The debts are quite large,' I pointed out.

'We have offers for the name alone that will cover the debts.'

'Just for the company name?'

'That's right. It'll be a lot of money, Natasha, more than you'll see in ten years working for those two old farts.'

I nodded thoughtfully. She pushed the document towards me. I picked it up and began to read, although it wasn't really necessary. From what I knew of Gilbert and Otto they would rather end up on the street than sell out to Orpheus Asset Management, while for me to accept the bribe would be a betrayal not only of them but of Percy as well. Lydia spoke up again before I was half-way through, her voice demanding and impatient.

'You have until the end of the week to get their signatures. Otherwise your share goes down to one and a half per cent.'

'I've already told you I can't rush them,' I protested.

'I'm sure you can if you try hard enough.'

'Look, seriously, not going to be easy. I need at least a month.'

'Rubbish. Use your body, Natasha. Take one of the old bastards to bed, or better still both of them. Once you can withhold their shags you'll be able to get them to sign their own death warrants.'

I made a face.

'Don't play the innocent with me, Tasha, I know what you're like, remember? They won't be the first dirty old men to have you, will they?'

She wasn't exactly keeping her voice down and I found myself blushing. I was also struggling not to smile, because she simply didn't understand the way I am; Lydia's incapable of seeing anybody except in her own terms. Biting my lip, I pushed the document back across the table.

'Three per cent, I'm allowed one month's grace, and I receive a goodwill payment on signature of . . . shall we say, ten thousand pounds?'

'That's not possible.'

'Take it or leave it.'

'Don't be silly, Natasha, you know it's a good deal and I don't have the authority to change it anyway.'

'Let me speak to somebody who has, then.'

Her eyes flashed fire and for a moment I thought she was going to threaten me. It was obviously important to her to make me sign without having to go to her boss, perhaps because she was at risk of losing out on commission, perhaps simply because to pass me up the ladder would damage her reputation as an evil little bitch who got what she wanted. I couldn't resist teasing, and leant across the table, speaking softly.

'What are you going to do about it, Lydia? Spank me? Go on, I dare you. I won't even put up a fight. Spank me, right here in front of all these people ... knickers down ... bare bottom. I'll love it, but you, Lydia, will get arrested.'

'Do try and be serious, Natasha,' she snapped. 'Look, I—'

'Take it or leave it, Lydia.'

She began to speak again, then made an angry face and started to gather her papers. For a moment I thought she was going to call my bluff, and I very nearly backed down, but then she spoke again.

'Very well. I'll put the proposal to the partners this afternoon. I'll meet you in Cirano's, seven o'clock sharp.'

I agreed, and would have been happy to sit and drink tea and chat for a while, but she was in a hurry. She left her cup half-empty and me feeling rather pleased with myself.

Seven

I turned up at Cirano's at a quarter to eight, after going home to shower and change, then twiddling my thumbs in a Soho coffee bar for a bit while Lydia got steamed up. When I came in I wondered if I'd left it a little too long, because she looked fit for murder, and her attempt to force a smile came out as an angry scowl. On the table was a document, which she pushed across to me as I sat down.

'There we are. I got what you wanted, but it wasn't easy. Now sign.'

'Daddy says I should never sign anything until I've read it, understood it and had it assessed by two independent experts.'

'It's all there. Now stop pissing about.'

I ignored her and picked up the document, read the first few lines, put it down and picked up the wine list. They had a Langhe Bianco, which was tempting, but Lydia was drinking gin and tonic and I didn't really want a whole bottle of white with my antipasto. I signalled a waiter.

'Do you have the Langhe by the glass?'

He belonged to the unreconstructedly macho school of Italian waitering and immediately began to flirt with me. I responded, enjoying teasing him almost as much as Lydia's increasing irritation, but I did genuinely need a drink and finally sent him away to get me a glass of Langhe, having insisted he open a new bottle. Only then did I go back to reading the contract.

It was more or less as I'd anticipated, accepting my terms subject to a long string of conditions, the most important of which was that I wouldn't get my advance payment until Orpheus had seen a letter from Gilbert and Otto agreeing to consider their offer. That was more than I'd expected, and there was no quibbling about my three per cent, although that made no real difference. All in all it was perfectly acceptable, but there was still a lot of fun to be had with Lydia, who was holding out a pen even as I put the contract back down on the table.

'I'll have to think about it,' I told her.

'What's to think about? That's our final offer.'

'You said that before.'

'This time I mean it, Natasha. For goodness' sake, you're behaving like a baby! This will make you rich!'

'I wouldn't say rich, and as it goes I quite like behaving like a baby. You ought to try it, especially being put in nappies. That feels wonderful.'

'You're a pervert, Natasha.'

'And you're not?'

'Not like you. Now come on, sign.'

'Hmm . . . no. You're going to have to make me. I always loved those films in which some dastardly villain tries to force the heroine to sign some damning document by threatening her with unspeakable things . . . only of course for me the dashing young hero doesn't turn up and I actually get the unspeakable things done to me.'

She drew a heavy sigh.

'Business first, Natasha. I'll take you to bed later, and believe me—'

'No. You're going to have to force me.'

'Tasha, look—'

'Lighten up, will you? I'll sign the stupid thing, but I want to play with you. Now have another drink and imagine all the horrible things you can do to me.'

She threw her hands up in exasperation, drained the remainder of her G and T, then buried her nose in the menu. I did the same, grinning to myself as I tried to decide what to have. If she was going to be rough with me later it was probably best not to have too much, or anything too rich, but all I'd had for lunch was a cup of tea, and there was a pasta with a complicated sauce of goat's meat and exotic mushrooms that I simply couldn't resist.

I ordered it as my main meal and tucked into the antipasto my waiter had brought. Confident that I would give in eventually, and now on her fourth or maybe fifth G and T, Lydia began to relax. The waiter, perhaps sensing that we were up for trouble, grew ever more flirtatious, introducing himself as Cristiano and telling us that our boyfriends were fools for letting us out on our own. Lydia came close to giving him a piece of her mind at that, but I winked at her before she could get her words in order.

'What makes you think we have boyfriends?' I asked.

'You have boyfriends,' he answered. 'How would it be otherwise? Two girls as beautiful as you.'

'Maybe we're lesbians?' I suggested.

He nearly dropped the bottle from which he'd been refilling my glass, but rallied.

'No, never on God's earth. A woman as beautiful as you does not need to be a lesbian.'

'You macho pig!' Lydia answered him. 'As a matter of fact we *are* lesbians.'

I kicked her under the table.

'Sort of lesbians. We like boys too. In fact . . .'

He had a bow tie on, the sort that fastens with elastic. I hooked a finger behind it and drew his head slowly down to the level of my mouth.

'... in fact, what we like best is for a nice, strong young man to watch us, and maybe ... just maybe, even join in.'

I let go of his bow tie, which snapped back against his neck, but I doubt he even noticed. He was staring like one of those goldfish with the bulbous eyes, while the bulge in his tight black trousers looked a great deal larger than it had earlier. The restaurant was quite dark, and nobody was looking, so I reached out and gave his cock a gentle squeeze, finding a fat, almost full erection. This time he dropped the bottle, which exploded on the tiles with a bang, drawing the attention of his superior.

The resulting spat of remonstrances and apologies, mostly in Italian, made it extremely hard to keep a straight face, especially with Lydia glaring at me. I got us a second bottle of wine for free and the incident left Cristiano deflated and me feeling full of mischief. By the time we'd finished I was up for anything, at least once my food had gone down a little, while I had Lydia wound up to breaking point as well as drunk and horny. As we left I gave Cristiano a smile and a flutter of my fingers, but when he made an urgent signal for us to come back and speak to him I simply walked away.

'You are such a bitch!' Lydia said with a laugh as we emerged on to the street.

'What, me? If I'd wanted to be a bitch I'd have said he could watch us later, then given him the wrong address. No, no, even better – go through with it, but pick up some bi-guy in one of the bars and then tell Cristiano he can watch us if he sucks the other man off!'

'You are evil, Natasha! What if he went for it?'

'Then he gets to watch us play.'

'I wouldn't do it, but I might make you suck him off.'

'Oh, yes, please. OK, mine or yours?'

'I warn you, Tasha, if we go home together you had better watch out.'

'Oh, that's fine. There's nothing like a bit of real anger to bring out the best in a sadist, don't you think?'

She answered with a despairing shake of her head and took my hand, leading me up Frith Street. There were quite a few people about, but I was too drunk and horny to care, also eager to get the best out of her.

'You can be as rough as you like,' I told her, 'but my bottom's a bit tender.'

'It'll be a lot more tender by the time I'm finished with you,' she answered. 'So what happened to you, slut?'

'They had me caned, Gilbert Hambling and some of his friends.'

'The dirty old bastards!'

'They spanked me too, one at a time, and they made me suck their cocks.'

'You've got to learn to hold yourself back, Natasha. If you let a man have you straight off it makes it a lot harder to control him later.'

'Not for me.'

'You're a slut, Natasha.'

'I know, and they really took advantage of that, but for real perverts the man I met in France was worse. The bastard tied me up and gave me a pussy enema, with my own wine, then left me in bondage. I think he was hoping I'd pee myself. I do seem to attract perverts, don't I?'

She laughed.

'It's not that you always meet perverts, Tasha. It's that everybody who gets you into bed realises it's their big chance to indulge whatever sick fantasy they've been too scared to try out with anybody less malleable.'

'In others words they're perverts.'

'Not necessarily. I'm sure he'd have been perfectly well behaved if it had been me instead of you.'

'Maybe,' I admitted. 'Let's get a cab, and you can make me suck the driver off for our fare, if you like.'

Again she shook her head, but stuck out her arm at the same time, signalling the second of a pair of black cabs just passing us. The driver was a middle-aged black guy with grizzled hair and a paunch, and I smacked my lips at the thought of having my head held down in his lap by Lydia as I licked and mouthed his penis, sucking and swallowing his spunk to pay a fare of a few pounds.

'Marylebone High Street,' Lydia ordered.

'Buxton Mews,' I added, 'just off Paddington Street. I'll pay you there, nicely.'

Lydia shot me a doubtful glance.

'Please?' I urged.

'I'm not sure . . .'

'Oh, OK, if you haven't got the guts.'

Her expression hardened and without a moment's hesitation she leant forward to the little window separating us from the driver's compartment.

'Cabbie, could we pay by having my friend suck you off?'

We were stuck in traffic and he turned around, looking none too pleased.

'I've got a living to make, girl, so either you pay, or you get your dirty bitch girlfriend out of my cab.'

'Spoilsport,' I told him.

Lydia had extracted a ten-pound note from her bag and passed it to him.

‘There, that should cover it, and if you want a suck anyway I’ll make her—’

‘That’s not the same . . .,’ I began, whining, but she wasn’t finished.

‘—and she’ll pay you. Twenty quid.’

I nearly came. It was bad enough prostituting myself in order to pay my cab fare, but to have to pay for the privilege of sucking the bastard’s cock was almost too much. My body had gone limp, barely controlled save for the desire to spread my thighs and open my mouth. As the traffic began to move again I was lying back in my seat, shaking at the thought of how I’d begged to be degraded. The play of shadows and yellow lights on Lydia’s face gave her a near-demonic cruelty.

The journey seemed to take forever, and my tension increased with every pause at a traffic light. By the time we got to the mews I was so far gone I’d have done it on my knees in the street, but fortunately Lydia had more sense, and made him park between two vans belonging to some hire company. I’d chosen the mews well: the hire company was just one of a row of premises that were all closed, and as the cabbie got into the back with us I knew there was very little chance of being caught.

‘Do it with your breasts out,’ Lydia ordered, her voice thick with sadistic pleasure.

I didn’t need to be told; my dress was already up above my waist and my bra raised to spill out my tits. The cabbie was a dirty bastard, leaning forward to grope me without bothering to ask if he could touch, and licking his lips as he squeezed my boobs and rubbed his big, coarse thumbs over my nipples. I unzipped him as he groped me, to find that he had no underpants on, his fat cock popping up from his fly the moment it was open. He was big, his skin hot and moist, his shaft heavy with blood. I pulled his balls out too, to leave the leathery black scrotum bulging obscenely from his open trousers and his cock rearing above it in my hand.

He pulled me forward by my tits, forcing me into an awkward position as he folded them around his shaft, jiggling them in his hands to get friction on his cock. My bottom was sticking out and Lydia quickly pulled down the back of my panties, letting the cool air get to my wet pussy and maing me feel more vulnerable than ever. If she ordered me to let him put himself up my cunt I knew I would do it, but that came later. For now it was time for me to suck cock.

I went down, taking him in, the thick male taste filling my mouth along with the meaty texture of his helmet. He took me by the hair, forcing himself deeper until his knob was pressed into my throat, making me gag. Lydia slipped a hand between my legs, exploring my pussy as I sucked, two fingers stuck up me. I wondered if she was getting me ready for fucking, and whether she'd make me pay extra for the privilege of surrendering my cunt to the over-eager bastard who was now fucking my mouth.

She began to spank me too, calling me a bitch and whore, laughing at the choking sounds I was making as the now rock-hard cock in my mouth was forced deeper. I could hardly breathe, and my eyes were watering so badly I could feel the tears running down my face, streaking my make-up and blurring my vision. Yet I wanted to come, my hands on my tits and my bottom wriggling on Lydia's intruding fingers, my head full of filthy thoughts. I wanted him to fuck me and then put his cock back in my mouth to make me suck up my own juices. I wanted him to make me hold my mouth open so he could spunk in it and watch me swallow his mess. I wanted him to bugger me and make me lick his cock clean while Lydia laughed at me and smacked my fat pink bottom for being such a slut.

I got none of it, but I did get something almost as good. He'd began to grunt and swear, calling me a filthy bitch and a whore as he fucked my throat. His grip was tight in my hair, painfully so, allowing me no chance of escape, so that when he suddenly jerked my head back there was nothing I could do but yield as he began to tug on his thick brown shaft, right in my face. My mouth was open, ready to be filled with spunk, my eyes tight closed. He began to slap his cock in my face, hard, as he masturbated furiously.

'Do it,' Lydia growled. 'Right in her face. Go on, come in her face and rub it all over with your cock.'

'Shut up, bitch,' the cabbie snapped, and he was there.

I felt the hot, wet come splash over my face and into my mouth, again and a third time, soiling my skin and hair, before he stuck his cock back into my mouth, slimy with spunk as he finished himself off down my throat. He'd done a lot, and I could imagine how I'd look, with my make-up smudged, my face dirty with streaks and blobs of thick white spunk, his fat brown cock shaft still stuck in my mouth as I sucked on him. I wanted to come, just as I was, soiled and humiliated, showing off to them as I rubbed my cunt over what they'd done to me. My hands went down, but Lydia slapped my bottom hard and pulled them away.

'Oh no you don't, not until I've finished with you, and no cleaning up either. Now pay the man.'

'Twenty pounds,' he reminded me.

There was a streamer of spunk over my left eye and I didn't dare open it, but my right was OK and I quickly found my bag and extracted a twenty-pound note. My fingers were shaking badly as I gave it to him, but even then there was no sympathy.

'Out,' he ordered. 'Some of us have got work to do.'

We climbed out, and Lydia helped me pull up my panties and adjust my bra and dress as the cabbie got back into the front. He drove off without another word, leaving me trembling and horny, my face still dirty with his come.

'Can I at least wipe my eye?' I asked.

'I suppose so,' she said, her voice full of cruel laughter. 'What a sight you are! Shit!'

I turned sharply as she spoke, realising that she'd seen somebody, but not expecting to find two men seated in the front of the nearest of the two vans. They'd been in darkness before, but one of them had opened the door, making the interior light come on. I backed away a little, scared and shocked by their sudden appearance. They could hardly have failed to realise what had been going on.

The man who'd opened the van door climbed out. He was tall, lanky and young, maybe still a teenager, darker-skinned even than the cabbie, and grinning. The other was still in the cab, a white boy a little older but a great deal less confident, his round moon face set in an expression of lust but also doubt and wonder, his mouth hanging open, a thin trickle of saliva drooling from one corner. He didn't look dangerous, but the first one was squeezing his cock through his trousers and there was aggression in his voice as he spoke.

'So what, you couldn't pay your fare, or you get off on sucking black guys?'

I already knew his cock was going in my mouth, maybe up my cunt, but all I could do was nod. Lydia spoke quickly, scared but determined.

'Not me. She does. She'll do you, if that's what you want.'

The man looked from her to me and back, shrugged, opened his trousers and flopped out a long, dark cock.

'Come on then. I'm Blake, the fat bastard's Lucas. He'll want to watch, or you can do him too.'

I barely heard him, my body on automatic, and I got down on my knees. The ground was hard, cold and dirty with oil, but I barely noticed as Blake stepped forward to feed his penis into my mouth. He was grinning and making obscene gestures to his friend as I began to suck, but he was less of a bastard than the cabbie, allowing me to suck the way I wanted to and not trying to force himself down my throat.

He was soon hard, just as my fear had soon given way to submission and lust. If I'd tried to turn him down he might have turned nasty, maybe, but now he had his cock in my mouth he'd be OK, and if he chose to fuck me I'd just have to take it. I was wishing he would, but he'd begun to toss himself into my mouth and it looked as if I'd be made to swallow.

Lydia had stepped away, her back to the second van, more worried about whether she'd be made to take a cock in her own precious mouth than about what I was doing. Not that Blake was likely to harass her, because I had his full attention, but it didn't look as if she'd try to control me; now I could come while I sucked. So I pulled up my dress and flopped out my tits for the second time within minutes, to rub them on Blake's cock and let him fuck my cleavage for a moment before taking him in my mouth again.

'Come on, man,' Blake urged, signalling to his friend. 'She's up for it.'

I nodded, beckoning to Lucas. As he climbed down from the van, still uncertain, I pushed a hand down the front of my knickers, masturbating as I rubbed my face against Blake's long, thin erection. Lucas came close, far from sure of himself, so I gave him some attention, unzipping him and pulling out his cock and balls. Now I had two cocks to play with, one white, one black, both erect – Lucas had obviously been playing with himself in the van.

My hand went back into my panties as I began to take turns with them, sucking one and tugging the other. Blake began to grope my tits and his breathing had started to get hoarse, but I was still taken by surprise when his cock erupted in my face while I still had his friend in my mouth. It went all over me, down my cheek and over my nose, on my tits too, and my dress. I got him back in my mouth before he'd finished, to swallow what I could before popping Lucas in again. My fingers were busy as my own climax began an instant later.

It was long and sweet and tight, my whole body locked in ecstasy as I sucked on the plump white cock in my mouth. I was still coming as Blake wiped his cock in my face, leaving me with a beautiful picture in my mind as I rode my orgasm, of myself kneeling near-nude on the dirty ground, my panties half down and my bare tits swinging in the cool autumn air, my mouth full of cock and my face smeared with streamers of spunk, used and degraded but still masturbating. Only at the very end did I let Lucas slip from my mouth and squat down, sore but satisfied, my head still hung in submission as he grabbed his cock, tugging furiously until he came all over my head.

Blake was laughing and clicking his fingers in delight to see what they'd done to me, and even the shy Lucas looked well pleased with himself. They still had their cocks out, and I thought they might be going to piss on me as a final horrid insult, but they simply climbed back into the van, still laughing. Only then did Lydia step forward, her voice shocked as she helped me to my feet and tugged my dress down to cover me.

'You filthy, filthy little bitch, Natasha! Come on, we'd better get you cleaned up.'

I nodded weakly, but instead of getting a tissue out she took my arm and led me quickly out of the mews. My door was only a few yards away and I kept my head down, but Lucas had spunked in my hair so I was sure somebody would realise what had been done to me. I was near to panic as I fumbled my key into the lock and I ran upstairs as fast as I could, Lydia following me and laughing. She was such a bitch, leaving me to cope with both boys and not even thanking me, but at least she was going to help me clean up.

So I thought, but when she led me into the bathroom, where I slipped my dress off, she began to tug at the loo roll, not to tear some off but to feed the paper into the bowl.

'What are you doing?' I demanded. 'You'll block the loo, Lydia.'

'I'm helping you clean up, silly. Now get on your knees.'

'Lydia! No! Come on, that's not fair!'

She flushed the loo, making the water rise and filling the pan with a deep pool of water, clean except little bits of pink loo paper.

'On your knees, Tasha,' she repeated.

I swallowed hard, near to tears as I looked down into the lavatory pan in which I was about to have my face washed, but too high on submission to resist. She gave a cruel, knowing chuckle as I knelt in front of the pan, my body shaking so hard that my tits were jiggling, while just the thought of having my head pushed down the lavatory was making me feel sick.

Lydia took me firmly by the hair and straddled my body, her weight pressing on my back as she pushed my head down. My face was just inches from the water and I could see my reflection, my cheeks stained with tear tracks where my make-up had run, my lipstick smeared, my skin soiled, blobs of spunk hanging from my nose and chin. I began to sob, bitterly sorry for myself but unable to fight back as Lydia tightened her grip in my hair.

'In you go, Tasha,' she said with a laugh. 'One . . . two . . . three!'

'No, Lydia, I—'

My voice turned into a pathetic bubbling noise as my face broke the surface of the water. She pushed my head well down, laughing as she rubbed my face in the soggy mess of loo paper at the bottom. I struggled to pull back, came up gasping and spitting bits of loo paper and spunk, only to have my head thrust back under water, filling my mouth and nose.

'You're not clean yet,' Lydia crowed, 'not by a long way.'

She'd got my head right down, jammed against the hard porcelain, and I was choking on a mouthful of half-dissolved loo paper, forcing me to fight back once more. This time she let me, holding me by the hair with my face an inch above the water as I coughed up what had gone in my mouth.

'Enough, please,' I begged. 'I think I'm going to be sick.'

'Don't be such a selfish bitch, Natasha,' she chided. 'You got yours, didn't you, rubbing yourself off like that? What about mine?'

Her skirt had ridden up, and I could feel the warm wetness of her pussy against my skin through her panties. She began to rub on me, using the bumps of my spine to get friction to her sex.

'I'm going to ride you until I come,' she told me, 'and while I do it I want to see you drinking out of that lavatory bowl.'

'No, please, Lydia,' I whined. 'I'll lick, and you . . . you can sit on my face if you like . . . I'll lick your bum too . . . I promise, Lydia, I'll be ever such a good girl, but please, not this.'

'Stop whining!' she snapped. 'Now do it, and I want to see you swallow. Come on, get your head in there!'

I began to protest again, but she was right. She deserved her turn, and what she wanted me to do was so, so dirty. I told myself I'd do it quickly, get it over with and let her come, but as my tongue pushed out to lap at the water in the lavatory bowl there was no denying the sudden tightening in my pussy.

'That's it, Tasha,' she breathed. 'Drink it up. More, Tasha, a good, big mouthful, and swallow.'

As she spoke she was rubbing her body back and forth on my spine, her pussy wet on my back through her knickers, her little soft bottom squashed against my skin. I tried to stop myself, knowing she was going to come anyway, but I couldn't. My face went down into the lavatory and I sucked up the water, filling my mouth until I could take no more. I turned my head to look up into Lydia's face and slowly, deliberately swallowed.

'Oh you filthy, filthy bitch!' she cried and she was there.

She screamed as she started to come. My head was jammed down the toilet one more time, sloshing water out over the rim, and kept there, my face pressed in to the mass of soggy loo roll as she brought herself off on my back. It seemed to last for ever, so long I thought she was going to drown me and began to panic, only for her grip to relax.

I came up gasping, loo water streaming from my mouth and nose, running down my breasts and on to the floor as she dismounted and I was finally allowed to kneel up. My head was spinning, dizzy with reaction and dirty thoughts, my craving too strong to be denied. I stuck a hand down my panties, pulling them out of my slit, and began to masturbate.

Lydia gave a soft, amused chuckle as she saw what I was doing. Her skirt was rucked up around her hips, showing off a pair of lacy black panties, the crotch slippery with her cream. She came close, pushing out her hips and tugging her panties aside to show off her bare pussy. I stuck out my tongue, eager to lick while I came, and got a faceful of piss for my trouble. As she urinated over me she began to laugh again, high and wild, thoroughly enjoying herself as she directed her stream first into my open mouth, then down over my breasts and belly, moving round to do my back and bottom, finishing off in my hair.

'There,' she told me, 'how's that?'

'Lovely,' I breathed. 'Thank you . . . thank you, Lydia . . .'

I trailed off, rubbing hard at my eager cunt as I teased myself towards orgasm, kneeling in a puddle of lavatory water and Lydia's piss, my body wet and slippery, my hair caked with bits of loo roll, my wet panties still tight up between my smacked bottom cheeks. Lydia could see my cane welts and I thought of her contempt for the way I'd allowed the old men to use me, contempt she'd expressed by washing my face in my lavatory bowl and pissing all over me.

The thought was too much. I came, screaming out her name as the orgasm hit me, my bottom splashing in the pee puddle as I bounced up and down in wild ecstasy, one fat wet breast clawed in my hand, my head thrown back and my mouth wide. Lydia laughed at me, setting off another peak, but I still wasn't finished. A moment to collect myself and I was rubbing again. Lydia walked away and I was left there, bog-washed, pissed on and masturbating furiously over my own degradation, to bring myself to orgasm after orgasm until at last my muscles failed me and I slumped down on the filthy floor.

Lydia had come back and was standing in the doorway, her contract in one hand and a pen in the other.

'If you've quite finished,' she said, 'perhaps you'd like to clean up a bit and then sign this?'

I nodded.

Eight

For the rest of the week I worked quite hard, talking to all the people I needed for my scheme to work, trying to convince Gilbert and Otto that it was the best way to go, ensuring that everybody involved received the information I wanted them to have but not the information I didn't want them to have. Oh, and sucking cocks.

Cocksucking seemed to be playing an increasingly important part in my scheme. I'd done Gilbert, Otto, Vernon and the entire kinky element of the Aviators club, Stubbs the commissionaire, Earle Hayes and Anton Yoshida, the black cabbie whose name I didn't even know, Blake and Lucas. In fact, by the end of the week I'd done many of them twice or even three times, most of them either making me swallow or doing it in my face. The sensation of having to suck a man's penis in order to try and influence a business deal was every bit as exciting as I'd anticipated, with all the delicious feelings of shame and obligation, but by Friday my jaw ached so badly I could hardly talk, and I was sure I had started to put on weight because of all the spunk I'd eaten.

I spent Friday night at home, eating Chinese food in the bath and drinking a bottle of Riesling while watching an old film. By morning I felt more or less ready for the world, and for Earle Hayes, although my cane welts still showed, as a set of lines just fractionally pinker than the rest of my bottom. That was enough to give me a frisson of embarrassment as I made my way to London City Airport and waited for the Bordeaux flight.

Earle had agreed to meet me at the airport, and turned up in a white suit, a hat and a bright-red shirt, with a thong tie fastened with an ostentatiously large malachite clasp. He caught the surprise in my face, despite my attempt to smile brightly, but simply laughed.

'I like to play up the American angle while I'm in France,' he explained. 'It keeps the growers off guard and it goes down well with the boys at home.'

He was in good humour, explaining how he adjusted his image to suit the circumstances, as he found me a trolley and wheeled it out to his hire car. That made it easy to relax, and as I settled back into the seat I was thoroughly looking forward to the weekend. I'd expected to be staying at a hotel in the city, and was surprised when he turned on to the ring road instead of following the *Centre Ville* signs.

'Where are we going?'

'Pomerol,' he told me. 'We're guests at Château La-Croix-de-Pignon.'

I nodded, impressed. La-Croix-de-Pignon was one of those few châteaux whose reputation had risen to the point at which only the super-rich could afford to drink the wine regularly, in no small part thanks to Earle.

'The new owners are determined to make a splash,' he explained, 'so they've invited a group of us to celebrate the release of their '05.'

'New owners?'

'Sure, didn't you know? When old man Saint-Cibard died his heirs couldn't agree on how to run things, nor on very much else by the sound of things. They ended up selling to the Blanquefort family, which really means Southern and Allied.'

'Oh. That's another fine estate down the pan, then.'

'Let's try it first, shall we?'

'You're right, of course, but their new Kavanagh *Cordon Noir* Cognac is a complete rip-off.'

He answered with a non-committal shrug and went quiet as he concentrated on passing a brace of lorries. When he spoke again it was to discuss the vintage. Apparently the dry start to autumn had allowed them to pick at least some grapes in reasonable condition, so it wasn't going to be the complete disaster I'd been expecting. Inevitably a lot of the growers were claiming a last-minute miracle and asking prices higher than the year before, among them several of the big names, but Earle was intending to be cautious and advise against rushing out to buy stock, an attitude that struck me as refreshingly honest in comparison to Anton Yoshida's.

Anton, I realised, was very likely to be there, which brought back the mixed feelings he'd inspired in me; anger, of course, but also a completely involuntary arousal. I told myself I'd keep my feelings carefully hidden and stick close to Earle, making it very clear that I wasn't interested, though I knew Yoshida was more likely to be amused than jealous.

We'd crossed the river before Earle finished his explanation, and as we climbed into the low hills of the Entre-Deux-Mers he fell silent for a while. When he did speak again there was a new tone to his voice, a hint of tension as he cautiously sounded me out.

'We have one of the best suites,' he said, 'the Louis Treize. They're all named after French kings, because they had enough called Louis to go around eighteen rooms. Ours is mighty fine, with a four-poster bed, nearly three hundred years old, apparently.'

'You'd better have me on a chair, then,' I joked. 'We wouldn't want to break the bed.'

He laughed, relaxed again, then went on.

'Say, it was good that first time, after the *Corkscrew* tasting, wasn't it? Took me right back that did, right back to my high-school days, parking up with some sweet little popsy . . .'

He trailed off with a sigh, but I could easily image the memories he'd be dwelling on. I wasn't sure how old he was, but he had to have been a teenager during the late 50s and early 60s, which meant he'd have been in some big, old-fashioned American car, beside a girl with a high pony-tail and her tight jumper pulled up over her tits while she tugged at his cock or, if he was very lucky or very pushy, sucked it.

I never cease to be amazed at my sexuality. In the previous month I'd taken so many cocks in my mouth I'd lost count, and yet the thought of being made to suck Earle off in his car still gave me a deliciously naughty thrill. We could recreate his memory, or my version of it, with my breasts out and the radio playing as I brought him to orgasm in my mouth and forced myself to swallow. Suddenly I needed it, badly, but my jaw muscles gave a twinge of protest and I decided to make my offer a little less generous.

'I suppose I'd better toss you off,' I told him, 'otherwise you might lose control and fuck me. Park up then, you dirty bastard.'

He understood immediately, grinning as he put his foot down. I didn't know the area, despite having driven up and down this motorway several times before, but he obviously did. Turning off at the top of the hill, he quickly found a track running between vineyards on one side and a thick wood on the other. The vines were shorn of their grapes and the yellow-brown leaves hung limply or were scattered on the ground. The growers were presumably all busy indoors working with barrels and vats. Nobody was about.

Earle parked at the very end of the track, where a circle of open ground, half-hidden in the trees, allowed tractors to turn. He backed in, positioning the car so that we'd get ample warning if anybody came our way, and turned the engine off, leaving us in silence.

'Get your dirty cock out then,' I told him and began to tug my top out from my jeans.

He didn't need telling, unzipping his fly as I pulled up my top and bra to bare my breasts. They felt lovely naked, very sensitive, with my nipples already stiff, but when he reached out for them I wagged a finger at him.

'Oh, no, you don't, mister. You can look, but you can't touch.'

He grinned, understanding. His cock was out, his balls too, bulging from the fly of his smart white trousers. There's something deliciously obscene about a man's genitals sticking out of his fly when he's otherwise fully dressed, even when he's limp. It's better still when he's hard, a nice stiff cock shaft rearing up above the sack of his balls: arousing, even a little bit frightening. I lost no time in taking him in hand, wanking slowly up and down, imagining what I was doing as a disagreeable but necessary task, disagreeable because no gentleman would ever make a girl play with his prick, necessary because if I didn't wank him off I'd get fucked.

I knew it was all nonsense, but it made a lovely fantasy as he slowly grew stiff in my hand, and as I grew more excited I let my mind wander to different and ruder permutations. Simply wanking off my boyfriend to avoid a rough fucking was nice, but it was better still to imagine myself a virgin, with the prospect of getting my hymen popped if I didn't manage to bring him off in my hand. He was a lot older than me too, allowing me to think of him not as my boyfriend but as my boss, some philandering bastard who'd lured me out in his car and given me a straight choice, get him off in my hand or have my virgin cunt fucked.

He was rock-hard, his eyes flicking lazily over my bare boobs as I wanked him. He was thoroughly in control, and I was just his dirty girl. I began to stroke and squeeze his balls, teasing him in the rising hope that he would lose control and fuck me. It was what I needed, but I had to be taken. When he let his seat down I thought he was going to do it, but he stayed as he was, lying back in comfort while I was forced to adjust my position, kneeling on the seat with my boobs jiggling as I went back to tossing his cock.

I popped the top button of my jeans, just to give him the idea of pulling them down, panties and all, and sticking his lovely cock right up me. Still he didn't respond, his face now slack with ecstasy and his breathing hard and deep. He was going to spunk in my hand, leaving me to frig off over my fantasy, which was nice but not as nice as a good rough fucking. I pulled down my zip, allowing him to see the little ribbon bow at the top of my panties, and went back to stroking his balls.

'You . . . you're not going to use me, are you?' I ventured, making my eyes as big as possible and giving my tits a little shake.

'Christ, but you're horny!' he swore, and got up.

There was nothing fake about my squeal of surprise as I was manhandled into position, spread out on his seat with my legs rolled up, my jeans and panties jerked unceremoniously down over my hips and bottom, baring me to his cock. He stuck it in with one, hard thrust and I was being fucked, just the way I'd wanted it, hard and crude. I couldn't get to my pussy or I'd have been frigging immediately, but it didn't matter.

With every push the broad, smooth buckle of his outsize belt pressed into me and I knew that would be enough to get me there. I was genuinely helpless, trapped beneath his weight, and I knew he wasn't going to stop. All I could do was cling on to the seat and push my hips up to increase the friction on my pussy, which made my position more awkward and painful, just as I wanted it to be.

In my mind he was my boss, some utter bastard who'd pressured me into sex, promising not to take my virginity if I tossed him off, but then fucked me anyway, my virgin blood trickling down my bum slit as I was pounded into the seat of his car. Worse, far worse, he could have been my uncle, tricking his innocent niece first into showing him her titties, then taking his dirty cock in her hand, only to lose control completely and fuck her . . . fuck me, strip me and fuck me, strip me and fuck me and spunk up me to leave me torn and pregnant.

I came, bucking furiously against his body as his belt buckle slapped on my clit and his cock drove in and out, ever faster. Three times he brought me to a peak before whipping his cock out at the last instant and jerking himself off between my bum cheeks. I felt the hot come spatter on my anus, and as it began to trickle down I was still imagining it as the blood from my ruined hymen.

Our session in the woods made an excellent start to the weekend. Château La-Croix-de-Pignon was every bit as magnificent as Earle had implied. It had apparently been converted in order to entertain wealthy clients and pundits, with no expense spared on either the ancient furnishings or the ultra-modern infrastructure. Never before had I seen a genuine Louis Quinze desk with a laptop built in, and although I guessed it would have given an antique collector apoplexy it was certainly both smart and convenient. The bed was better still, with satin sheets, and had I not drained Earle half an hour before he would have had me then and there while I changed out of my jeans into a dress.

We spent the early afternoon being shown around and introduced to people, including many I'd have been more than eager to meet when I'd first taken up my job. None of that really mattered now, but it was still useful and I stayed on best behaviour, smiling and flirting a little when the situation called for it. As I'd suspected, Anton Yoshida was there, and his arrogant smirk as he greeted me was the only unpleasant moment until the time came to taste the newly bottled '05.

I'd expected a tour of the winery but they were altogether too grand for that, instead presenting the 'oh-five vintage in a magnificent drawing room looking out across the lawns and vineyards towards Vieux Château Certan. Everybody smacked their lips and made approving noises, although at a release price well in excess of £1,000 a bottle I wouldn't be bothering to put any down myself. Anton Yoshida seemed to think otherwise, and made a long and unctuous speech about the legendary status of the vintage and the great potential of the wine, citing it as a rival to Pétrus itself and an excellent investment opportunity. A good many of our fellow guests were wealthy businessmen, many from the Far East, who took him at his word and made out presumably enormous cheques on the spot.

That was my second bad moment, because the amount of money changing hands, if perhaps not quite enough to pull Hambling and Borse around, would have been a major step in the right direction. It was exactly the sort of transaction I had imagined myself conducting, or at the least influencing, but thanks to Anton Yoshida I'd been firmly locked out. I'd been abused and humiliated into the bargain, and the worst of it was that the memory sparked a sudden surge of excitement, quite involuntary and so strong it hurt.

I turned to the window in an effort to hide my emotions, wishing I had better control of them, although I knew perfectly well that it was that very inability to resist that gave the greatest pleasure. Yoshida was just feet away, assuring some Chinese bigwig that he was making a sensible choice, and I did my best to shut out his voice. A lorry was visible beyond some trees on one side of the vineyard, moving in among a cluster of low, modern buildings half hidden by foliage, evidently the actual winery. I could see why we hadn't been taken there. No doubt brand-new and state-of-the-art, it lacked the air of mystique that was essential for charging prices out of all proportion to the sensual pleasure of the wine. Not that the buyers cared, because they almost certainly wouldn't drink it themselves but would sell it on at a profit, a point underlined as Yoshida's voice forced itself back into my reverie.

'. . . a very sound investment indeed, I assure you. Prices have been rising at an unprecedented rate and there is every reason to believe that they will continue to do so. Of one thing you can be certain, Château La-Croix-de-Pignon will receive excellent publicity, as will this particular vintage.'

He wasn't even attempting to appear independent, promoting the wine for all he was worth, and I wondered if Southern and Allied were actually paying him or if he intended to make a killing by buying stock himself and talking it up, or both. I bit my lip in irritation, wishing I had a fraction of his influence, or could at least enlist Earle to my cause, and I had to remind myself forcefully that I'd chosen a different path.

I was still staring resentfully out of the window when a hand was laid gently on my shoulder. Expecting Earle, I turned with a smile, only to find myself looking up into the cool, haughty face of Anton Yoshida.

'You're very good at getting yourself into prestigious events,' he remarked. 'In fact, I didn't know they invited shopgirls at all.'

'I'm here as Mr Hayes's guest,' I told him, keeping my voice as cold as I could manage.

'Oh,' he said. 'I do apologise, not a shopgirl then. I didn't realise you were Earle's tart.'

I felt the blood rush to my face, and restrained myself with difficulty from planting my knee in his crotch as he went on.

'Isn't he a little old for you? A little straight-laced too, I would imagine?'

'Not at all,' I said icily. 'He is a very considerate lover, which is more than can be said for some people.'

He laughed.

'Ah, yes, I tied you up and left you for a while, didn't I? But you mustn't be resentful. I only did it to teach you a lesson, and you did rather enjoy it, didn't you?'

'No, I did not!' I snapped, but my face was crimson and we both knew I was lying.

He responded with a knowing smirk, so smug, so superior, that for a second time I had to fight down the urge to hit him. I was close to tears as well, and he must have realised, but he wasn't finished with me.

'You did,' he said, 'and, as it happens, so did I, so once you've put Earle to bed with a mug of cocoa and let him jerk off over your fat, white, Anglo-Saxon breasts or whatever it is he likes to do to you, why don't you come up to my suite for something more worthwhile? A little bondage perhaps, in a kneeling position, I think. I'm in the Louis Quatorze.'

'I'd sooner have sex with a diseased warthog!'

'Hmm . . . well, I'm not certain I can manage a warthog, but Monsieur Blanquefort has a magnificent Great Dane who could probably be persuaded to mount you. Perhaps I could even persuade some of my friends to come and watch.'

'Pig!'

'If you insist, although I understand that their cocks are rather small, and having had the experience of your cunt I expect the Great Dane would be a better fit.'

This time I couldn't stop myself. My leg came up, as hard as I could, but he was too quick, or more likely he was used to girls trying to knee him in the balls. I missed, nearly fell over and only kept my balance by grabbing the curtain, which fortunately was sturdy enough to hold me. Anton pretended to offer an arm as he made a quick apology to the little knot of guests who'd noticed.

'She is a little drunk, I'm afraid, but we must forgive her. I don't suppose a girl her age has the opportunity to drink wine of such quality very often, if at all.'

The men were all from the Far East and bobbed politely in response, but I was left with my face and chest blushing red-hot, furious and with tears coursing down my cheeks. I could have cheerfully killed him, but with an immense effort of will I managed to bring myself back under control, and was about to give him my opinion of his behaviour, quietly but without reserve, when Earle appeared.

'Are you all right, Natasha?' he asked, with a nod for Anton.

'My heel,' I said hurriedly, 'it got caught in the ventilator and I twisted my foot.'

'I see. Anyway, Anton, I see you're keen, and I confess that it has structure and balance, as any respectable wine from the vintage should, but I'm not convinced it's greatly superior to its neighbours.'

'I think the market will agree with my verdict,' Anton responded, every bit as arrogant towards Earle as he had been to me, if less rude.

'The market will follow your verdict, don't you mean?' I said, determined to at least try and puncture his ego. 'Even up to ten times the sensible price.'

He merely shrugged.

'I am influential, it is true, and justly so. People rely on my opinions, as they do on Mr Hayes's, but you clearly have no understanding of how these things work. These are not wines to be compared like for like, as you might when deciding which of two *vins ordinaires* you intend to use to wash down your roast beef. The price represents the wine's prestige, and without that prestige it is nothing. Do you suppose Mr Zhang over there would entertain his clients with a bottle costing ten pounds, or even a hundred pounds? The concept would be unutterably shameful to him. No, prestigious wines must be expensive, and be seen to be expensive. Hence the price.'

'But why Château La-Croix-de-Pignon?' I asked, hoping he had such a low opinion of me that he'd admit to being, to all intents and purposes, bribed.

He was not to be caught so easily.

'It is the best,' he said, 'or, at least, one of a handful which can compete for the title of the best each year.'

I'd expected Earle to say something in my defence, but he remained silent, his nose deep in his glass.

'How can you be so certain?' I demanded. 'Have you tasted the '05 from every property in Bordeaux, or even Pomerol?'

'I taste only the best.'

'That doesn't make sense. How can you know what the best is until you've tasted it?'

'By the technique and quality of viticulture and vinification,' he replied airily. 'Why should I trouble to taste a wine I know to be badly made? Besides, the *petits châteaux* cannot afford to make great wine.'

'Fifty years ago La-Croix-de-Pignon was considered a *petit château.*'

'Exactly, but it has the land, which is why M. Blanquefort has chosen to invest, an investment which in turn justifies the price.'

'But you just said the price was a function of . . . oh, never mind.'

He was making me cross and I could see he thought it was funny. Nor was Earle going to help, as I discovered when he finally withdrew his nose from his glass.

'Mr Yoshida is right,' he said with infuriating complacency. 'The trade at this level has very little to do with the simple, sensual pleasures you appreciate so much and everything to do with supply and demand. Mr Yoshida and I ensure that what is presented as the best really is the best. Without us, goodness knows what horrible stuff the wealthy would be drinking.'

'*Cordon Noir* Cognac?' I suggested in what I knew was a pretty feeble sally.

'The economics are not easy to understand,' Yoshida said, openly implying that I was stupid.

Both men nodded. I gave up, angry and embarrassed. Cask samples of the '06 had been set out on a side table and I went over, intrigued to find how the château had coped with a poor year. I hadn't had a chance to taste any, but I'd read the vintage reports, which dwelt on bad weather leading to thin wine with harsh tannins. Both Gilbert and Earle had said that Pomerol had come off best, but only those producers who'd been rigorous about discarding all but the best grapes had managed to make good wine.

The wine was curious: big, rich and fruity, with very little of the sharp acidity or bitter tannin I'd been expecting, and entirely different from my experience of Pomerol in poor years. Nevertheless, given it blind I wasn't sure I'd even have recognised it as Bordeaux, and it was far inferior to the '05 in quality – though not price, which had been reduced by only fifteen per cent. Most extraordinarily of all, it was going to be ready in four or five years. I was forced to admit that there might be something in what Anton Yoshida had said. No producer without a lot of money behind them could have afforded to make such a good wine in such a poor year.

I turned to look out of the window while I finished my glass, found myself staring at the biggest, blackest dog I had ever seen and turned quickly back – to find myself staring at Rhiannon, an altogether more attractive sight, despite being painted purple and having vine leaves and bunches of grapes in her hair. Her dress was a sort of Roman tunic, tightly belted but loose at chest and hips, also purple and extremely short.

She was giving out brochures to the guests, making a little curtsy as she handed each one over. A good many of the men present were giving her surreptitious glances, a few admiring her openly, and I could see their point. Despite the silly costume she looked enchanting, and if she bent even slightly she was going to be making a show of her bottom. I walked over, delighted to see her despite the hideously embarrassing circumstances of our last meeting. She smiled, bobbed and spoke quietly as she handed me a brochure.

'Hi, nice to see you.'

'You too. Why are you purple?'

'I'm supposed to represent the spirit of the vine, but I'm not supposed to chat with the guests. See you later, yeah?'

She moved off, leaving me with my interest piqued. Her voice had been quiet and oddly shy, but also a little excited, unless that was just wishful thinking. Things hadn't worked out in Paris, and she definitely came under the heading of unfinished business, but I hadn't expected to see her again. Now, with her pretty legs twinkling as she walked and her little round bottom bobbing under her skirt, she looked infinitely desirable, and her sweet, shy attitude only enhanced her charm.

Being with Earle made things awkward, because while I'd have been perfectly happy with a threesome the suggestion would almost certainly scare her off. The only other possibility seemed to be to try and seduce her as fast as I could and hope to grab a quickie or two over the course of the weekend, but that was neither certain to work nor particularly satisfying. What I really wanted was several hours alone together so that we could thoroughly explore each other, but that didn't look like being feasible.

I promised myself that I'd catch up with her if I could, and went back to my wine, now feeling frustrated as well as irritable. Earle was still talking to Anton Yoshida and they were now the centre of a knot of businessmen, all tasting the '06 and listening politely. I thought of going into the garden, remembered the Great Dane and changed my mind. With nothing better to do, I went to watch the sun set, dwelling on what the coming night might bring as the vineyards were splashed with gold and rosy pinks that couldn't help reminding me of the colour of smacked bottom flesh.

It was announced that dinner would be in half an hour, and I hurried upstairs to change. The meal proved to be an extraordinarily drawn-out affair. M. Blanquefort at least had better taste than the

Kavanaghs, serving a brilliant succession of wines from the family estates, beginning with a fresh, dry crémant, through Entre-Deux-Mers and white Graves, Fronsac, Château La-Croix-de-Pignon itself from the '66 and '70 vintages, Margaux, St-Estèphe and finally a luxurious old Sauternes. Each wine was accompanied by a suitable delicacy, and with Earle very much the centre of attention at our table I was left pretty much to myself, save for having to flirt a little with the ancient Chinese businessman to my left.

Rhiannon was one of the waitresses, along with several others in the same purple outfit, and as the wine did its work on me it grew harder and harder not to watch her, especially as each time she bent to serve, her dress would lift just enough to show the double curve of a beautiful little peach and a triangle of purple panties clinging lovingly to her cheeks. I wanted to pull them down and spank her, to smother my face in her hot bottom and lick her to ecstasy from behind, to have her sit it in my face and laugh at me while I licked her anus.

None of it was likely to happen, but by the time M. Blanquefort had got through the toasts and people had begun to disperse I was feeling impossibly horny. Cognac, coffee and chocolates were being served in the drawing room in which they'd held the tasting, with Rhiannon serving. In different company I'd have had her on the floor, but while I'm sure most of the men would have enjoyed the show it was obviously out of the question. Even speaking to her privately was next to impossible, but I finally managed it, hissing a question as she filled my coffee cup while Earle was distracted.

'Where are you staying?'

'The girls' dormitory block, across the main courtyard, room twelve.'

Her answer was shy and uncertain, but also breathless, giving me a sharp pang of desire. I made to speak again, but M. Blanquefort himself was approaching and a moment later the head waiter had told her off to fetch fresh coffee, leaving me more frustrated than ever, and more expectant. She had to be game, I was sure of it, or almost sure, but I was going to try my luck anyway, whatever the consequences.

Nine

I made a hasty, and drunken, plan, intending to tell Earle I was going out for a breath of fresh air and then sneaking across to the dormitory block. Rhiannon had been on duty for at least six hours, maybe longer, so surely had to get off soon. I'd meet her and her friends in the courtyard as if by accident, get her alone in her room, tease her out of her clothes, suck her pretty little breasts, spank her gorgeous bottom, have her return the favour, go down on her and finish off queened on her face with her tongue well in up my bumhole . . .

'How about an early night, Natasha?'

It was Earle, breaking into my fantasy and destroying it with a single remark. I could hardly refuse, and as I was led from the room I tried to console myself that at least I was going to get a good fucking. We passed a group of which Anton Yoshida was part and I stuck my nose in the air, but there was no escaping the amused disdain of his expression and I found myself blushing as we climbed the stairs. He knew Earle and I were going to bed, and it was pretty obvious we'd be having sex too. I could imagine what he'd be thinking, about me getting it the way he'd suggested, with my tits out while I milked Earle all over them – my fat, white, Anglo-Saxon breasts, as he'd called them. Exhausted, Earle would fall asleep, and I would sneak over to the Louis Quatorze suite, where I'd be made to strip nude, tied up in some awkward and humiliating position, beaten, penetrated and spunked on, before he went to fetch M. Blanquefort and a few others for the real show.

It wasn't going to happen, it just couldn't, and yet I wanted it, all of it, too drunk and vulnerable to pretend otherwise. I told myself I'd go to Rhiannon instead, but suddenly the thought of her sweet, inexperienced caresses seemed inadequate beside the horrible fantasy Anton Yoshida had planted in my mind. My only hope was that Earle would keep me busy, and he was at least eager, fumbling for his fly even as he closed the door of our suite behind him. I bounced down on the bed, watching as he produced his cock and balls, just the way he had done earlier, with everything hanging out but his trousers still done up.

'How would you like me?' I teased, hoping to slow him down a little and make it last at least long enough to let me come and get some of the awful thoughts out of my head.

'Wide open, honey,' he told me, pushing his cock at my mouth.

'OK, but not for too long,' I replied.

Just in time, I stopped myself explaining, realising that he almost certainly wasn't the sort of man who would get off on knowing that the girl who was about to take his precious cock in her mouth had sucked so many men off during the last week that her jaw still ached. He knew I was no angel, but like most of his sex he appreciated experience while wanting innocence. I took him in as deep as I could, trying to concentrate on the cock in my mouth instead of imagining myself in tight bondage as I was mounted from the rear, with a dozen Oriental businessmen laughing at my plight and placing bets on which of my two well-lubricated holes would be used.

'That's good,' Earle sighed, rescuing me from my nightmare. 'You are one beautiful little cocksucker.'

Earlier in the day, when we'd parked in the woods, his remark would have worked on me well, making me feel small and dirty at the same time; a compliment, in a sense, and yet implying that all I'm good for is my looks and my ability to get men off in my mouth. Now it was wholly inadequate, because Anton Yoshida had already made me feel tiny, while what he'd threatened me with went far beyond merely sucking cock, which just about everybody does after all. Earle was nearly stiff anyway, and I was going to get fucked, hard and rough, but it just wouldn't be enough, or so I thought until Earle rescued me with a single question.

'OK, I'm ready. On your knees with you, and tell me how your uncle spanks you while we do it.'

It was as if he'd flicked a switch. Suddenly what Percy had said came back to me, and the full extent of my filthy fantasies earlier that day, so dirty it made me choke to think of it. Now I could get off the way I like to, over something truly filthy: not some tepid piece of sex anybody might have, but something that would make my supposedly liberated friends go pale. I bounced over on the bed, exhibiting my bottom beneath the deep red satin of my evening dress, with my back pulled in tight and my knees a little apart to make myself as enticing as possible for him.

'You're a bastard, Earle, but OK, I will, if that's what you want. First . . . first he tells me off, when I've been naughty, and . . . and if I complain and tell him it's not right he always says the same thing. He says he's my uncle, and he has a right to spank me, and that it doesn't matter that I'm grown up, because I'm still a naughty girl and I still need to be spanked, spanked regularly, and spanked on my bare bottom. He always get me bare-bottom, always. He bends me across his knee and he pulls down my trousers or lifts up my dress. Like this, Earle, watch.'

He didn't need telling, his eyes bulging as I reached back, raising one knee at a time to lift my dress, showing my nylon-clad thighs and the soft ring of flesh above my stocking tops, my straining suspender straps and the seat of my red satin knickers pulled taut over my bulging cheeks. His hand was on his cock, wanking furiously as I exposed myself.

'Always bare-bottom,' I repeated, my voice now husky with my own emotion. 'He always gets me bare-bottom. It doesn't matter now much I plead. It doesn't matter how much I kick and wriggle and howl. It doesn't even matter if I cry. He says bad girls have to go bare-bottom, so my knickers come down, every time . . . every time, Earle, at my age, a grown woman, and this is what he shows off, Earle.'

I'd put my thumbs in the waistband of my panties and, as I spoke, I'd begun to ease them down, ever so slowly exposing my bottom, the top of my crease, the fullness of my cheeks, the rude, dark star of my bumhole, the pouted shape of my pussy lips and the wetness between, and, of course, my cane welts.

'Jesus!' he breathed.

'I know,' I sobbed. 'The last time he caned me. He took me across his knee and pulled my panties down the way he always does, and spanked me, spanked my bare bottom until I was all pink and hot, and crying too. But he still said it wasn't enough, so he made me touch my toes, still with my bottom all bare, and he caned me, my own uncle.'

I burst into tears, overcome by my own story, for all that it was completely made up. He should have felt guilty, maybe he did, but that didn't stop him. He was growling curses as he climbed on to the bed, his cock in his hand as he got into position behind me. I felt his helmet push at my flesh, against one thigh, then on target and up me. The breath was driven from my body as my pussy filled and he began to pump into me, furiously hard, and as he rode me he slapped my bottom.

'Christ, what a bastard!' he gasped. 'What a bastard, but you know . . . you know, I can't say I blame him, not with a niece like you, 'cause if ever a girl needed spanking it's you, Natasha . . . spanking and fucking, and, by God, am I the man to do it!'

All the while he'd been pushing into me so hard that it took all my concentration to brace myself and take it, but I needed to come and what he'd said was just right. If I'd been his niece he'd have spanked me and fucked me, which was exactly what he was doing. I imagined myself as before, his innocent niece, only not seduced into taking his cock in her hand and then fucked when he got carried away, but spanked for being a naughty girl and then mounted on her hot bottom because he couldn't resist her.

It was perfect, or it would have been if he hadn't suddenly paused to grab his hat from the side table where he'd put it earlier. He began to beat me with it, slapping my hip and bottom as he thrust into me, breaking my fantasy of a hand-spanking over his knee followed by a rough, uncontrolled fucking. I'd still have made it, as soon as I'd got my hand to my pussy, but he went off at a tangent, shrieking and slapping my bottom with his hat as he fucked me.

'Ride 'em cowboy!' he yelled. 'Oh yeah, this is the way, on your knees and whupped like some crazy bronco!'

My fantasy disintegrated, and I'd have burst into giggles if he hadn't been jamming himself in and out of me so hard I was fighting for breath. I reached back, still determined to try and get myself off, but his next thrust knocked me sideways. His cock slipped out, was very nearly jammed up my unlubricated bottom hole, slid between my cheeks instead and erupted a fountain of spunk all over my expensive satin evening dress. I collapsed on the bed, feeling thoroughly put upon as he finished himself off over my bottom and into my knickers, still whooping with delight and gibbering about cowboys and broncos.

I suppose I should have found it thoroughly humiliating, both to be referred to as a horse and to have my clothes spunked all over, but I'd been too focused on my own fantasy. Unfortunately, he was straddling my legs, pinning me to the bed, making it impossible for me to masturbate. By the time he got off I'd given up, intending to wait until he'd recovered and have him spank me while I brought myself off.

He wasn't going to do that while my bottom was sticky with spunk, and I was keen to save my dress, so I skipped into the bathroom and quickly cleaned up. As I did so I was sorting out my fantasy in my head, wondering if it would be best to carry on as before or try and mix in his cowboy fetish, perhaps imagining myself as a girl spanked by her uncle at a rodeo, perhaps in front of the men she'd been flirting with to earn her punishment.

It would have worked too, but when I came out of the bathroom Earle was in bed, snoring gently. I threw my dirty knickers at him in frustration, but they fell short, leaving me standing there boiling with frustration and rising worry. Earle had come over me and immediately fallen asleep, just as Anton Yoshida had predicted, except that it was my bum rather than my tits he'd spunked over. Now all I had to do was walk across the passage to the Louis Quatorze suite and I'd get what I needed: roped, abused, fucked . . .

I was not going to do it, but I was going to get my fun, with Rhiannon. With my jaw set firm I pulled on a fresh pair of panties and my coat and slipped my mobile into my pocket in case I was locked out. Then I let myself into the passage. People were still up and I could hear a faint buzz of voices and laughter coming from the direction of the stairs. I had no wish to be seen, especially by Yoshida, who for all I knew was still up, and going into his room to wait for him would have been even more humiliating than finding him ready. I went the other way instead, along the passage to where a smaller staircase led me down to the ground floor. I came out near the kitchens, and let myself out of the scullery door into the main courtyard.

The night was cold, and my breath showed in the air where an old-fashioned lamp illuminated the back door. My shoes crunched on the frosted gravel. Doubts had begun to assail me. Maybe she didn't want me at all, at least not sexually, and while she had told me where she was staying she hadn't actually invited me to come over, especially not around midnight. If she did want me, maybe she'd be horrified by the sort of filthy fantasies I need to explore in order to get off. Yet I had to try.

Her dormitory block was easy to locate, a modern two-storey building next to the château's cellars, or *chai*, and half hidden by trees. Some of the lights were still on, but as I approached the door I saw that not only was it covered by a CCTV camera but it opened to a code pressed into an intercom panel. I hesitated, wondering if a late-night visit from a guest would get her into trouble. On the one hand they'd had her running around half the night showing her legs off to a load of middle-aged businessmen, who were sure to make passes at her, and she *had* invited me to come over. On the other, Southern and Allied seemed to be pretty strict with their employees and I knew she wasn't supposed to talk to guests while at work. More importantly, if I was caught on camera M. Blanquefort might find out, and possibly even Anton Yoshida or Earle.

I decided not to risk it and went around the back, carefully avoiding the camera. The windows were quite high, out of my reach, the curtains closed, so I couldn't see in at all. She'd said she was in room two, which was probably the first window on the right, so once again I hesitated, before deciding that if I got the wrong girl I'd just have to ask. I picked up some gravel and threw it at the window, and after a moment of agonising suspense the curtain was drawn back and a face appeared. Rhiannon.

'Hi,' I whispered, my voice thick with embarrassment. 'It's me, Natasha. Can I come in, please?'

She glanced down, more nervous and shy than ever, then shook her head. A rush of disappointment hit me, so strong it made me feel sick, but then she spoke, in an urgent hiss.

'I wish you could.'

She wanted me. I tried not to giggle as my sick disappointment vanished under a wave of euphoria.

'We're not allowed visitors after six,' she explained, 'and there's CCTV over the front door and in the passage.'

'What is this, Colditz?'

'Something like that, and my contract says I'm not to do anything that might bring Southern and Allied into disrepute, which includes shagging.'

'I'm not going to shag you, although I would if I had the equipment.'

She giggled, removing the last shred of doubt from my mind.

'Help me up,' I demanded, reaching up.

'I can't, I share my room! Evaline's in the bathroom.'

'Will she mind?'

Rhiannon burst into giggles.

'Of course she'll mind!'

I shrugged, more than happy to accommodate Evaline, who was presumably one of the other waitresses. Rhiannon spoke again.

'I'll come down. She won't tell on me.'

I was going to object, but she was already climbing out and I saw that she was still in her waitress outfit, allowing me to see all the way up her skirt as she swung one pretty leg out of the window. I tried to help, and the thrill as I touched her flesh made my throat tight with desire, especially when I tried to take her weight and her thigh and the curve of her bottom pressed to my face. At that moment she lost her grip and dropped the last couple of feet. I tried to catch her, fell over and we collapsed in a giggling heap on the frost-covered grass. The feel of her in my arms was too much and I kissed her, my hand slipping down under her tiny skirt to cup one resilient bottom cheek as our mouths opened together. I would have had her, right there, but she pulled away, speaking in a hoarse whisper.

'We'll get caught, Natasha, and it's bloody freezing!'

'Well, if you were dressed properly,' I joked and slapped her bottom.

She gave a little purr, and after that I'd have had her even if Anton Yoshida, M. Blanquefort and the Great Dane had all turned up together. I tugged her bodice down, baring small upturned breasts, her nipples straining to erection in the cold air. She squeaked and giggled but pulled away once more, protesting.

'Natasha, not here! Let's go to your room.'

'We can't . . . unless you fancy letting Earle Hayes join in?'

'You're with a man?'

'Yes,' I began, and stopped, embarrassed to admit my companion was almost twice my age. 'Never mind him, though, it's you I want. I don't know, maybe he won't wake up, or maybe he can watch?'

She gave me her shy smile and shook her head. Like me she was drunk and horny, but not enough to go for what might be her first lesbian encounter in front of a strange man.

'We have to go somewhere,' I pointed out.

Her response was an urgent nod and to set off along the side of the dormitory block, beckoning me to follow. We came to a gateway, let into the high stone wall of the *chai*. The rusty gate stood open, and a pathway led among old stone buildings, creating a confusing patchwork of angular shadows and splashes of dim light. Rhiannon took my hand and drew me to one of the buildings and in at a door. As it closed behind us she switched on a light, revealing a windowless room, evidently a disused part of the *chai*, to judge by the rusty, cobwebbed wine-making equipment at one end. Nearer to us were chairs and a table with an empty mug, a used ashtray and a French magazine on it. An old-fashioned gas stove warmed the room.

'Some of us come here to cadge cigarettes off the lorry drivers,' Rhiannon explained in a whisper. 'And other things.'

I could well imagine it. The air was warm and smelt of strong cigarettes and male sweat. No doubt the drivers were more than happy to entertain the girls from the dormitory, and to keep their indiscretions secret. I was already picturing the two of us kneeling on chairs, kissing and playing with each other as half a dozen men took turns with us from behind, something I very much doubted she could have coped with.

'What if they come back?' I asked.

'No lorries, no drivers,' she pointed out.

I was going to ask why the stove was on, but she was smiling and beckoning me forward again. At the other end of the room, half concealed by the old machinery, there was a door, and beyond it a storeroom, empty except for some old bottles and cans and a big, stained mattress. She closed the door, slid a bolt home and we were alone.

'Neat, huh?' she giggled. 'A lot of the girls come here to . . .'

She went suddenly quiet and looked down, once more unsure of herself. All we had to see by was the faint light coming in through a big keyhole and under the door, but I could imagine her pretty face and the shy look that turned me on so much. I took her in my arms to guide her gently down on to the mattress, kissing her and stroking her skin. She responded as before, unsure what to do but making no effort to stop me as I gently eased her bodice down over her breasts and tucked up her skirt to get her bare behind. I could feel her shivering, no longer with cold but with apprehension, but her mouth was open under mine and she had allowed one hand to sneak down to the curve of my bottom.

I needed more, far more – urgent, rude, filthy sex, with fingers and tongues up pussies and in bumholes – but I forced myself to hold back, kissing and exploring until she'd begun to sigh and cling to me in her rising pleasure. Only then did I take down her knickers, easing her out of them and gently spreading her thighs. She gave a little, abandoned sob as her legs parted, perhaps as much in surrender as in pleasure, but there was no doubting the ecstasy of her sigh as my tongue found her pussy. I added a pair of fingers, meaning to penetrate her while I licked her out, but she went suddenly stiff.

'No,' she gasped, 'not that. I . . . I've never been—'

She broke off, but I knew what she meant and suddenly everything about her made a lot more sense. I touched her and felt the tight arc of skin around the mouth of her pussy. She was a virgin, a discovery that sent a delicious thrill through me. I'd seduced a virgin, introducing her to lesbian sex before she'd ever had a man, making her my own sweet playmate, who'd be licking me in turn just as soon as I'd brought her off.

I needed it desperately, but didn't dare push her too hard, so I licked her gently and stroked her thighs until her hand found my hair and pulled me in more firmly. Now I had her, and I began to lick harder and allow my hands to stray down to her bottom, teasing her cheeks, and between. She gave a little mew of protest when I found her bumhole, but she didn't try to stop me. I couldn't see, but her hole felt tight and sweetly formed, making me want to lick it and see how far in I could get my tongue, but she was already starting to flex her thighs and push herself into my face, obviously close to orgasm. Her bumhole began to squeeze and I slipped my finger in a little way, feeling her tiny ring tighten to the contractions of her muscles, her virgin pussy too, as she came against my face, sobbing out my name over and over again in what might even have been her first-ever climax.

When she was done I moved up to take her in my arms, kissing her once more and cuddling her close. She was shaking and sobbing, maybe struggling to come to terms with having come under another woman's tongue, maybe just overwhelmed by her orgasm, but in any case needing to be held. It took all my self-control just to let her cling to me, because the feel of her body in my arms was both frustrating and arousing, but I knew I had to let her take things at her own pace. What I wanted was her bottom in my face, to savour her sweet little bumhole and virgin pussy while she licked me to ecstasy, but I knew I couldn't just lie down and ask her to climb on top. She need cajoling into it, slowly and carefully.

'My turn, yes?' I said, speaking very softly and stroking her hair.

She nodded and her trembling abruptly increased.

'How would you like me?' I offered.

'I . . . I don't know. You choose.'

'Head to tail? That's nice, and your body is so lovely.'

'If you like,' she answered, so sweet and shy and nervous that her words alone made my tummy tighten.

She was going to do it, to lick me to ecstasy with her pretty little bottom right in my face. I was shaking as much as she was as I hitched my dress up to get at my panties, only to stop, realising how much more fun it would be to have her pull them down for me. She'd seen me tied up, she knew I was kinky, so maybe I could even persuade her to spank me before we went head to toe. I had to ask.

'Rhiannon? Would you mind doing me a little favour?'

'What's that?'

'Would you . . . do you mind spanking my bottom first?'

My words had come out in an embarrassed rush, but she burst into giggles immediately. I knew I was going to get it, and I could hold back no longer.

'Over your knee please,' I asked, twisting myself into position. 'Lift my dress, and take my knickers down, and spank me hard, even if I kick and squeal, even if I cry.'

'Naughty Natasha!' she giggled.

I was across her lap, my bottom lifted to let her bare me, in such ecstasy I couldn't stop myself squeezing my thighs and bum cheeks in anticipation of what I was about to get: a good, firm spanking across my lovely new playmate's lap, followed by her bum in my face as she brought me off.

'Very naughty,' she said as she began to turn up my dress, 'very, very naughty. You need spanking, Natasha.'

She was playing, but her every word brought me a fresh jolt of pleasure. Once my dress was up, her hands found my panties and eased them down. As I was stripped I was sobbing with ecstasy, and I couldn't help but push my bottom up, drawing the satin tight against my cheeks as it drew slowly across my skin, exposing me to the cool night air – my cheeks, my bumhole, my pussy, all bare, ready to be smacked and teased and touched while she told me off in her soft Irish lilt.

'Naughty, naughty Natasha. You do like to be spanked, don't you, you bad girl? Bad, bad girl, and now . . .'

She lifted her hand, ready to bring it down on my bare, quivering bum cheeks, and I broke completely, gasping out my words as I begged for punishment.

'Please, yes, Rhiannon, like that. Tell me off while you spank me. Tell me what a bad, naughty girl I am while you smack my bare bottom, smack me . . . spank me . . . spank me like the naughty little girl I am . . . oh, please . . . fuck!'

Her hand had come down on my bottom, hard, but that wasn't why I'd sworn. The building was shivering to the low rumble of a powerful engine and it could only be one thing, a lorry. We both froze, Rhiannon with her hand lifted to apply the second smack to my bare cheeks, me with my hips still stuck high to receive my spanking. From outside we heard the crunch of gravel, a grinding noise and the hiss of released pressure. The lorry had parked directly outside our hiding place. I scrambled up, cursing, but not as bitterly as Rhiannon, who seemed scared.

'It's one of the drivers, Natasha! If he finds us he'll—'

'No he won't,' I assured her, 'but what the fuck does he think he's doing at this time of night?'

'I don't know,' she said, and now there was no mistaking the fear in her voice, 'but they're really rough men. Martine came in here with one of them and he made her do his mate as well, in her mouth while she got it from behind!'

It sounded fun, but Rhiannon obviously didn't think so. I gave her a hug and lowered my voice to a whisper as we caught the sound of the lorry door slamming shut.

'Don't worry, darling. I'll cope with him, and as soon as we're gone you nip back to the dormitory. I'll see you tomorrow, OK?'

She nodded immediately, happily allowing me to abandon myself to my fate, but then, she was genuinely scared and I didn't mind. I also needed to come, with a desperation I'd seldom experienced, and if that meant sucking off a French lorry driver while I played with myself it was a scene straight out of my fantasies. It was also something I'd done, more or less, altogether too often in recent days, and licking Rhiannon hadn't helped; I was rubbing my jaw as I put my eye to the keyhole.

The driver had just come in, a short, burly man in *bleu de travail*, the clothes baggy save for where his paunch pushed out the front. He had a thick black moustache and greasy hair with a curl, a big Roman nose but quite dark skin. I was sure I could handle him by flirting a little until he thought he was going to get it, then releasing Rhiannon and returning to the dormitory with her, but that was not what I wanted.

I quickly adjusted my knickers and dress, then stepped through the door. He looked up in surprise, but his broad, weather-beaten face immediately split into a grin. I smiled back, letting my hips do the talking as I came close. He greeted me, his Catalan accent so thick I struggled to understand. Not that it mattered, because we weren't going to need instructions. Seeing no reason to beat about the bush, I sat down on his lap and put an arm around his shoulder, then bent close to whisper my proposition into his ear.

He was surprised, to say the least, and hesitated, perhaps wondering if I had some peculiar ulterior motive. I did, in a sense, but nothing he needed to worry about, so to encourage him I pushed up under my bodice to pop my boobs out, right in his face. That got his attention, and after a mumbled exclamation and a glance at the door he fastened himself to my tit. He was rough, biting at my nipple, while his moustache tickled dreadfully, but I shut my eyes and clenched my teeth, concentrating on the thought of having my tits bare for a man whose name I didn't even know rather than on the physical sensation. I was also aware that Rhiannon almost certainly had her eye to the keyhole and I was keen to show that I was making a sacrifice for her rather than simply playing the slut.

I did want it, though, and I knew that if I went down on him I'd soon be masturbating, and that if he fucked me over the table I'd be unable to hide my pleasure. Right now I had to let her escape. So I pulled back but left my breasts bare as I stood up, beckoning him with one crooked finger as I suggested that the cab of his lorry might be a better place to have me. He agreed and we hurried outside to where a big silver tanker stood parked.

As I'd already guessed, it was a proper long-distance rig, with a sleeping compartment in the cab, into which he led me, boosting me up with a hand on my bottom. I shrugged my coat off and crawled up, my nose wrinkling at the thick masculine scent. The interior light came on, revealing an unmade bed and several tacky posters of busty girls showing off their tits or spread-legged to expose both their breasts and the pink of their cunts. He grinned as he saw what I was looking at and made what was supposed to be a flattering comparison of my own breasts with those of the girls he liked to wank over. I forced myself to smile and bounced them in my hands, showing off to him as he climbed up to join me.

He took me then and there, no kissing, no conversation, just a one-handed grope of my boobs while he unzipped and fumbled his cock free, tugged my dress up, removed my panties and shoved his cock unceremoniously up my hole. I let him have his way, knowing my turn would come, although it was impossible not to feel a certain conflict, even with him thrusting in and out of me: I was supposed to be with Rhiannon, spanked and then licked to heaven while I enjoyed her lovely bottom, not on my back with my thighs spread to a hulking French lorry driver.

I thought he'd do a jack-rabbit on me, a moment of furious pumping, his load up my pussy and me left to take the pleasure of my fingers while his mess dribbled down between my cheeks. Fortunately he wasn't that bad, or maybe he'd had a wank earlier during a rest stop, enjoying his busty French tarts while he tugged on his cock. That set me off, imagining myself on a beach somewhere in southern France, my bikini pulled up to show off my boobs to a photographer for a few euros so that hundreds of men could masturbate over my naked body.

He pulled out with a sudden grunt and for a moment I thought he'd come, only to be ordered brusquely to roll over. I obeyed happily, scrambling on to my knees with my bum stuck up for rear entry and my boobs lolling down under my chest. He got on top, clambering on to my back, doggy-style, with his big, sweaty hands cupping my tits. Now I could come, and I was fighting to get my dress out of the way even as he probed for my cunt. I grabbed his cock, guided him in, squeezed his balls as he slid himself back up me, and began to masturbate.

I had a lot to come over, not least imagining myself as a soft porn model, tits out for men to toss off over, then caught by one of the men for a doggy-style fucking with those same big tits in his great grubby hands. Men like me that way, kneeling with my bum stuck up to show it all off and my boobs dangling bare and heavy under my chest. Earle had done me the same way, making me tell him how Percy liked to spank my bare bottom while he rode me cowboy style. All that was good, and as I rubbed at my clit and the driver's thrusts grew harder and deeper my mind was flicking between them, only for my concentration to go at the last instant. My mind slipped to what Anton Yoshida had threatened to do to me: tie me kneeling in his room and have me mounted in front of his business friends.

Suddenly the scene was crystal-clear in my head: me kneeling on the floor, my dress up, my boobs flopped out, my wrists tied to my legs to leave me utterly unable to defend myself. There'd be ten – no, twenty, forty businessmen watching me, Japanese, Chinese,

Taiwanese, M. Blanquefort too, and Earle, and the staff, even a few random peasants they'd picked up, all laughing at my plight as I was prepared for my fucking, my panties pulled down, my bumhole and cunt lubricated. Anton would be behind me, sneering down at my helpless body, and I'd get mounted, the audience jeering and clapping, taking photographs and filming me too as my slippery cunt filled with fat red cock.

How I screamed, again and again as my orgasm tore through me, and just at the perfect moment the lorry driver spunked inside me. I felt his mess squash out of my hole as he thrust himself deep once more, and imagined that same filthy sight recorded on camera as I was given a public fucking in tight bondage, with the man who'd done it to me crowing with delight.

Ten

I woke from a dream in which I was having my bottom iced by a demented dwarf to find that it wasn't so very far from the truth. There was no dwarf: the inconsiderate bastard of a lorry driver had pulled the covers off me, although my dress was rucked up and I still had no panties, leaving my bare bottom thrust out into the freezing air.

The cab had been warm the night before and although I'd intended to leave, the drink, sex and simple exhaustion had caught up with me. I remembered lying back, telling myself I'd relax for a little before taking my leave, and that was all. My next thought was the embarrassment of explaining myself to Earle, but with luck it wasn't too late. Dawn was only just breaking over the wall of the *chai*, and with any luck I could be safely tucked up beside him before he woke up. Our suite would also be a great deal more comfortable.

I was stiff and sticky, also thirsty and desperate for a pee. Extricating myself from Vilaró, who'd finally condescended to tell me his name after he'd fucked me, I hurried into my coat and took a swallow from a bottle that proved to contain some revoltingly bitter cordial. A brief search for my knickers discovered them clutched in his hand, which was held against his face as he sucked one large and grubby thumb. I decided to abandon them, sure he'd appreciate a trophy, made a brief and unsuccessful attempt to clean the oily paw marks from my boobs, then climbed down from the cab.

The frost was rock-hard, covering the ground, the stones of the wall and the nearby building and every branch and twig of the trees. Vilaró had parked in a narrow gap, so that the tanker was concealed from all but one direction, something I was grateful for as I nipped behind it and squatted down. Dress up, thighs wide, let go, sighing in bliss as my pee gushed out to splash on the packed gravel, melting the frost and forming a long yellow puddle. It smelt quite strong, but not strong enough to overwhelm the scent of grape juice filling the air. After a moment I realised that the hem of my coat was in a small pool of it that had dripped from the tanker. I swore under my breath, quickly lifted my coat, slipped and sat my bottom down in a mingled puddle of chilly grape must and warm pee.

My dress had got wet too and I was cursing violently as I struggled to sort myself out, only to stop as the implications of the situation sank in. Vilaró was Catalan, and he was driving a long-distance tanker with southern plates. The *département* number was thirty-four, Hérault in the south of France, and the deep red grape juice dripping slowly on to the ground smelt of nothing so much as blackcurrants. I caught a drop on my finger and tasted exactly the bitter-sweet fruit I'd expected. I smiled.

The dawn was now bright in the east, my eyes fully adapted to colour. Soon people would be up and about, so there was no time to lose. Using my mobile I took a series of photos of the tanker, making sure to get in recognisable parts of the *chai* and as much of the roof of the château as I could. I still needed a sample, and took time to nip into the room where Rhiannon and I had played, to find a bottle and a cork. I collected an inch of juice in the bottle, took a last photo and fled, nipping through the gate Rhiannon had shown me and across the yard.

If the back door had been locked I'd have been in trouble, but the kitchen staff were up and very nearly caught me as I slipped in and up the stairs. The corridor was empty, our suite dark and deliciously warm after the freezing dawn air. Earle was asleep, still snoring, in almost exactly the position I'd left him in. I nipped into the bathroom, stripped, washed as quickly and as silently as I could, thrust my dirty clothes into my case along with my sample and climbed into bed.

I should have slept – I was tired enough – but my mind was racing. Vilaró's tanker was full of southern French Cabernet-Sauvignon must, brought in at dead of night and parked where nobody could see, or so they thought. That could only mean one thing, that Château La-Croix-de-Pignon '07 was going to be stretched with some nice ripe juice from the sunny south. No wonder they could make fruity wine in a bad vintage; that surely explained the taste of the '06, while Southern and Allied were so big they'd have no trouble in fudging the paperwork. All of it was highly illegal and, better still, it would make a mockery of Anton Yoshida's claims of mystical excellence, or at least it would if he gave the '07 a good write-up. For that I'd have to wait until fermentation was finished, because I had no proof that the '06 was dodgy.

For the next half hour I was grinning to myself as I imagined ever finer scenarios in which I exposed Yoshida as a fraud, and I was so happy that when Earle finally woke up with a nice fat morning erection

I gave him the blowjob of his life without worrying about my aching jaw. That put him in a good mood in turn, but what really put the gloss on it was walking downstairs hand in hand and meeting Anton Yoshida. I gave him a smug grin and a wink, which left him looking puzzled; he obviously thought he'd crushed me completely. Suddenly I remembered what I'd come over, the night before, and the blood rushed to my face, but by then we were past him and he didn't see.

There was a reception of some sort in the morning, but we were under no obligation to be there and Earle wanted to visit some other châteaux. Directly after breakfast we set off on a whistle-stop tour of the district, first Pomerol itself, then the backwoods around Montagne and Lussac, finishing with St Emilion. It was heavy going, one achingly tannic young wine after another and the same story at every stop of how careful selection had been necessary. By lunchtime I could barely taste my food, but what had become very evident was that Yoshida's snotty comments about the smaller wineries not being able to afford to make good wine were rubbish. All the growers had done their best, small and large, and the only thing that linked them was Earle's good opinion, which was no surprise, as he'd been visiting the district since before I was born.

Not that I gave my full attention to the tastings, because my head was crammed with what I'd learnt that morning and ideas about what I was going to do with my information. The photos themselves were pretty damning, and nobody could deny that I'd been at La-Croix-de-Pignon on the date recorded with the images. I could come forward as a righteous whistle-blower and all hell would break lose. The only disadvantage was that I would be at the centre of the storm and might get more attention than I wanted, maybe with certain bits of my past being raked up.

Alternatively I could put my case together in as much detail as possible without giving away my identity and send everything to the press – including Pia Santi. It didn't matter that she wasn't in the country; in fact it was for the best, because it would be easier for me to remain anonymous, and she was such a cold, mercenary little bitch that she could be guaranteed to milk the scandal for every penny it was worth. With any luck she would ruin Yoshida's reputation, a very satisfying thought indeed.

By the time we got back most of the guests had gone, including Anton Yoshida, moving on *en masse* to another of the Southern and Allied properties, in the Médoc. I wanted to speak with Rhiannon, and caught her just in time before she and her fellow waitresses were loaded into a minibus. Even then we only had time for a brief word, assuring each other that we'd been all right the night before, and a hug, assuring each other that what had happened between us was good, and might happen again. I gave her a card and she promised to call when she was in London later that month.

I watched the minibus leave, feeling more than a touch of regret, because for all the fun we'd had together she was still very much unfinished business, and if my feelings for her before had been pretty much pure lust, now they were more complex. Back indoors I joined Earle, M. Blanquefort and a few others for a very English tea. We spoke of this and that, mainly wine, and when M. Blanquefort expressed surprise at the depth of my knowledge I admitted to working for Hambling and Borst. He immediately went into raptures, demanding to know how they were and telling a series of stories about his times with them when he'd been a junior broker in the family firm, long before their association with Southern and Allied. I hadn't really talked to him before, and on the previous day he'd seemed rather stiff, but I now found myself liking him and grateful for his hospitality, which presented me with a problem. If I exposed the fraud he was quite obviously involved in, he would get the worst of it, certainly more so than Anton Yoshida, whom I could only hope to make look a fool, not a criminal.

By the time we'd finished dinner my dilemma had been resolved. It was a very different affair from the night before, with just M. Blanquefort, his family, two French wine writers, Earle and myself. The wines were better still, including their own '61 and the legendary '45. As the last drop of that exquisite wine slithered down my throat I knew I could not possibly expose the man who had allowed me to taste it. It would have been a betrayal – and really, if a lot of wealthy businessmen with no taste wanted to pay vast sums for a mixture of unripe Merlot and southern French Cabernet Sauvignon, what business was it of mine?

The conversation was also a great deal more open, the older men discussing the way the trade had changed over the last forty years or more and openly cynical about the huge prices wines were fetching. I was included as part of what was to all intents and purposes a conspiracy, and by the time I'd swallowed an ancient Cognac and nibbled my last chocolate we were all as thick as thieves.

That night I got the cowboy treatment again, but this time I thoroughly enjoyed it, naked on my knees while Earle rode me and spanked my bottom with his hat. He even brought me off with his cock, on my careful instructions, rubbing it on my pussy from behind until I'd reached climax and finishing himself all over my bum as he had the night before. Unlike then I went to sleep beside him, warm and content.

The morning was a rush: breakfast, hasty goodbyes, the drive back through frost-coated vineyards, Bordeaux airport, the flight, home. By the time I got back to my flat all I wanted to do was put my feet up and sip a hot cup of tea. Earle had kept his word about not talking shop, but had asked for a meeting the following day, which I could hardly refuse. I was still going to have to turn him down, but I wasn't looking forward to it.

I went into work the next day feeling glum but determined. Gilbert, Otto and Vernon Flyght greeted me with an open bottle of Patrice Beauroy's Champagne, all three of them congratulating me heartily as I accepted it.

'Your idea is truly brilliant, my dear,' Gilbert said warmly.

'More brilliant than you realise, perhaps,' Otto added. 'We have been speaking to our accountants, and the tax incentives alone are too tempting to resist.'

'You're accepting my proposal?' I asked.

'Of course, my dear,' Gilbert assured me.

'All of it?'

'In its entirety. Vernon here and a select group of friends and acquaintances with, shall we say, certain shared tastes, have agreed to invest in what we have decided to call the Linnet Club. A nice touch, don't you think?'

'You're naming it after me?' I was flattered.

'Who better?' he responded, grinning all over his basset-dog face. 'You conceived the idea and you are a paragon of our founding principle.'

'Which is that girls should have their bottoms smacked on a regular basis,' Vernon added unnecessarily. 'But seriously, it really is an excellent solution, Natasha.'

I nodded, accepting my due. Hambling and Borst would now be broken up, and the premises would become one more of St James's already numerous gentlemen's clubs, but with a difference. Membership would be restricted to shareholders, including Gilbert and Otto themselves, Vernon and some or all of his kinky friends from the Aviators, Percy as an honorary member, and, as the sole female member, myself. The stock would become the club cellar, or at least most of it would.

'And I get the name?' I asked.

'Absolutely,' Gilbert assured me, 'although what you want with it I cannot imagine.'

'It has its uses,' I assured him. 'How about the right to pay for bottles from the cellar by getting spanked?'

'Oh, of course,' Vernon laughed. 'An amusing little clause, we thought, although naturally the lawyers will have to be careful how it is worded.'

'But I can pay for bottles by offering myself for spanking?' I insisted.

'Absolutely,' he assured me, 'and officially, once all the documents are signed, which should be by the end of the week. Unofficially, should you feel the need for a trip over my knee before then, please don't hesitate to ask.'

I smiled and looked down, feigning embarrassment in an effort to hide the triumph I was sure would show in my eyes. They had gone for it, hook, line and sinker, accepting my terms without a quibble, including the little piece of dodgy dealing I had disguised as an erotic game. Everything was coming together very nicely indeed.

As I left the building an hour later with a rosy bottom under my skirt and a large cheque in my handbag I felt well pleased with myself, but with a touch of disappointment. I had succeeded, and all that remained were a few simple tasks; informing Earle and Lydia of the situation, collecting my due and attending the opening party of the club, an event sure to be even more painful and humiliating for me than my visit to the Aviators. I knew what the problem was: except in one or two minor details, there would be no sense of obligation. The next time I had my bottom smacked, or a man demanded that I suck his cock, or I offered, it would be a simple matter of whether I felt like it or not, with nothing important hanging on my choice. That would take a lot of the excitement away . . . still, I knew there would be other pleasures; there always were.

As well as the cheque in my handbag I had a document signed by both Gilbert and Otto, making over the company name to me. I called Lydia, suggesting she come to dinner and telling her to bring a signed cheque from her boss. She made me speak to him, photograph the document on my mobile and email them the picture. Once that was done they agreed, and Lydia waited until her boss was out of earshot before assuring me of an excellent evening and ordering me to wear a plug in each hole for the rest of the day, which put a big grin on my face as I turned my steps towards the bank.

When I arrived at the restaurant where I'd agreed to meet him, Earle was already there, inspecting a glass of Alsace with anticipation. I greeted him, sat down and poured myself some wine, nervous but determined to say what I had to and to get it over quickly.

'I have bad news, I'm afraid,' I told him. 'I did my best to persuade them to take up your offer, but they've decided to go with an alternative. A private consortium is buying them up, to convert the building into an elite gentleman's club. I'm sorry.'

'Don't be,' he said. 'There are other names I can use, not quite so grand perhaps, but still good. So they're closing down, huh? Did you manage to salvage anything from the wreck?'

'Nothing of any use to you,' I told him, 'but I did pick up a present.'

I dug into my handbag to pull out the Bonnes-Mares '62 from Clair-Daü that I'd selected as payment for the spanking Gilbert, Otto and Vernon had given me earlier. They didn't know what I'd chosen, and even if they did know that they had any of this remarkable wine left, they had no idea how many bottles, which was just as well. Earle took a moment to realise what I'd handed him before his expression turned reverent. He shook his head in wonder.

'Well, that's something you don't see very often these days! Thank you, Natasha, that's very thoughtful of you, very thoughtful indeed.'

'It's nothing,' I assured him, 'just a token of my appreciation and a thank-you for the nice weekend.'

He nodded, thanked me again and put the bottle very carefully into his briefcase. I picked up the menu and selected a goat's cheese salad to suit the Riesling we were drinking. Earle began to talk, reminiscing about his early days in the trade and I listened, sipping my wine and feeling content. He'd taken the news a lot better than I'd expected, so well in fact that I began to wonder how much of his interest had been in buying out Hambling and Borse and how much in getting into my knickers. That he had done, and he clearly wasn't finished with me, because he suggested we meet again soon. I accepted, although I knew I would soon be back on the island.

With that he left. We parted on good terms, although in my case also a touch of regret. He'd been nice, if not entirely to my taste, but I consoled myself with the rest of the bottle and the thought that it was always possible I'd see him again. After all, a few short weeks before, Lydia had been a distant memory – and now I was going to meet her for dinner and have horrible things done to me. That would be fun, rather more fun than she expected, and as I left the restaurant, now a little drunk as well as happy, I was grinning so broadly that I got funny looks in the street.

Lydia had told me to put plugs in, and I was tipsy enough and horny enough to want to do it. Soho was only a few minutes' walk away and I went straight there, rejecting the first two sex shops because there weren't enough people in them and finally choosing one where they had dirty videos playing and a large audience of sleazy men. I spent ages selecting my plugs, a thick cock-shaped dildo for my pussy and a slim pink one for my bottom hole, all the while with the men's eyes flickering over my body.

I went to a pub to put them in, ordering a large gin and tonic before making for the Ladies' loo with a sachet of mayonnaise pinched from their food bar. In the cubicle I hitched up my skirt and pushed my tights and knickers down, deliberately exposing my bottom and pussy as I unwrapped the plugs, my excitement rising all the while. With my bare bottom stuck out I applied the mayonnaise to my anus, rubbing it well in before sticking a finger up to make sure I was slippery enough to take the plug.

It went up easily enough, but to feel my ring stretch around the hard plastic and close again on the neck was almost too much. I knew how I'd look from behind too, with the base of the plug sticking out between my cheeks to make it quite obvious what I'd done to myself. Just to know that was enough to make me want to come, and by the time I'd got the dildo unwrapped I was so wet it slid up with ease. In fact it would have fallen out again if I hadn't pulled up my clothes to hold it in place.

I'd done as Lydia said and it felt deliciously dirty, both to be under her orders and to have my pussy and bottom filled. As I sat down, back in the bar, they pushed deeper up me, making me gasp and drawing a very odd look from the barman. I gave him a smile, wondering what he'd do if he knew, but determined not to make a pass at him. By the time Lydia got to me I wanted be so high I was ready for anything, and I knew full well that once I'd got my hands on the barman's cock there would be no holding back.

While I drank my gin and tonic I sent Lydia a text to tell her I was plugged and got one back calling me a slut and telling me to be in my flat by six o'clock. That was more than four hours away, and I wasn't at all sure I could hold out. I was going to try, though, if only to torture myself, although I was already fit to burst.

Knowing I was relatively safe in the pub, I ordered another gin and tonic, trying not to wriggle in my seat as I drank it, my mind running over the possibilities of what might happen later. I had no idea why Lydia wanted me plugged, but it was sure to be filthy. Possibly she was bringing her boss with her and wanted me good and ready for fucking, not just up my pussy but my bottom too. I could just imagine it, some silky, sleazy businessman whose name I didn't even know . . . I'd be obliged to strip for him, show off my naked body with the twin plugs protruding from between my cheeks as I bent over, suck him hard while Lydia played with me, kneel as the dildo was pulled out and replaced with his cock.

Maybe it wouldn't be her boss but the two delivery

boys I'd had to suck off the last time she'd had me, Blake and Lucas. She knew where they worked, and it was hardly going to be difficult to persuade them to use me. That would mean a cock in each hole, probably my mouth and pussy, with the thrusts from whoever was in me from behind jamming the smaller plug in and out of my bottom.

Not that Lydia really needed a man, or men. She would bring a strap-on, a great big fat one that would really stretch me out. I'd be fucked first, naked on my knees while I sucked on the dildo she'd just taken out of my hole. Next would come my bum, with the plug extracted and stuck in my mouth so that I could taste myself while I was buggered with her monster strap-on.

A violent shiver ran through me at the thought, and if I hadn't been in the pub that would have been it. My hand would have been down my knickers in an instant, to rub at my bump until I hit my now desperately needed climax. I tried to turn my mind to something else, but even the TV was against me, showing some rap artist loaded down with bling and surrounded by girls, all black or Hispanic and all with voluptuous figures. In an instant I was imagining myself among them, only naked and plugged, with the girls laughing at the state I was in as I was made to suck their man erect.

'You all right, love?' the barman asked.

'Fine, thank you,' I lied, blushing furiously.

I was sure he knew, or at least had guessed something of what was going on, so I drained my drink and left, burning with embarrassment and arousal as I set off up Dean Street. With every step I could feel the plugs moving inside me, keeping me acutely conscious of my penetration and making it next to impossible not to wiggle my hips as I walked.

Men were starting to look at me, and I was sure that despite my smart business suit I would be mistaken for a tart and propositioned at any moment.

At that thought I realised a new possibility. Perhaps Lydia wanted me to disgrace myself? After what had happened with the cabbie, Lucas and Blake it seemed quite likely. I stopped, wondering if I should go back and proposition the barman after all. He was at work, but the pub had been almost empty and he had seemed interested.

Five minutes later I was on my knees among the beer kegs in his store room with his thick pink cock in my mouth while I played with my pussy through my knickers and fiddled with the ends of my plugs. He was quick, spunking down my throat almost as soon as he was properly hard, but by then I'd already come.

Not that it helped much. I was still dizzy with arousal as I started north once more, not just because of the plugs inside me but because I'd been so dirty. My mouth tasted of him and I wanted more, much more, cock after cock after cock until my belly was bulging with spunk and I was dripping from my soiled mouth, my aching pussy, my buggered bumhole. I had to go slowly, though, or the base of the plug up my bum would make me sore in the wrong way.

By the time I got to my flat I simply couldn't stop myself. I stripped to my knickers and crawled on to the bed, where I played with the plugs in my bottom and cunt while I brought myself to a second orgasm and a third, more leisurely. Only then did I extract the plugs and climb into the bath, telling myself I had plenty of time to get ready for Lydia. Timing was everything, and she needed to find me ready and willing, so that she could start on me without asking any awkward questions.

Once I was dry I put the paperwork in the bottom drawer by my bed and covered it with clothes. I was warm, drunk and tired, so it was all too easy to flop back naked on my bed. There were still over two hours before Lydia turned up, and as I closed my eyes I was telling myself I'd have a nap, then be fresh and ready when she arrived.

The next thing to penetrate my conscience was the insistent ringing of the doorbell. I took a moment to realise what was going on before it all came back in a rush. Jumping up from the bed, I scampered across to the intercom, babbling an excuse about being on the loo in response to Lydia's angry demand to be let in. I pressed the release button, ran for the bathroom, grabbed my plugs from where they'd been soaking in the sink and tried to stick the dildo up my pussy, only to discover that I wasn't ready. I grabbed for my moisturising cream and squeezed.

A gush of air spattered a few pathetic flecks of cream over the head of the dildo. Normally my cupboard would have been full of creams and gels, including proper lubricant for my bottom, but I'd used them up while playing with Percy. I cursed, and was about to run to the kitchen for some butter when I remembered that it was in the fridge and would be rock-hard. At that moment the bell went, immediately followed by a rap on the door. There was only one thing for it.

Grabbing my toothpaste, I squeezed two fat, stripy worms on to the heads of the plugs. I knew it would sting, but I was determined to be ready for Lydia. Squatting down, I put the dildo to my pussy, rubbing the head between my lips until I began to open up, then sliding it deep. Another, more insistent rap sounded at the door, followed by Lydia's voice demanding to be let in. I called back, promising to be quick as I stuck out my bottom and pressed the anal plug to my hole. Taking things up the bum should never be rushed, and I spent a moment probing myself until my hole began to open, then pushed. Lydia was banging on the door again, but I allowed myself to enjoy the moment, my eyes shut and my mouth wide as my ring spread slowly to the pressure, opening until at last I felt the widest part push in up my anus.

'Coming!' I called again, and dashed for the door.

My pussy and bumhole had already begun to burn, and I was wriggling as I opened the door. Lydia saw that I was naked and responded with a cruel smirk, then glanced down as I began to tread my feet in a vain effort to dispel the rising heat of my penetrated holes.

'Are you all right? I thought you said you'd just been to the loo?'

'I have. It's the plugs! Ow!'

I shut the door hastily before any of my neighbours could see me. Lydia put down the bags she was carrying and shrugged off her coat, casting the occasional curious glance at me as she did so. My eyes had started to water and I grabbed the heads of both plugs, easing them in and out to soothe the pain, or at least to spread it out a little.

'I used toothpaste to lube myself up,' I explained.

'You really are a glutton for punishment, aren't you?' she laughed. 'OK, let's get on with it. Into the bathroom with you. Kneel on the floor.'

I hastened to obey, getting down on the cool, hard tiles as she pulled out my dressing-gown cord.

'Arms behind your back,' she ordered, stretching out the cord.

As I crossed my wrists for her to tie I looked back over my shoulder. The bag she'd put down beside her handbag contained something large and round, a football maybe. I was fairly sure that not even Lydia would attempt to stick something that large up me, but

I was feeling more than a little nervous as she lashed my wrists firmly together. She pushed me down a little too, forcing me to bend forward and show off the plug in my bottom hole, which she took hold of, making my burning ring pout as she tugged on the base.

'You're tighter than I expected,' she remarked, 'perhaps some more toothpaste?'

'I . . . I get loose quite easily,' I assured her, but she ignored me.

She took the tube of toothpaste from the cupboard and held it over my bottom, which I'd stuck out, knowing that resistance would only make it worse. She squeezed hard, emptying almost the entire tube between my cheeks, and began to play with my butt plug, making my hole pout once more. I was already sobbing with reaction, my pussy and bottom hole already on fire, the fresh paste in my slit starting to burn.

'I need you good and open,' she said, and pulled out my plug.

I gasped as my hole gave way, and again as she began to stuff it with toothpaste, using the tip of the plug to feed it up me. It felt squashy and cool until the burning sensation returned, now so hot I was left shaking my head and panting for breath. When she finally stuck the plug back up my bum it went in without difficulty, and I could guess that I had about half the tube of toothpaste in my rectum.

The rest went up my pussy and between my lips, smeared on with the dildo until I was burning from my mound to the top of my bum slit. She put some on my cheeks too, squeezing out the very last of the tube and rubbing it in to give me a warm glow not unlike the aftermath of a spanking. By then my pain had begun to give way to pleasure, and I managed to find my voice.

‘What are you going to do to me?’

‘You’ll see,’ she told me. ‘Just stay still and shut up.’

She stood up, crossed to the loo and began to feed the paper into the bowl, just as she’d done the day she’d washed my face in it.

‘Not that, Lydia!’ I begged. ‘Not again!’

‘Shut up,’ she repeated. ‘I have something else in mind, but actually, since you mention it, and since I rather enjoyed washing your face in the loo, and you won’t shut up, come here.’

‘Lydia . . . ow!’

She’d taken me by my hair, pulling hard to force me to crawl across to the loo, where she positioned my face over the pile of paper she’d made. I really hadn’t wanted my head stuck down the lavatory, and I was cursing myself for reminding her, but I still had no idea why else she would want to fill the loo with paper.

Not that it mattered what I thought, or what I wanted. All I could do was try to make the best of it, concentrating on the choking humiliation in my head as she climbed on my back, just as she had before. Her skirt had rucked up and I felt her pussy squash on my spine, hot and wet through her panties.

‘Head down, Tasha,’ she said cheerfully, and my face was pushed against the still dry loo roll.

She began to feed paper down the toilet once more, tugging vigorously on the roll and not bothering too much about her aim, so that it began to pile up on my head as well as fill the bowl. I tried to shake it off but only succeeded in knocking the loo seat, which landed on my head, trapping me in place and sending Lydia into such gales of laughter that she nearly fell off my back. There was so much paper down the loo I was sure it would overflow.

‘Lydia, it’s going to go everywhere!’

‘Oh, shut up.’

'Lydia! What if it floods the flat below?'

'Then you'll just have to explain how you had to be bog-washed, won't you? Now get your head in there properly!'

She pushed down hard on the loo seat, forcing my face deep into the folds of paper.

'Here goes,' she crowed. 'One bog-washed tart!'

I heard the click of the lever. Cold water exploded around my head and for one ghastly moment my face was underwater and my head trapped in place by the seat, forcing me to fight back before once more abandoning myself to her cruelty. She obviously didn't care, laughing at me as I coughed up what had gone in my mouth. It had been done, my head flushed down my own lavatory, an awful thing to do to anybody, so awful it had me sobbing and fighting back the tears as she finally lifted the seat – but only the upper part, leaving me trapped by my neck as if I was wearing a yoke. She saw the state I was in but didn't care, laughing at me as she once more took a firm grip in my hair.

'Hang on,' she told me, 'the cistern has to fill.'

'Not again, Lydia! Please?'

'Yes, again, as many times as I like. Now shut up.'

I obeyed, sobbing bitterly as I waited for my horrid punishment to be repeated. She'd begun to rub herself on my back, just gently, and to twist her fist in her hair, thoroughly enjoying my degradation. Admittedly, I was too. My pussy was now so inflamed from the toothpaste and so wet with my own juices that the dildo squeezed out and fell to the floor. Lydia ignored it and I was left gaping behind, the cool air making my open hole burn hotter than ever.

'That should do,' she said. 'Down you go.'

She pushed and I shut my eyes and mouth just in time as my head was jammed down the lavatory again.

The water swirled up, covering my ears and soaking what little of my hair was still dry, only to drop suddenly as the blockage gave way. Once more I was left gasping and spitting, with loo water running out of my nose and ears, my face plastered with bits of soggy pink toilet paper, my hair hanging down into the bowl in a bedraggled curtain.

'Drink some loo water, Tasha,' Lydia ordered, and once more began to rub herself on my back.

'I can't!' I sobbed. 'There's no water, Lydia.'

'Oh, bugger,' she laughed, 'it's all gone. Hang on.'

The loo had drained, leaving only a great soggy mass of paper. Lydia gave a cluck of irritation as she pulled my head aside to see what was going on. My neck was still trapped in the seat, sticking through the hole. She stuck my head back down a little, twisting her hand hard in my hair to keep me firmly under control, all the while rocking gently back and forth on my back.

'Eat some bog paper,' she demanded, 'That'll be a laugh.'

'Lydia!'

'Eat!' she snapped and thrust down hard.

My head went into the lavatory again, only this time not with a splash but with a squelch as my face hit the soggy paper. She held me down, rubbing hard on my back.

'Eat it, you little bitch!' she yelled. 'Eat it, or I swear I'll piss on your head, Natasha, I will.'

I tried to answer, but I could only make stupid burbling noises. She reached back to grab the base of my butt plug, tug it out a little way and push it back up, making me gasp as my hot, slippery ring spread and closed, spread and closed.

'Come on,' she urged, 'I want to see you with a mouthful, and I want to see you swallow it. You can do it clean or you can do it pissy. Your choice Tasha.'

'I can't!' I wailed, forcing my head up and around. 'I'll be sick!'

'Just fucking do it!' she screamed, and slapped me.

She caught me on the side of my face, a single, stinging blow. My resistance snapped, my face went back into the bowl and I took a mouthful of the wet lavatory paper. Lydia gave a peal of laughter and began to rub herself harder, still with her hand twisted into my hair.

'That's right,' she crowed. 'Eat it. Take a good, big mouthful and swallow it down. Swallow, bitch!'

I did it, the tears streaming from my eyes as I forced myself to gulp down my revolting mouthful. She saw and her laughter grew yet more demented and her rubbing harder still.

'Good girl!' she called. 'Oh, you filthy, filthy bitch Natasha. That's right, have some more . . . get it down you . . . fill your belly with it, you dirty little whore! Here, have something to wash it down!'

She pulled the lever and cold water spurted out to cover my head and spill over the edge of the bowl, soaking the floor. Some went in my mouth and I swallowed it, on purpose, no longer able to resist her. She was swearing at me, twisting my hair viciously, slapping my bottom and hips, all the while grinding her pussy on to my spine. The loo had blocked, creating a pool of water filled with bits of pink lavatory paper, into which she pushed my face again and again as she rode me.

I struggled to be a good girl, gulping down the water as best I could, mouthful after mouthful, deliberately drinking from a lavatory bowl to help her get off, with my tummy already full of loo paper. She was riding me so hard my tits had begun to slap against the hard porcelain of the loo bowl, and I knew I was going to come. It was just like the time before, when she'd used my body for her amusement. I turned at the last moment, showing her my wet face and a piece of paper hanging from between my lips, and at that she came.

It hurt, but I held my place, reduced to her sex toy and in ecstasy for having it done. Not that she appreciated my submission, taking her time over her orgasm and giving me a resounding slap on my bum when she finally got off and let go of my hair. I tried to get up, assuming it was over and eager to stretch my aching limbs before bringing myself to orgasm in front of her. In response I got another smack.

'Stay as you are,' she told me. 'No, not with your head down the loo, you slut. I want you to watch.'

I nodded my acquiescence, but she wanted to be sure and looped some of my wet hair around the loo seat, tying it in a crude knot, leaving me helpless. Then she took the cardboard tube from the loo-paper holder. I knew where it was going, and would have hung my head in shameful acceptance if that hadn't meant putting it back down the loo. Instead I made myself as comfortable as I could, resting my shoulders on the loo, parting my knees and sticking my bottom out.

'Good girl,' she said as she pinched one end of the loo roll shut. 'That's exactly the position I want you in. Knowing little slut, aren't you?'

She was right, but that didn't stop me making a face as she got down on her knees behind me. Taking hold of the plug in my bumhole, she drew it gently out to leave me gaping wide as she pushed the tip of the loo roll in up my bum. I was slippery, but not slippery enough to take the absorbent cardboard, and she had to leave me like that while she went and rummaged in one of her bags, returning with a tub of butter.

I stayed in position, my head trapped in the loo seat, my bottom thrust high and open, as she carefully greased the loo roll, easing it up bit by bit and using my butt plug to open the tip out. At last I was ready, with a tunnel leading in up my bottom, ready for whatever she'd decided to fill me with. I could guess what it would be, although after my bog-washing the last thing I was going to do was tell her and end up getting something she hadn't planned in advance. It would be chocolate cake mix, a couple of pounds of it, then into panties and an embarrassingly short skirt, out into the night where she'd keep me walking until I could hold on no more. I'd fill my panties in the street and be forced to walk home like that, with a big, fat bulge under my skirt for everybody to see, and they wouldn't know it was only cake mix.

'Open wide,' Lydia said, holding my butt plug to my mouth.

I'd have been surprised if she didn't make me suck it and obeyed readily enough, wondering if I could get my hands free and sneak a frig while she was in the kitchen. After all, she couldn't very well take me out in the street tied. She stood up, her hands on her hips as she looked down at me with an expression of pure malice.

'Suck on it,' she ordered. 'I won't be a moment.'

My tummy went tight as she left the room and I realised I'd been right. I twisted my head around and watched as she dug again into the plastic bag and produced not a bowl and some instant cake mix but a large ball of translucent blue plastic. I'd been wrong, but something was going to happen to me, although it was obvious that the thing couldn't possibly be accommodated in either of my holes.

'That won't fit up me,' I protested, spitting out the butt plug. 'It must be a foot across!'

'I'm not going to put it up you, silly,' she laughed. 'It's what's in it that goes up you.'

I didn't understand, until she was close enough for me to see inside the ball, in which a small, furry object lay among some shredded newspaper – a hamster. She was going to felch me.

I was babbling immediately, in a state of utter, blind panic.

'Lydia, no! You can't, not up my bum! You can't, you fucking psychopath! Lydia, no! It's not fair on the hamster!'

She had opened the ball as I spoke and dipped her hand in, her face contorted with a malicious humour I'd never imagined possible for a human being.

'No you don't, you fucking maniac!' I shouted and tried to get up, struggling to pull the knot in my hair loose. 'No, Lydia, you really can't, not a felching! No, no!'

I was screaming, but she just laughed at me, a cackling so demented that I wondered if she really was insane, and as she reached down towards the open tunnel into my rectum I began to kick and thrash and scream my head off, determined not to let her do it, begging her to let me off and swearing at her in the same breath. My bladder went in my fear and I wet myself all over the floor, spurt after spurt of urine gushing out backwards to pool around her shoes. She merely grinned, then spoke.

'Look, it's not even a real hamster.'

She held her hand to my face and uncurled it, revealing a little furry cat toy.

'You bitch,' I breathed, 'you utter bitch!'

She laughed and planted a ringing slap on my bottom, making my ring contract on the cardboard tube. I collapsed, spent, as if I'd just come but without the pleasure. She was still laughing, thoroughly pleased with herself at what she'd done to me. Utterly defeated, I hung my head down into the lavatory bowl, and when I spoke my voice was faint.

'That's enough, Lydia. Be nice to me, please? Just make me come, then let me go.'

'No,' she said. 'You can do it yourself.'

'Lydia, please?' I begged. 'I'm tied up. I want to be tied while I come.'

'Your hair's still tied to the seat,' she pointed out, 'and you were very rude to me.'

'I'm sorry,' I answered her. 'Please? I'm begging you, Lydia.'

'No,' she repeated. 'Rub your own dirty cunt. I've had my fun.'

'Please?' I wailed, but she had already left the room.

I noticed she'd sat down where she could see me, though, and that she was watching as she began to eat grapes from my fruit bowl. She wanted me to complete my degradation by coming in front of her, and I couldn't stop myself. It took me a while to wriggle my hands free of the knot she'd made with my dressing gown cord, but they went straight to my sore, gaping pussy. She gave a quiet, contemptuous chuckle as I began to masturbate.

A couple of touches and my bumhole began to squeeze on the lavatory roll holding me open, my pussy too, squashing out a mixture of toothpaste and juice, which I rubbed in eagerly. I was going to come, so soon that it was hardly going to be possible to dwell on all the awful details of what she'd done to me, but I couldn't stop myself or even slow down. I'd been made to wear plugs for hours, one up my pussy and one up my bum. I'd got so excited I'd sucked a stranger's cock in a pub toilet, and even after that I'd masturbated twice more before I was content. I'd used toothpaste to lube myself up, leaving my flesh sore and swollen. I'd had my hands tied behind my back and been made to crawl naked on my bathroom floor. I'd had my head stuck down a lavatory that was flushed repeatedly. I'd been made to eat wet loo paper while she rode me to orgasm. I'd had a loo roll stuck up my bottom to hold me open and been threatened with felching, scaring me so badly I'd wet myself . . . and that was what I came over, my own fear, so strong that I'd lost control of my bladder and pissed all over the floor in front of the smug, vicious little bitch who was still watching me with her pretty face twisted into a look of vindictive evil.

It took me ages to clear up, and all the while Lydia just sat in my armchair sipping a glass of wine. My legs felt weak and I was sore in a dozen places, my bumhole worst of all, but even that couldn't detract from my rising excitement as I thought about what I was going to do. She looked so pleased with herself, and was happily telling me how much money she and Orpheus Asset Management were going to make from the Hambling and Borst name. I let her talk, answering only to tell her how clever she'd been and how easily she'd manipulated me.

'Percy will be over in a few minutes,' I said, all innocence. 'Are you ready to play again?'

'Percy?' she demanded. 'What did you invite him round for?'

'To play with us, of course.'

'What the fuck are you talking about!? I'm not playing with any of your dirty old men!'

'Oh,' I said, crestfallen. 'I thought you might like a good spanking for a change.'

'No, I would not.'

'Oh . . . um, you'd better go then, because I told him you'd be up for it and he'll be over any minute.'

'I don't care what he thinks. He's not coming anywhere near me!'

'Yes, but . . . the thing is, I said you liked to make

a fight of it and that he shouldn't take any notice of your protests, you see—'

'Natasha, for fuck's sake! OK, I'd better go. Have you got the paper?'

'Sure, just let me throw some clothes on and I'll see you out.'

It had worked like a dream, her reaction exactly as I'd expected. I took my time dressing, while Lydia grew increasingly annoyed, until at last Percy rang the bell, four minutes late. I took the envelope from the chest of drawers and passed it to her and we went downstairs together, Lydia hurrying and nagging me about my inappropriate behaviour. Percy was at the door, beaming and, of course, utterly unaware of what was going on except that he was taking me out to dinner.

'Are you ready?' he asked. 'Good evening, Lydia.'

'Fuck off, you filthy old git!' she spat, and stalked off down the pavement, leaving Percy staring after her in astonishment.

'How very rude,' he remarked.

'She's a little upset,' I explained, 'but not as upset as she will be when she opens that envelope.'

'Why so?'

'She thinks she's bought Hambling and Borst, but what I've actually sold her is their holding company, Monterprise Ltd.'

Eleven

I didn't expect Lydia to take it lying down, so I gave up my flat and spent the rest of the week with Percy, coming into Hambling and Borse each day to sort out the cellar and, on the Friday, to witness the signing of the papers making the property over to the Linnet Club. Lydia excepted, everybody was extremely pleased with me. Gilbert and Otto not only no longer had to worry about debt but had enough to see them comfortably through retirement, as well as a ready supply of fine wines to drink and girls to spank. Percy too was pleased, basking in reflected glory as he received congratulations for having put me forward, along with an associate membership of the club. Vernon and his friends were delighted with the arrangement, even the filthy Stubbs, who had accepted the job of commissionaire.

It was all great fun, and there was one last act to play, but I couldn't help feeling a touch of despondency. The inaugural party was on the following Saturday and I was due to be thoroughly roasted, but that would be it, job done – but not properly. Just thinking about Anton Yoshida simultaneously made my blood boil and filled my head with filthy fantasies. I also wanted Rhiannon quite badly. I was even tempted to stay in London, but with Lydia about it really wasn't advisable. She knew altogether too many of the people I did, and if she got together with somebody like Pia Santi I might end up in real difficulty. Then there was the situation with Earle, because it could only be a matter of time before he discovered that my so-called Uncle Percy not only still spanked my bottom but spent his time rogering me silly.

I was still interested to see how M. Blanquefort's little piece of jiggery-pokery with the '07 Château La-Croix-de-Pignon worked out. Each morning I would search the net, reading the cautious articles as wine writers began to commit themselves on the quality of the vintage, until on the Tuesday Anton Yoshida made his initial pronouncements. At first he was as cautious as any, more so if anything, admitting that it would be a difficult year at best and advising on which châteaux had been most conscientious and were therefore likely to make the best wine. The list was largely predictable but contained one or two surprises and so seemed likely to be honest, or at least more honest than his promotion of Kavanagh's *Cordon Noir* Cognac. However, Château La-Croix-de-Pignon was included in the list with a five-star recommendation for quality, which was a joke, and a five-star recommendation for value, which was insane. That meant he was either a fool or a liar, and for all my low opinion of him I had to admit that he was no fool.

As I sat back from my screen I was biting my lip in consternation. It was such a shame not to expose him, but I couldn't. I was just going to have to swallow my pride, for the time being at least, and put down my experience with him as a solitary defeat in a war I'd won. That wasn't easy, not when every time I tried to masturbate, and even when Percy was in me, my head would fill with what he'd threatened to make me do.

An added humiliation was that he had no further interest in me, but had said what he had purely because he knew it would get to me . . . or so I thought until my mobile rang later that afternoon. I recognised his arrogant drawl immediately.

'What do you want?' I demanded.

He laughed.

'Temper, temper, Natasha. I have a little proposition for you.'

'Well, you can take your proposition and—'

'Now, now, Natasha, I think we know who'll come off best if you start that again. Besides, from what I hear you need work. Hambling and Borst are giving up the game, are they not?'

'Yes,' I admitted cautiously, wondering how much he knew.

'Not before time either,' he continued. 'I'm sure even you can see that they were dinosaurs?'

'You want the stock, don't you?' I responded. 'It's not for sale.'

'The stock? A few bottles of mediocre Bordeaux and some Burgundies that should have been drunk twenty years ago? Don't be foolish, Natasha. What I want is you.'

'Well, you can . . . hang on, you're offering me a job?'

'After a fashion. Certain of my friends wish to enjoy a discreet entertainment, for which you would be perfect. You are pretty, albeit in a rather bovine way, busty and you have a big bottom—'

'No I do not, and if—'

I stopped, knowing that my anger and embarrassment would only amuse him, but I couldn't cut the connection without saying something to get back at him. He carried on, his voice as calm and smug as ever.

'Not gargantuan, perhaps, but like so many Anglo-Saxon girls you do rather tend to run to fat around the hips and buttocks, so very different from the elegance shared by the French and the Japanese. One friend of mine, when watching you walk, said it reminded him of two piglets fighting under a blanket, and the general consensus is that your body is highly erotic, if in a rather vulgar way. Anyway, enough flattery. Do you know what a bukkake party is?'

My mouth opened to answer, but no words came out. I knew perfectly well what a bukkake party was, as I'd had it done to me more than once and thoroughly enjoyed it, but for him to suggest it after the way he'd treated me was so outrageous I was bereft of speech.

'No?' he queried. 'I'm surprised. The essence of it is that one girl entertains a great many men, in her mouth and hands, the idea being to get as much spend as possible in her face.'

'I know what a bukkake party is, Mr Yoshida,' I managed, trying to keep my voice cold and hard but failing miserably, 'but if you think I would attend one for your perverted friends let me assure you . . .'

'That you would rather have sex with a warthog?' he interrupted. 'I did tell them you'd enjoy that, but it's not really to their taste and they are the ones who're paying. A thousand pounds was the sum mentioned.'

'No. Not for a thousand pounds. Not for ten thousand pounds. I am not a prostitute, Mr Yoshida.'

'No? You must excuse me, but English is such a mongrel language and I sometimes get lost in its complexities. What do you call a girl who accompanies wealthy men on exclusive trips on the understanding that she spreads her legs on demand?'

'You . . . you utter, fucking . . . no, you are not going to get to me, Mr Yoshida. If you and your perverted friends want to get off on covering some poor girl with spunk you can look elsewhere. I am not for sale.'

'Oh I'm sure you are,' he replied, 'but haggling is so sordid, don't you think? So I'll tell you now that we're prepared to go to two thousand, no more.'

It was not the time to admit that I had plenty of money. With him a show of pure pride would be far more effective, not to mention good for my battered ego.

'No,' I told him, 'and no, Mr Yoshida, means no.'

'Fifty pounds then, if you prefer to think of yourself as a cheap tart.'

'No! Not for any amount of money.'

'No? You surprise me. In fact, I doubt you're being entirely honest with yourself. For free then?'

I'd been about to cut the connection, but stopped, amazed by his sheer arrogance.

'Free?' I demanded. 'Why would I do it for free, Mr Yoshida?'

'Because you like degrading yourself, as we both know. Come, come, Natasha, give in to what you know you want. I intend to have you, you realise that? After all, there are very few girls as dirty as you, and if we hire a girl who's only in it for the money she'll either be unable to cope or, if she can cope, she'll be bored or, worse, try to pretend she's enjoying herself.'

'I have given you my answer, Mr Yoshida.'

'Very well, as you appear to have more pride than a girl like you can really afford, my guess is that it extends to other people. It's a little awkward, you see, if you're going to be so uncooperative, to keep on a girl who broke her contract of employment by having lesbian sex with a guest—'

'You bastard!' I broke in. 'Leave Rhiannon out of this. It's nothing to do with her! Anyway, we didn't—'

'Please don't insult my intelligence, Natasha. You were caught on the security cameras, crossing the yard and going back again the next morning. We know you spent the night in her room.'

'You're a blackmailing bastard, Mr Yoshida, but it won't work. Now fuck off!'

I broke the connection and hurled my phone into a chair. My anger was so hot I felt as if I was going to be sick, while tears were welling in my eyes. I bit my lip, struggling not to cry and telling myself that what I needed to do was think, and hard. He might have been bluffing about Rhiannon, and she was probably better off in another job anyway, considering how Southern and Allied treated her. Yet he'd implied that he could influence their decision, which suggested he was pretty closely tied up with them.

Again I considered exposing him. All I had to do was turn my pictures into a well-presented file and perhaps wait for the results to come back on my wine sample. I could send copies to Pia Santi, the French authorities, the EC even. At the very least Yoshida would be severely embarrassed, but I'd hurt a lot of other people as well, mainly ones I didn't know at all, but also M. Blanquefort. I needed to get at Yoshida personally.

For a long time I sat brooding in my armchair, only to realise that the solution was staring me in the face, just so long as I had the courage to go through with it. Yoshida understood my sexuality quite well. Perhaps he even thought he understood me better than I did myself. Certainly he was arrogant enough, and at least he realised he had a strong effect on me. Even though I'd managed to resist so far, he wasn't going to be surprised when I gave in, especially as he'd brought Rhiannon into the equation. I rang him back.

'Ah, Natasha, I'd been expecting you to call.'

His smug, syrupy voice made me want to retch, but I did my best to sound resentful but defeated rather than angry as I answered him.

'OK, I'll do it, but you don't have to be such a bastard about everything.'

He laughed.

'Oh, but I do, Natasha, as I expect you know very well. It wouldn't be nearly as exciting otherwise, would it?'

'No,' I admitted, 'but you definitely don't have to blackmail me. Leave Rhiannon alone.'

'That was merely a bluff, in case you needed it as an excuse. So, would you like to prostitute yourself, or will you do it for free?'

My voice was cracking as I answered.

'I . . . I'd like to prostitute myself.'

Again he laughed.

'I rather thought you might. Two thousand pounds then, on the understanding that you are properly compliant.'

'I will be, but I'd rather the men paid per head, and on the spot.'

'Ah ha, I quite understand, how crass of me not to have realised. You can strip for us first and I'll tell everybody to put their money in your underwear. They'll enjoy that.'

'OK. A hundred pounds a head?'

'I expect that can be arranged. You will wear . . . let me see, a tight dress, high heels, stockings, matching panties and bra, all in red.'

'Yes.'

'Good. I am so glad we understand each other, Natasha. Most of my clients are still in France, so I will arrange the event for next Saturday, in the afternoon. I will tell you where to come once I've chosen a suitable venue.'

He rang off.

Saturday was the same day as the inaugural party at the Linnet Club, which was a nuisance but something I'd just have to put up with. The most important thing was to make sure Blake and Lucas did as they were told, so I invited them up to my flat for a private party. By the time they'd finished with me, fat Lucas from behind with his belly resting on my upturned bum and Blake in my mouth, I had them both eating out of my hands. They were also the right men for the job, as I'd been sure they would be. Being asked to drive to Weymouth in the early hours of the morning didn't faze them at all, but their appreciation of wine stopped at knowing there was alcohol in it.

That meant making some very careful arrangements, but by Thursday I was ready, allowing me to spend Friday preparing myself for the experience of being put in a ring of men and come over until I was so sodden with spunk I was unrecognisable. Had it been Monty Hartle and his friends, or some of the local lads on the island, I'd have been nervous and excited, but with a group of Oriental businessmen, only one of whom I knew by name, my sense of anticipation was stronger by far. Again and again I had to tell myself that I could cope with it, and with what would come later, but that night I barely slept for erotic nightmares, and so I was still in bed at eleven on Saturday morning when Anton Yoshida called to tell me that the party was in a conference suite at one of the big five-star hotels on Park Lane.

All my life I've never really had to work, because even while I was making a living as a wine writer I knew that if it all went horribly wrong Daddy would be there to catch me. Yet I've often wondered how it must feel to have no choice but to work, and, for a pretty girl with no qualifications, how it must be to cope with the knowledge that you can always sell yourself. As my cab threaded its way through the London traffic I wondered if a high-class call-girl felt any different from me, knowing she was to be paid to entertain men with her body: perhaps ashamed, perhaps excited, perhaps a little afraid, as I was? Or perhaps I'd got it all wrong and after a few times she'd simply be bored.

I very definitely was not bored. All I had on was a smart red leather coat over a set of expensive and matching scarlet underwear: bra and panties, stockings and suspenders. Lipstick-red high heels and a big scarlet flower in my hair completed the ensemble, making me feel how I looked, a tart – admittedly a very expensive tart, but nonetheless a tart. Even the cabbie realised, his eyes flicking with an odd mixture of desire and contempt, and he dropped me at a back door of the hotel.

That suggested there was some sort of protocol, but I wasn't sure what to do, so stood there on the pavement looking conspicuous until the doorman noticed me. He exchanged a knowing look with the cabbie and beckoned me in through a small rotating door. I smiled my thanks and had my bum squeezed for my trouble, adding to my rising sense of sexual vulnerability as I rode the service lift to the fifteenth floor. The suite was easy to find, but only after getting more dirty looks, this time from a pair of cleaners pushing a trolley piled with sheets. As they passed me and carried on down the passage they were whispering together, and I caught a single word – 'whore'.

The lump in my throat was threatening to choke me as I knocked on the door. I was eager to get to work, humiliated and aroused by my encounters but too vulnerable to want any more. The men at least understood, and were there to get their pleasure just as I was there to give it, so the suite was a sanctuary – or so I thought until the door was opened by a girl with a black bob and mischievous, upturned nose: Rhiannon.

'What . . . what are you doing here?' I stammered as the blood rushed to my face and chest.

'I'm the waitress,' she replied, 'and . . .'

She trailed off, her big green eyes wide in shock, her pretty mouth ever so slightly open. It was obvious she knew, because it was obvious that Anton Yoshida had hired her on purpose, no doubt telling her that a call-girl was coming up to entertain the men but not that it was me. I couldn't think what to say, and I was burning with embarrassment and shame, so hot that I was close to tears as I entered the suite. There was no time to explain the truth, and I was very sure Yoshida would have primed her with care and skill. My sweet, virginal Rhiannon now thought I was a call-girl. I very nearly lost my cool, but the shock as I glanced around the huge living room of the suite burst the bubble of my anger. Yoshida himself was there, and the men, lots of them, so many that my mouth came open in automatic protest.

'I . . . I can't, not all of you!'

'Forty-seven?' Yoshida answered me. 'Surely that's not too many for a girl of your experience?'

I shrugged, lost for words, my head so full of conflicting emotions that I didn't know what to say or do. All forty-eight of them were looking at me, Rhiannon in shock, Yoshida in cool amusement, the businessmen bobbing their heads and smiling. For a long, hideously embarrassing pause nobody spoke at all, until Yoshida himself broke the silence.

'What are those?'

'I, er . . .' I began, holding out the pile of shiny red presentation packs I'd made up so carefully, 'I . . . I thought you might all like a memento. I had some pictures done, of me.'

There was an immediate buzz of appreciation and more polite nodding from the businessmen. I put the folders down and opened the top one, showing a large glossy print of me kneeling in nothing but a pair of minuscule yellow bikini bottoms with my head bowed and my naked breasts held up for inspection. Again came the buzz of appreciation.

'There won't be enough to go around, I'm afraid,' I admitted. 'I only did twenty. I . . . I thought you said twenty, Mr Yoshida?'

'You proved to be rather more popular than I anticipated,' Yoshida answered, 'but never mind, you can have some more folders made up later. Very well then. First of all, gentlemen, there is the matter of payment, for which Natasha has come up with rather a sweet idea. She will dance for us, and you are to tuck your money into her underwear, as if she were a lap dancer in a strip club, as she was for a couple of years before she became a call-girl.'

It was an outrageous lie and my mouth opened in angry denial, only to close again. I needed to stay in control, or I might as well just leave, in which case it would all have been for nothing and I definitely wouldn't get a chance to explain to Rhiannon. Instead I smiled and stepped forward to the middle of the carpet, feeling more vulnerable than ever. The view through the huge picture window was of Hyde Park, but it might as well have been another world.

I bowed, because it seemed the right thing to do, first towards Mr Zhang and the group around him, then to each side of the room. Rhiannon had gone to fetch drinks from the kitchen. The men seemed anonymous and interchangeable, but I couldn't shake her presence from my mind. I had to do it, though, and do it well, so I simply let my body take over, imagining I was performing for Percy and his friends as I let my coat slip from my shoulders and began to dance.

It wasn't hard; it never is. I've danced for men often enough to know what they like, plenty of boobs and plenty of bum, peeks of pussy and occasional eye contact, a little bit of tease and a little bit of brazen display. The most important thing is to go all the way, otherwise they feel cheated. Men like to feel they own a girl who's stripping for them, that they know her every secret. Hold back a little and they get off on your shyness, hold back too much and they feel dissatisfied.

Not that it mattered this time, as they were guaranteed their satisfaction, all over me, and any clothes I left on were sure to be ruined. Still I did my best, just out of pride, teasing and flirting as I gradually exposed myself, making very sure they all got their fair share and that long before I was finished each and every one of them was familiar with every curve of my waist and hips, every intimate contour of my boobs and bottom, every fold and crease of my shaved pink pussy and the wrinkled brown star between my rear cheeks.

They loved it, clapping and cheering, exchanging lewd jokes in several languages I didn't understand, pushing their bundles of money into my underwear while I still had any on and wedging them into my cleavage and between the cheeks of my bottom once I was nude. I didn't even try to count but just let it all pile up, until the floor was littered with scraps of scarlet material and banknotes of every denomination. All the while Rhiannon distributed beers, whisky and glasses of Champagne, walking among the men with quick, dextrous movements, clearly nervous and fearful of groping hands and pinching fingers. None of them touched her, or not that I saw, and she was able to retreat to the kitchen unmolested while I stood in the centre of the room, as naked as the day I was born, my hands on my head, my feet set apart among my discarded clothes and the money I'd been paid for my services.

'Put your clothes and money over there in the corner, Natasha,' Yoshida ordered. 'Then go into the small bedroom' – he gestured towards a door – 'and bring the plastic sheet you'll find in the bathroom. Spread it on the floor.'

His voice was so calm and authoritative, the atmosphere of male privilege and female submission so strong that I found myself bowing to him by instinct and hurrying to obey. The bedroom he'd sent me to was only small by comparison with a normal hotel, and *en suite*. I quickly found the sheet and scampered back to spread it on the floor, my heart hammering at what I was about to do.

The men were joking among themselves, and the more senior ones clustered around me. I knelt, a position that seemed shamefully appropriate to what I was doing, looked up and opened my mouth. They wasted no time, and were far less concerned about exposing themselves than a group of British men would have been. Mr Zhang simply flopped his cock out of his trousers, straight into my mouth. Others had also unzipped and I took a cock in each hand, while one man began to fondle my breasts as he masturbated and another to rub his cock in my hair.

I was still painfully aware of Rhiannon, who was peeping from the kitchen door with a look of horrified fascination, but I couldn't have stopped myself if I'd had the chance. My instincts had taken over, and yet my mind was still clear enough for me to be astonished by my own behaviour as I tugged and sucked and flaunted myself for their pleasure. One man ducked down to grope my bottom and I found myself wanting to stick it out in the hope of getting an exploratory finger up my pussy. When Mr Zhang pulled his cock free and pressed his balls to my mouth I took in as much of the fat, leathery sack as I could, rolling his balls over my tongue, as dirty and subservient as Yoshida could possibly have wanted me.

Soon I was surrounded by a forest of hard cocks, fat and thin, long and short, all sticking rudely out of their smart suits, most with their balls bulging out below. The air was thick with male scent and I'd started to juice and squeeze my thighs, while my nipples were sticking up like little corks. When the first man spunked on me it gave me a sharp jolt of pleasure, even though he'd only done it in my hair and across my forehead. I began to suck more eagerly, jammed another man's cock in beside Mr Zhang's and set up a fast rhythm with the two in my hands, one of whom came on the instant, erupting spunk down my cheek and over my shoulder and one tit.

They were laughing at my eagerness, and passing comments in their own languages and English, all utterly indifferent to my feelings. They said I was beautiful and called me a slut. They said I was pretty and how they'd like to spunk in my face. They said I looked nice and laughed as one spunked in my eye and the mascara began to run down my face. They said how big and firm my boobs were and how they'd like to fuck my cleavage. They said I had a fat bottom and pointed out the now faint marks from my caning. They said I had a pretty bumhole and asked me to stick my bum out to show it off.

I obeyed, lost in my own arousal, wiggling my hips to make my cheeks shake and encourage them to touch. They took the invitation, a finger sliding in up my wet pussy just as Mr Zhang reached his orgasm, holding me by my jaw so that he could wank into my open mouth and let everybody see the pool of spunk he'd laid on my tongue. As soon as he let go I swallowed his mess like a good girl and took another man in. Four, maybe five, had already come on me and the rest were waiting their turn, either standing or seated, with their cocks out ready for my mouth and hands. All except Anton Yoshida.

He just watched and sipped his Champagne, more amused than aroused as I gave in to the appalling degradation he'd planned for me. I saw him smile when I deliberately gaped wide to let a man spunk in my mouth, but at the same instant I got a load in my other eye, and from then on I couldn't see at all. Both my eyes were stinging with sperm, but I got no mercy, only another load splashed over my tightly closed lids. Now utterly helpless, I could only let them take control, guiding my hands to their cocks and twisting my head about by the hair to make me suck.

I shivered at every splash of sperm on my body. One man did it all over my tits, another down my back and in my hair, a third over my bottom. My pussy was straining to an entire fist, and I was sure I'd be fucked, but it never happened. They did what they'd paid to do and spunked on me, one after another after another, until my face was plastered and my belly had begun to bulge from what I'd swallowed, and I was sure that if just one more did it in my mouth I would be sick. That didn't stop me wriggling my bottom in the slimy puddle underneath me as soon as the man who'd fisted me had relieved his cock all over my hip. I had to come, but I knew I'd never get enough friction from the splash mat, so the moment they began to slow down a little I stuck a hand between my thighs and began to rub.

They cheered and clapped as they saw I was masturbating, but that didn't stop me. Instead it almost got me off, because I knew they were watching and enjoying my reaction. I spread my thighs for them, rubbing hard on my bump, all thoughts of decency forgotten, no longer even caring that Rhiannon was watching me. She could like it or lump it, that was all, I had to come, and come immediately. One man was still in my mouth, another rubbing his cock on my slimy tits, a third tickling my bumhole.

Spunk splashed in my cleavage, down my belly and on to my hand as well. I rubbed it in, sucking urgently and squirming on the finger that was now a little way into my slippery bumhole, right on the brink of orgasm ... and then I was there, my whole body jerking and shaking as spasm after spasm ran through me. One of them spunked in my ear, another full in my face, both driving me up to another peak, and at the final, choking, breathless summit of my ecstasy the man in my mouth jammed his cock deep and spunked down my throat.

It was too much. My belly gave a single huge lurch and I threw up at least a pint of spunk all over the man's cock, down my own tits and on my legs and cunt. A second lurch and I'd done it on the man between my knees, but they were still around me, still wanking over me, even as I squatted in my own filth, a thick, slimy mat of spunk covering my body, sticking in my hair and running slowly down my face and breasts to soil my belly and thighs, smearing my bum cheeks and my open hole, into which the very last of them had just ejaculated.

Not that I realised he was the last. I couldn't see, I couldn't hear properly, I could barely breathe. Forty-six men had come on me, most of them not even bothering to use my mouth, but I hadn't been fucked at all and I'd had only one cock in my bumhole, and that was no more than a finger's width. My jaw ached, my throat hurt and my tummy felt raw, but that was it: it was over. I felt an odd sense of disappointment as the men backed away, clapping and congratulating me on my performance.

I managed a smile through my mask of spunk and tried to climb to my feet, only to slip and sit down again in the mess, theirs and mine. That made them laugh, but they did at least help me, moving me and the mat very carefully into the small suite, where I was made to lie down, rolled up in the mat and plonked down in the bath, where I wasted no time in turning on the taps.

The first thing I did was clean my eyes, to discover that the men who'd helped me had left, except Anton Yoshida. He was in the bedroom, sitting in an armchair he'd positioned so that he could watch me through the open bathroom door. In one hand he held a glass of Champagne, while with the other he was toying with his cock and balls where they hung from his open fly. He nodded when he saw that I was watching, then spoke.

'You were very good, Natasha, really very good. I particularly enjoyed it when you were sick down your chest . . .'

I could well believe it of him, and forced a rueful smile as he went on.

'. . . although I suspect that Mr Kweon, whose cock you were sucking at the time, and who got a good deal of it on his trousers, was less pleased.'

'I'll apologise,' I promised.

'Good,' he said. 'You're learning. I knew you'd be the girl for this job, Natasha, once I'd brought you out of yourself a little. So, what shall I do with you?'

'You . . . you can do anything you want,' I told him. 'You know that.'

'Yes, I do, and I'm glad you've come to understand. It's the only way for a girl like you, isn't it, to accept a man as master?'

'Yes,' I admitted.

'Very good. Finish cleaning yourself up and come to me, crawling.'

I nodded and began to soap myself, taking my time as he watched. My entire body was soiled, but the real problem was my hair, which was badly matted and needed to be rinsed and shampooed several times before I was satisfied. He didn't rush me, but sipped his drink and watched, his eyes drinking in my naked body as I moved in the bath and stood to get under the shower. Finally I was clean, and as I towelled myself dry I was wondering why nothing had happened. It looked as if I would have to suck him off after all.

There was an assortment of body lotions and powder, courtesy of the hotel, so I made an elaborate show of creaming my skin and powdering my pussy and anus, all in full view. There was even a hair-dryer, but that really was going to take too long, so with my hair still wound up under a towel I got down on my knees. He watched, quite calm but with his eyes and the corners of his mouth betraying the cruelty and arousal I knew he felt.

I hadn't meant it to go so far, but I was still turned on and seemed to have little choice. Extending my tongue, I began to lick his balls, making myself his obedient little dog as I knelt naked between his open thighs. I wanted to masturbate again, and for a few seconds my pride held me back before I gave in and began to tease myself. My pussy felt smooth and powdery, just a little wet in the middle, very different from the state I'd been in earlier.

I took Anton's cock in my mouth and began to suck in earnest, my arousal rising apace with my humiliation as I gave a willing blowjob on my knees to a man who'd treated me like dirt, a man who got his kicks from seeing me gag on a cock and puke all over my breasts. He really was an utter bastard, and yet there I was, stark naked at his feet, mouthing eagerly on his cock as I masturbated.

I was going to come too, at any second, certainly before he did. My bum cheeks were already beginning to clench and my pussy to tighten, and I remembered how it had felt to spew up a mixture of spunk and my lunch, hot and slimy on my boobs and tummy, all over my legs, soiling my cunt. On that thought I came, and I knew it wouldn't be the last time I got off on what ranked among the filthiest and finest memories of my life.

'Dirty bitch,' Anton chuckled. He tugged my head hard back by the hair, grabbed his cock and with a few quick jerks tossed himself off in my open mouth.

All of it went in and I swallowed it quickly, spent a few painful seconds trying to keep it down, then rocked back on my heels.

'May I fetch you another drink, please?' I asked.

He held out his glass, not bothering to reply. I got up, still a little unsteady on my feet, and left the bedroom. I was wondering what was going on in the living room, but I needn't have worried. Mr Zhang and the others were standing in little clusters, all urgently discussing the contents of the folders I'd given them. One or two asked questions, which I did my best to answer as I slipped into my knickers and shoes before gathering up the money and stuffing it into my handbag.

There was no sign of Rhiannon, and the realisation that she would probably never want to speak to me again took more than a little of the gloss off my pleasure as I pulled on my coat and buckled it tight to make sure I didn't give anyone an accidental flash in the street. My stockings, suspenders and bra went into one pocket and I was done – as was Anton Yoshida.

It had seemed reasonable to assume that Mr Zhang and his colleagues had a strong sense of honour, and also that they would object to being cheated. Only the top two sheets of each folder were pictures of me, while the rest was a very carefully constructed exposure of his corrupt methods, including as much evidence as I'd been able to cite without leaving M. Blanquefort in danger of criminal prosecution. It had been enough, of that I could be sure from the black fury on Mr Zhang's face as he demanded that Yoshida come out of the bedroom.

I left the same way I'd come, down by the service lift and out at the back. All the while I was wishing my black mood would lift, but by having Rhiannon witness my submission Yoshida had ruined what should have been a moment of triumph. I'd seen the horror on her face as she watched, and though I'd soon been too far gone to stop myself my bad feelings were flooding back. Worst of all, the state I'd got into while they gave me bukkake was a deep part of me, and something Rhiannon would never have been able to accept. As I came out of the hotel I was biting my lip, close to tears.

Then I saw her, standing on the other side of the street, her hands folded in her lap, her head lowered. She looked up and I crossed to her, an apology trembling on my lips, only for her to speak first.

'Are you OK?'

'Yes. Look, Rhiannon—'

'You are so brave, Natasha! I so wish I was like you.'

'Like me?'

'Like you, to just handle men the way you do, like they were nothing, like you can take them all and come out laughing.'

'Oh. Well, I suppose you could put it like that . . .'

'How else? What did you earn just now?'

'I don't know, about five thousand, I think.'

'Five grand! In what, just over an hour? It takes me nearly six months to earn that.'

She had me completely off guard, and I very nearly pointed out that I could arrange another bukkake party for her with Mr Zhang before I stopped myself, realising that however much she admired me it was something she could never bring herself to do. Instead I shrugged and waved my hands in a meaningless gesture as I struggled for something to say. Her next question caught me by surprise.

'Do you really like men?'

I knew the answer to that, not the truth, necessarily, but the only sensible thing to say.

'Not as much as I like girls, especially the girl who's standing in front of me now.'

She smiled and blushed. I held out my hand, she took it and as we began to walk all my bad feelings vanished, to be replaced by a glow of triumph. I'd dealt with Lydia, I'd dealt with Anton Yoshida and I was holding hands with Rhiannon. The only flaw was that I had just a few hours before I had to be in St James's, not nearly enough time to do justice to her, and my aching jaw and the raw feeling in my tummy weren't going to help. I really needed to rest, but it was my only chance.

'I hope you're not working this afternoon?' I asked.

'No. That was a special booking. My contract's finished.'

'Contract?'

'I was on a three-month contract with Southern and Allied Food Products. Mr Yoshida said you'd lost your job. I'm sorry.'

'It's not like that. Like you, I was on a short-term contract, that's all. In fact, there's a leaving party of sorts this evening. I'd much rather be with you, but as it's for me I really have to go.'

'Oh. Maybe we could meet up afterwards? Or could I come along?'

‘Er . . .’ I stopped, embarrassed. ‘. . . um, the thing is, it’s a bit like the other . . . what just happened. They expect to spank me, you see, as, um . . . a sort of going-away thing.’

I was blushing hot, which was ridiculous when she’d just watched me strip and get bukkake from forty-six businessmen. She giggled.

‘You’re terrible, Natasha! And are you going dressed like that?’

‘I was going to change. This is much too overt for their taste. They’d rather I was in my business suit or, better still, school uniform. You know what dirty old men are like.’

‘No, I don’t.’

‘Well, if you come with me you’ll find out!’

She fell silent for a while, leaving me once more conscious of my appearance and the way people were looking at us, or rather at me. My mood had changed, and had it not been for the cold November wind I’d have been tempted to flash my tits at the more intrusive of them, particularly an elderly woman with a miniature poodle who looked at me as if I’d just risen from hell.

As we reached Berkeley Square Rhiannon suddenly began to talk again, her words tumbling out so fast that with her accent I could barely understand what she was saying.

‘You’d have hated my life, Natasha and that’s the truth. I’ve been so shut up, always shut up, in convents and at home, with everybody always on my case telling me I have to be pure and I have to be good or else I’ll go to hell, or get raped because every man always wants to fuck and doesn’t care, and I don’t want to be like that, Natasha. I want to be free. That’s why I went to Paris and signed up with the agency, just to get away, but I can’t, not in my head, not yet, but maybe with you, if you'd help me? I . . . I'd quite like to watch.'

I squeezed her hand, taken aback by her sudden explosion of emotion, because I could tell that she was close to tears. She'd always seemed vulnerable but now more so than ever, and younger.

'How old are you, Rhiannon, if you don't mind me asking?'

'Eighteen.'

A year less and she'd have been close to half my age. I felt a sudden pang of guilt for what I wanted to do to her, but it didn't last long. She wanted it, and if she was ever to enjoy her sex life, she needed it. Besides, if I didn't take her she would no doubt succumb to some fumbling oaf or smooth-talking bastard, so it was really for the best.

'OK,' I told her, 'you can come, and I promise I'll look after you.'

Twelve

Rhiannon and I spent the rest of the afternoon clothes-shopping, partly because I was going to need some things until Percy could send on my luggage and partly to get kitted up for the evening. Gilbert, Otto and company had only ever seen me in a smart business suit, and while that seemed to appeal I was definitely due for a change.

After first buying a pair of cheap jeans, a baggy top and a jumper so that I wouldn't freeze to death, we began to try options. I considered a nurse's uniform in one of the medical supply shops off Harley Street, a fully correct bottle-green school outfit in Selfridges and red, white and blue cheerleader's gear in the American Boutique in Carnaby Street. None of them were right, but it was fun trying them on, especially as Rhiannon grew gradually bolder after watching me dress and undress so many times. I took the opportunity to have a snog and a squeeze in the American Boutique, after which she told me that whatever outfit I chose she would dress to match.

What we eventually chose was sheer mischief, and better designed to earn me a spanking than the shortest of skirts or the tightest of panties. Selecting a gent's outfitters just on the wrong side of Regent Street, we converted ourselves into parodies of the men themselves. First came male briefs, the smallest size they had available, which clung to our bottoms but bagged at the front, then white shirts and silk waistcoats to accentuate our breasts, particularly mine, which looked as if they were doing their best to burst free. Sensible brogues and diamond-pattern socks served for our feet, while the herringbone twill suits we selected might very well have come from the wardrobe of the Right Honourable Vernon Flyght himself, except that they were several sizes too small. They also had the effect of showing off the roundness of our bottoms, which peeped out from beneath the hems of our jackets in a way I knew Percy for one would find irresistible, as he would the implied mockery of our style.

The shop assistant certainly thought so, his manner remaining frigid despite my liberal dispensations of cash. I paid for Rhiannon, as each outfit cost several hundred pounds, and that put her in an ecstasy of gratitude as we walked south. By then I no longer felt even remotely guilty about my decision to have her. It was what she wanted, and it was what she was going to get.

We were still half an hour early, so we stopped at a bar for a couple of large gin and tonics. I was sure Rhiannon needed a drink and I certainly did, because for all my careful planning there were a dozen things that could go wrong. First was having the right man on the door, and I relieved to see Stubbs standing there in full uniform, right down to the sergeant's stripes on the sleeves of his crimson jacket. I gave him a smile and a surreptitious squeeze of his crotch, to which he returned a knowing wink.

Second was the location. I'd suggested the tasting room on the first floor, the largest in the building, because although it looked out over St James's there were heavy shutters that could be closed to ensure absolute privacy. They'd taken my advice, adding to the atmosphere by having only the central chandelier lit, while each of the tables placed against the walls supported a large, polished brass candelabrum with deep-red candles. Most of the men were already there, Gilbert with a glass of Champagne in his hand at the door. He greeted me with a smile that changed to an enquiring look as he took in my outfit and my companion.

'Rhiannon, this is Gilbert Hambling, my ex-boss,' I explained. 'Gilbert, this is Rhiannon, who has volunteered to pass the drinks around this evening.'

'Delighted, I'm sure,' Gilbert responded.

'She's very experienced,' I assured him, 'so you can leave everything to her, but she's not to be touched, except, just possibly, by me.'

His great bushy eyebrows rose a fraction and I gave him my cheekiest smile before moving further into the room. Otto was there, and Vernon, along with most of the men who'd enjoyed me at the Aviators. I now knew all of them by name, but I remembered them from the way they'd behaved at that first encounter: the cold one, the one who liked girls to put up a fight, the one who'd pulled my boobs out. Now it was time for another round, and in front of Rhiannon, and I was filled with nervous excitement as I accepted their compliments and congratulations, as well as several remarks on my choice of costume and what the consequences were likely to be. I accepted it all, trying not to keep looking at the clock above the door as they gradually assembled, with Percy turning up last of all.

'Shall we begin, then?' Gilbert suggested.

There was general agreement, and I stepped out into the middle of the room, where the traditional single chair had been placed at the centre of the carpet.

'OK, boys, who's first?' I asked.

Vernon gave a polite gesture towards Gilbert, who in turn cocked an eyebrow at Percy.

'No, no. I enjoy the privilege nightly,' Percy insisted.

'You're too polite, you silly old buffers,' I said with a laugh.

'I'll show you who's an old buffer!' a fat, silver-haired man wheezed, and he began to get to his feet.

'That seems as good a way as any,' I said. 'We'll do it by seniority, oldest first.'

'Old I may be,' the man said, advancing, 'but not too old to take a saucy little brat like you to task, Natasha.'

He sat down, making a lap for me to climb over. I undid my fly buttons to make it easier for him and draped myself across his knees, the tweed of my trousers now tauter than ever across my bottom. He turned my jacket tails up on to my back and began to fondle me, grunting softly to himself as he explored the shape and feel of my cheeks, apparently in no hurry whatsoever to actually spank me.

I closed my eyes, concentrating on the exquisite humiliation of my position, bum high over some dirty old bastard's knee as he molested me in front of his friends and my own girlfriend. By the time he decided to get me stripped I was fighting the urge to let my thighs come apart, and I couldn't repress a sigh as my trousers were tugged down to expose the white briefs beneath. He patted my bottom, traced one finger slowly down to push my pants into my crease, adjusted each leg hole to ensure that my cheeks were perfectly exhibited in their tight white cotton casing, spent a long moment simply admiring the view and at last took hold of my waistband.

My bottom was stripped, something I've always enjoyed, but this time it was pure bliss just to know that they were all watching, especially Rhiannon, as my briefs slid slowly down to expose my cheeks, full and bare for spanking. I'd deliberately pushed myself high to make my cheeks spread and let them all see the tight brown knot of my bumhole. He made a good job of me too, tucking my briefs right down to make sure I lost every last scrap of modesty.

'Good heavens, it's a girl!' he remarked as my pussy came on show to the room.

Everybody laughed and my face flushed hot as I imagined what I was showing behind, every soft pink fold of my sex in plain view. At last he began to spank, just gently, calling me a saucy little minx as he smacked my bottom and pausing occasionally to touch me up. I couldn't help but react, sighing and wriggling in my growing excitement as my cheeks grew slowly warmer and my pussy wetter.

By the time he'd finished I had completely surrendered. The next man made me put my hands on my head while he opened the front of my clothes, unbuttoning my shirt and waistcoat just far enough for him to lift my tits out and leave them dangling awkwardly and slapping together as I was spanked across his knee. The third put a finger in me and made me suck it, while the fourth made a point of inspecting my bottom slit and remarking on the brownish colour of my anal flesh. The fifth man spanked hard; he was the first who seemed to want to punish me rather than humiliate or take advantage of me. The sixth was Gilbert, and when he stepped up to the chair I saw that he was holding a small wooden box.

'Something to keep you warm,' he remarked in response to my curious gaze, then opened the box.

Inside was a small fruit knife, a wrapped pat of butter and a large piece of fresh root ginger. He was going to fig me.

'Over you go, my dear,' he instructed, sitting down.

I got into position, wondering how Rhiannon felt about girls having things put up their bottom holes as I braced my feet as far apart as my lowered clothes would permit and stuck my hips up. It was a thoroughly rude position, showing everything, and Gilbert took immediate advantage, squashing the pat of butter into my anus so that it began to melt, lubricating me as he carved the fig. I could feel the butter, moist and slippery as it pooled in my anus and trickled slowly down into my pussy hole and over my lips.

He took ages, with me holding my position all the while. I could see Rhiannon serving drinks and repeatedly glancing at my spread bottom. Her emotions were hard to read, and seemed to keep changing, but they were certainly strong, which made mine stronger in turn, and when the neatly carved plug of ginger root was finally inserted in my bumhole I was sobbing with shame. Thirty seconds later I was sobbing for a quite different reason as the heat in my penetrated bumhole grew to a powerful burn and Gilbert smacked my naked bottom to add to my woes.

I couldn't hold myself still, but kicked, wriggled and squeezed my bum cheeks, to the delight of my audience. Gilbert took his time as well, not only adding to the already hot glow of my bum but taking my trousers and briefs down to my knees so that he could smack my thighs and make sure everybody behind me got a good view of the fig in my penetrated anus.

When he'd finally finished I felt dizzy and didn't try to stand, but fell to my knees on the floor. The next man stepped up, and I was given a firm but rather short spanking and put back on the floor. Then Otto got to his feet. He too was holding something, and he spoke as he tucked me across his knee.

‘I also have a little surprise for you,’ he said, holding up a long, weather-beaten box. ‘Well, not so very little perhaps.’

He opened the box, causing a ripple of laughter and a few muttered remarks as he showed the others what it contained. I twisted around, eager to find out what was to be done to me and expecting a dog quirt or some equally painful and humiliating implement. What he had was an enormous thermometer, the old-fashioned kind with a glass bulb full of coloured alcohol and a long calibrated shaft. I knew exactly where it was going, up my bum, as it wouldn’t be the first time some pervert had inflicted his fetish for medical humiliation on me; but the horrible thing was at least four times the size of any I’d had used on me before.

‘It is’, he explained as he once more began to stroke my bottom, ‘a relic of the days when our deliveries were done by horse and cart, and is intended, as you may therefore have deduced, to measure the rectal temperature of a horse. However, no doubt it will do equally well when inserted between the cheeks of Natasha’s somewhat perter and prettier bottom.’

‘You’re a bastard, Otto,’ I muttered, but I hung my head in submission and braced my feet to lift my bottom back into full prominence.

His fingers delved between my bum cheeks to grip the base of my fig and extract it, leaving my bumhole open and slippery. Keeping my cheeks spread, he pushed the big, round thermometer bulb in without difficulty and lodged it well up my rectum. The fig went up my pussy, making me gasp and my eyes water as the heat built in my sex. Then he began to spank me, the thermometer waggling in my bottom hole at every slap. He only gave me a couple of dozen, then took hold of the thermometer and eased it free, once more leaving my bumhole gaping to the audience.

'Normal,' he remarked as he inspected it, 'for a horse at least. For a human she is a little warm, but that is perhaps not surprising.'

He chuckled and went back to spanking me, only to pause so that he could place the thermometer on Rhiannon's tray and ask her to wash it, which I found almost as shameful as having it stuck up my bottom. I couldn't help lifting my head to watch the rotation of her cheeks beneath her boyish trousers as she left the room.

After Gilbert came Percy, who made me eat my fig and wouldn't stop spanking until I'd swallowed every last bit, then Vernon, who made me run on the spot with my tits bouncing wildly and my bum jiggling, just long enough to make sure that Rhiannon had a good look when she came back into the room. He spanked me in nappy-changing position, rolled up on my back with my legs held up to ensure that every lewd detail of my sex was flaunted as he smacked my already fiery cheeks. After that they started to compete, each man doing his best to spread me out in some even ruder or more inventive position: bent down with my head jammed between one's knees, with my thighs open across another's knee to make my pussy rub on his trousers as he spanked me, thrown over a third's shoulder like a flour sack, with my bum the highest part of my body.

As the men became more excited, again and again I'd have an erection rubbing against my body as I was reduced to a kicking, wriggling tantrum with my hair flying and tears streaming down my face. Several of them fingered me or had a rub of my pussy, but it was Stubbs who made me come, spanking me hard with one hand while the other cupped my pussy and masturbated me to a long, shame-filled orgasm that left me panting and sweaty on the floor, my bare red bottom stuck out to the room and the juice trickling slowly down one thigh.

Percy helped me up and Rhiannon pressed a glass of Champagne into my hand. I drank it at a gulp and took a second glass before pausing to rearrange myself. They'd all been thoroughly enjoying the show and were now talking animatedly among themselves, so I sat down to refresh myself and check that Rhiannon was OK. It had taken about an hour for me to be passed around: not quite as long as I'd liked, but we were far from finished. After my third glass of Champagne and a kiss for Rhiannon I stepped back to the centre of the room and raised my hands for silence, which I eventually got.

'Gentlemen,' I called out, 'I have a special treat for you. If she agrees, and only if, I am going to spank Rhiannon in front of you. Rhiannon?'

She nodded and swallowed, shy but determined, which sent a sharp thrill of lust through me. I sat down on the chair, my own bottom hot and tender in my briefs. The men were turning their attention to us, their interest growing as I went on.

'I'm not going to hurt you,' I told her, 'and unlike some gentlemen I could mention I won't play any nasty tricks, but you are going to be bare-bottom, is that clear? Now, gentlemen, before I start I think you should all know that Rhiannon is only eighteen. Come down across my knee, darling.'

She gave one last worried glance at the ring of expectant male faces and draped herself across my lap, her bottom lifted, the tweed of her trousers tight over her cheeks, just as mine had been. I reached under her tummy to undo her fly, loosened her trousers a little, lifted my leg and took her firmly around the waist to make her pull her back in and ensure that everyone got a good view.

'Better still, this will be her virgin spanking,' I said, and took her trousers down.

Rhiannon had shaken her head as her briefs came on show, but I wasn't sure what she meant and she didn't try to get up, so I stuck my thumbs into the waistband of her pants and pushed. She gave a single, hard sob as her bottom cheeks came bare, small and sweet and rounded, each chubby little cheek bulging out, so full and firm you'd have thought she'd been pumped up, which gave her a very rude rear view indeed, with the tiny, dimpled star of her anus on full display and her cunt too, neat and pink and virgin. Every eye in the room was on her now, bulging from their reddened faces as they drank in the beautiful sight of her exposed bottom and sex, stripped for men for the first time.

She was trembling, and so was I, scarcely able to hold back my desire for her. Yet I knew I had to take it slowly, because she didn't have spanking fantasies and if I did her too hard she never would. The most she knew was what it meant to have to show her bottom in front of dozens of men, and even then in panties, not bare. So I took my time, caressing her, squeezing the meat of her cheeks and running my nails across her skin, patting her ever so gently until the first pink flush had begun to creep over her bottom.

Only then did I begin to spank her, not hard, just enough as if I was trying to give her a lesson without really hurting. At that she began to kick a little, and her breathing was growing fast, so I kept apace with her and fought down the rising desire to spank the gorgeous little brat until she howled. That would come another time.

I stopped and helped her to her feet. The men began to clap, saying what a brave girl she was and complimenting her on her bottom as I took her in my arms. She clung tight, trembling, and I saw that she had begun to cry, a tear moistening each cheek. I kissed them away, thanked her and again drew her close, holding her until she chose to pull back, but even then only a little, while she seemed unable to stop herself kissing me.

Everybody in the room was watching us. I knew what I owed them, but that was just going to have to wait. Rhiannon was on heat and that mattered more than their pleasure. I stood up, still holding on to her as I spoke.

'If you would excuse us for a few minutes, gentlemen. Percy?'

They began to mutter among themselves as we left the room, Rhiannon still with her clothes loosened and her pink bum cheeks showing beneath her shirt-tails. Percy followed a few paces behind as I climbed to what had been my office. The moment I'd locked the door behind us I took Rhiannon in my arms again, kissed her passionately and pulled at her clothes. She responded, still nervous but not unwilling, allowing me to strip her out of her jacket and waistcoat, her shoes and trousers, her shirt and at last her briefs to leave her nude but for her little diamond-pattern socks.

Percy had sat down at the desk, watching and waiting, knowing better than to interrupt, for all that he looked fit to burst. Rhiannon had glanced at him repeatedly as she was being stripped, but she'd said nothing and made no resistance, even when her briefs came off. I wasn't sure if she'd guessed her fate, or if she'd accept it, but I had to tell her.

'He's going to fuck you,' I said, my voice gentle but firm, my words deliberately unambiguous.

Her mouth opened a little, her lower lip trembling, but she said nothing.

'Get your cock out, Percy,' I ordered. 'Don't worry, darling, it won't hurt. His cock's quite small, and he's the perfect gentleman.'

She responded with a weak nod and I gave her an encouraging smile. Percy was doing as he'd been told, leaning back in the chair and extracting his cock and balls from his trousers. He was already stiff, his erection a little pink spike rising above his oversized scrotum, just right for puncturing Rhiannon's hymen.

'It's nice to have a smacked bottom first,' I told her, patting her. 'Now climb on.'

Again she nodded, completely acquiescent to my will. I got down on the floor as she swung one shapely leg across Percy's lap, watching as she positioned herself above him, her virgin pussy directly over his erection.

'Let me,' I demanded, crawling close.

Her bum was right in my face, her pink cheeks open to display the tight wrinkle of her anus and the mouth of her sex, moist and ready but closed by the pink arc of her hymen. I poked out my tongue, took hold of Percy's cock, and licked her as I wanked him and rubbed his helmet on her clit. She soon began to moan and I saw that she was clinging on to him, her breasts in his face. I rubbed harder, to make her think I was going to bring her off, only to suddenly press his cock to her virgin pussy and pull down on her hips.

At the same instant he pushed. I saw her hymen stretch, heard her gasp of pain and surprise, saw her flesh split and his cock disappear up her cunt. Blood began to trickle from her ruptured maidenhead as he fucked her, holding her tightly in his arms to prevent her escaping and make sure she got it properly. I buried my face at the junction of his cock and her freshly penetrated cunt, tasting her virgin blood, rich and salty in my mouth, as it trickled down his shaft and over his enormous balls.

She was crying softly, and whimpering, but we held her firmly in place until at last her pleasure got the better of her and she begun to bounce on Percy's cock. We had her, and I let myself go, licking between her bum cheeks to taste her anus and lapping up the mixture of blood and juice now coating his balls. I had to come, and my hand went down my trousers and briefs as I licked, to find my wet, ready pussy.

I was licking Rhiannon's bottom as I began to masturbate, my head dizzy with delight at what I'd done with her and the pleasure she was getting from both her spanked bottom and her penetrated pussy. Maybe I was a bitch, but it was what she'd wanted and I was licking her bum to make up for it. Did it make any sense? I didn't care any more, too close to orgasm to worry about morals as I licked Percy's balls and tongued Rhiannon's bottom, pleasuring them as they fucked.

Percy came suddenly, and his hot spunk exploded from Rhiannon's cunt into my face and mouth. I just licked all the harder, cleaning up the mess of blood and spunk and pussy juice as my own orgasm kicked in, so long and hard and high that I came close to fainting. Three times I peaked as I mouthed Percy's scrotum, all the while with Rhiannon's bottom squashing in my face, and then a fourth time with my tongue stuck as far up her bumhole as it would go.

Even then I wasn't finished, but jerked Percy's cock free and stuck it in my mouth to once more taste Rhiannon's blood before I buried my face in her newly fucked cunt, determined to bring her to orgasm. She didn't need encouragement, wriggling her bottom in my face and begging me to lick harder as she clung to Percy with an animal desperation, his face smothered in her chest. I was still masturbating, and as she began to buck and writhe and scream out her ecstasy I was coming again, together with her in the perfect climax.

* * *

Things weren't quite going to plan, but they were close enough. I hadn't factored Rhiannon into my programe, which meant that I was left with nearly two dozen dirty old men expecting their cocks sucked, to say nothing of Stubbs, Blake and Lucas. Percy was also a problem, if a minor one, because he was blissfully unaware of what I was up to.

I just had to get on with it, because there was no choice. Any funny business and they might get suspicious, which would be a disaster. So into the broom cupboard I went, a tradition Vernon had insisted on, to suck cock after cock after cock until my tummy was so bloated with spunk it was a relief to have to kneel on the chair and let Stubbs do it up my bum. By then everybody else was sitting about chatting, and they weren't in the least surprised when I announced that I was off to a hotel room with Rhiannon and told them not to expect me back.

The van was where I'd said it should be, with Blake and Lucas sittting in the cab grinning. A quick check in the back confirmed that they had done as I'd told them and taken only the cases marked with a blue splash. Lucas had to go, as Rhiannon was coming and there was no room in the cab, but I was kind and gave him his thank-you blowjob in the back of the van anyway. That left Blake, but I made him wait. Rhiannon and I cuddled beside him as we drove west, not stopping until we reached a lay-by just outside Weymouth. There, sore but happy, with the cream of the contents of the Hambling and Borst cellar now mine – which I'd very definitely earned, even if my rate of exchange in bottles per spanking was a trifle more generous than they might have wished – I sat him down on a case of Clos de Tart 1955, pulled out his fat black cock and gave him what I hoped would be my last blowjob for a very long time. A week, at least.

The leading publisher of fetish and adult fiction

TELL US WHAT YOU THINK!

Readers' ideas and opinions matter to us so please take a few minutes to fill in the questionnaire below.

1. **Sex:** Are you male ☐ female ☐ a couple ☐?

2. **Age:** Under 21 ☐ 21–30 ☐ 31–40 ☐ 41–50 ☐ 51–60 ☐ over 60 ☐

3. **Where do you buy your Nexus books from?**

☐ A chain book shop. If so, which one(s)?

____

☐ An independent book shop. If so, which one(s)?

____

☐ A used book shop/charity shop
☐ Online book store. If so, which one(s)?

____

4. **How did you find out about Nexus books?**

☐ Browsing in a book shop
☐ A review in a magazine
☐ Online
☐ Recommendation
☐ Other __________________________________

5. **In terms of settings, which do you prefer? (Tick as many as you like.)**

☐ Down to earth and as realistic as possible
☐ Historical settings. If so, which period do you prefer?

____

☐ Fantasy settings – barbarian worlds
☐ Completely escapist/surreal fantasy
☐ Institutional or secret academy

☐ Futuristic/sci fi
☐ Escapist but still believable
☐ Any settings you dislike?

____

☐ Where would you like to see an adult novel set?

____

6. In terms of storylines, would you prefer:

☐ Simple stories that concentrate on adult interests?
☐ More plot and character-driven stories with less explicit adult activity?
☐ We value your ideas, so give us your opinion of this book:

____

____

____

7. In terms of your adult interests, what do you like to read about? (Tick as many as you like.)

☐ Traditional corporal punishment (CP)
☐ Modern corporal punishment
☐ Spanking
☐ Restraint/bondage
☐ Rope bondage
☐ Latex/rubber
☐ Leather
☐ Female domination and male submission
☐ Female domination and female submission
☐ Male domination and female submission
☐ Willing captivity
☐ Uniforms
☐ Lingerie/underwear/hosiery/footwear (boots and high heels)
☐ Sex rituals
☐ Vanilla sex
☐ Swinging
☐ Cross-dressing/TV
☐ Enforced feminisation

☐ Others – tell us what you don't see enough of in adult fiction:

8. Would you prefer books with a more specialised approach to your interests, i.e. a novel specifically about uniforms? If so, which subject(s) would you like to read a Nexus novel about?

9. Would you like to read true stories in Nexus books? For instance, the true story of a submissive woman, or a male slave? Tell us which true revelations you would most like to read about:

10. What do you like best about Nexus books?

11. What do you like least about Nexus books?

12. Which are your favourite titles?

13. Who are your favourite authors?

14. Which covers do you prefer? Those featuring:
(Tick as many as you like.)

- ☐ Fetish outfits
- ☐ More nudity
- ☐ Two models
- ☐ Unusual models or settings
- ☐ Classic erotic photography
- ☐ More contemporary images and poses
- ☐ A blank/non-erotic cover
- ☐ What would your ideal cover look like?

___

15. Describe your ideal Nexus novel in the space provided:

___

___

___

___

16. Which celebrity would feature in one of your Nexus-style fantasies? We'll post the best suggestions on our website – anonymously!

___

THANKS FOR YOUR TIME

Now simply write the title of this book in the space below and cut out the questionnaire pages. Post to: Nexus, Marketing Dept., Thames Wharf Studios, Rainville Rd, London W6 9HA

Book title: ___

NEXUS NEW BOOKS

To be published in December 2008

THE GIRLFLESH CASTLE
Adriana Arden

Vanessa Buckingham has discovered strange contentment in the bizarre and secretive underworld of commercially organised slavery. Having accepted her own submissive nature, Vanessa is now happily working for the powerful Shiller Company as a 'slave reporter' for *Girlflesh News*. She has also found a lover in the form of the beautiful slavegirl Kashika. But there are forces at work that wish to destroy Shiller's carefully run 'ethical' slave business. Shiller's rival and arch enemy – the media mogul, Sir Harvey Rochester – has not given up trying to take over the operation. Having failed to use Vanessa as his unwitting pawn to expose Shiller, Sir Harvey now turns to more extreme methods.

£7.99 ISBN 978 0 352 34504 2

To be published in January 2009

WICKED OBSESSION
Ray Gordon

Eighteen-year-old Anne has always been jealous of her attractive and successful older sister, Haley. Feeling second best is something she has grown used to. But when a handsome young man rejects her advances and takes a shine to Haley instead, it is one humiliation too many. Seething with envy, Anne decides to take revenge the only way she knows how – by using her young body and sexual charms to destroy Haley's relationship. Before long behaving wickedly becomes an obsession and Anne relishes the rewards of her promiscuous behaviour. Prepared to go to any extreme to trump her sister, Anne makes plans to seduce Haley's future husband on the night before the wedding.

£7.99 ISBN 978 0 352 34508 0

To be published in February 2009

NEXUS CONFESSIONS: VOLUME 6

Various

Swinging, dogging, group sex, cross-dressing, spanking, female domination, corporal punishment, and extreme fetishes . . . *Nexus Confessions* explores the length and breadth of erotic obsession, real experience and sexual fantasy. This is an encyclopaedic collection of the bizarre, the extreme, the utterly inappropriate, the daring and the shocking experiences of ordinary men and women driven by their extraordinary desires. Collected by the world's leading publisher of fetish fiction, these are true stories and shameful confessions, never-before-told or published.

£7.99 ISBN 978 0 352 34509 7

If you would like more information about Nexus titles, please visit our website at www.nexus-books.co.uk, or send a large stamped addressed envelope to:

Nexus, Thames Wharf Studios,
Rainville Road, London W6 9HA

NEXUS BOOKLIST

Information is correct at time of printing. To avoid disappointment, check availability before ordering. Go to www.nexus-books.co.uk.

All books are priced at £6.99 unless another price is given.

NEXUS

☐ ABANDONED ALICE	Adriana Arden	ISBN 978 0 352 33969 0
☐ ALICE IN CHAINS	Adriana Arden	ISBN 978 0 352 33908 9
☐ AMERICAN BLUE	Penny Birch	ISBN 978 0 352 34169 3
☐ AQUA DOMINATION	William Doughty	ISBN 978 0 352 34020 7
☐ THE ART OF CORRECTION	Tara Black	ISBN 978 0 352 33895 2
☐ THE ART OF SURRENDER	Madeline Bastinado	ISBN 978 0 352 34013 9
☐ BEASTLY BEHAVIOUR	Aishling Morgan	ISBN 978 0 352 34095 5
☐ BEING A GIRL	Chloë Thurlow	ISBN 978 0 352 34139 6
☐ BELINDA BARES UP	Yolanda Celbridge	ISBN 978 0 352 33926 3
☐ BIDDING TO SIN	Rosita Varón	ISBN 978 0 352 34063 4
☐ BLUSHING AT BOTH ENDS	Philip Kemp	ISBN 978 0 352 34107 5
☐ THE BOOK OF PUNISHMENT	Cat Scarlett	ISBN 978 0 352 33975 1
☐ BRUSH STROKES	Penny Birch	ISBN 978 0 352 34072 6
☐ CALLED TO THE WILD	Angel Blake	ISBN 978 0 352 34067 2
☐ CAPTIVES OF CHEYNER CLOSE	Adriana Arden	ISBN 978 0 352 34028 3
☐ CARNAL POSSESSION	Yvonne Strickland	ISBN 978 0 352 34062 7
☐ CITY MAID	Amelia Evangeline	ISBN 978 0 352 34096 2
☐ COLLEGE GIRLS	Cat Scarlett	ISBN 978 0 352 33942 3
☐ COMPANY OF SLAVES	Christina Shelly	ISBN 978 0 352 33887 7
☐ CONCEIT AND CONSEQUENCE	Aishling Morgan	ISBN 978 0 352 33965 2
☐ CORRECTIVE THERAPY	Jacqueline Masterson	ISBN 978 0 352 33917 1
☐ CORRUPTION	Virginia Crowley	ISBN 978 0 352 34073 3

☐ CRUEL SHADOW	Aishling Morgan	ISBN 978 0 352 33886 0
☐ DARK MISCHIEF	Lady Alice McCloud	ISBN 978 0 352 33998 0
☐ DEPTHS OF DEPRAVATION	Ray Gordon	ISBN 978 0 352 33995 9
☐ DICE WITH DOMINATION	P.S. Brett	ISBN 978 0 352 34023 8
☐ DOMINANT	Felix Baron	ISBN 978 0 352 34044 3
☐ DOMINATION DOLLS	Lindsay Gordon	ISBN 978 0 352 33891 4
☐ EXPOSÉ	Laura Bowen	ISBN 978 0 352 34035 1
☐ FORBIDDEN READING	Lisette Ashton	ISBN 978 0 352 34022 1
☐ FRESH FLESH	Wendy Swanscombe	ISBN 978 0 352 34041 2
☐ THE GIRLFLESH INSTITUTE	Adriana Arden	ISBN 978 0 352 34101 3
☐ THE INDECENCIES OF ISABELLE	Penny Birch (writing as Cruella)	ISBN 978 0 352 33989 8
☐ THE INDISCRETIONS OF ISABELLE	Penny Birch (writing as Cruella)	ISBN 978 0 352 33882 2
☐ IN DISGRACE	Penny Birch	ISBN 978 0 352 33922 5
☐ IN HER SERVICE	Lindsay Gordon	ISBN 978 0 352 33968 3
☐ INSTRUMENTS OF PLEASURE	Nicole Dere	ISBN 978 0 352 34098 6
☐ JULIA C	Laura Bowen	ISBN 978 0 352 33852 5
☐ LACING LISBETH	Yolanda Celbridge	ISBN 978 0 352 33912 6
☐ LEAH'S PUNISHMENT	Aran Ashe	ISBN 978 0 352 34171 6
☐ LICKED CLEAN	Yolanda Celbridge	ISBN 978 0 352 33999 7
☐ LONGING FOR TOYS	Virginia Crowley	ISBN 978 0 352 34138 9
☐ LOVE JUICE	Donna Exeter	ISBN 978 0 352 33913 3
☐ MANSLAVE	J.D. Jensen	ISBN 978 0 352 34040 5
☐ NEIGHBOURHOOD WATCH	Lisette Ashton	ISBN 978 0 352 34190 7
☐ NIGHTS IN WHITE COTTON	Penny Birch	ISBN 978 0 352 34008 5
☐ NO PAIN, NO GAIN	James Baron	ISBN 978 0 352 33966 9
☐ THE OLD PERVERSITY SHOP	Aishling Morgan	ISBN 978 0 352 34007 8
☐ THE PALACE OF PLEASURES	Christobel Coleridge	ISBN 978 0 352 33801 3
☐ PETTING GIRLS	Penny Birch	ISBN 978 0 352 33957 7

☐ PORTRAIT OF A DISCIPLINARIAN	Aishling Morgan	ISBN 978 0 352 34179 2
☐ THE PRIESTESS	Jacqueline Bellevois	ISBN 978 0 352 33905 8
☐ PRIZE OF PAIN	Wendy Swanscombe	ISBN 978 0 352 33890 7
☐ PUNISHED IN PINK	Yolanda Celbridge	ISBN 978 0 352 34003 0
☐ THE PUNISHMENT CAMP	Jacqueline Masterson	ISBN 978 0 352 33940 9
☐ THE PUNISHMENT CLUB	Jacqueline Masterson	ISBN 978 0 352 33862 4
☐ THE ROAD TO DEPRAVITY	Ray Gordon	ISBN 978 0 352 34092 4
☐ SCARLET VICE	Aishling Morgan	ISBN 978 0 352 33988 1
☐ SCHOOLED FOR SERVICE	Lady Alice McCloud	ISBN 978 0 352 33918 8
☐ SCHOOL FOR STINGERS	Yolanda Celbridge	ISBN 978 0 352 33994 2
☐ SEXUAL HEELING	Wendy Swanscombe	ISBN 978 0 352 33921 8
☐ SILKEN EMBRACE	Christina Shelly	ISBN 978 0 352 34081 8
☐ SILKEN SERVITUDE	Christina Shelly	ISBN 978 0 352 34004 7
☐ SINDI IN SILK	Yolanda Celbridge	ISBN 978 0 352 34102 0
☐ SIN'S APPRENTICE	Aishling Morgan	ISBN 978 0 352 33909 6
☐ SLAVE OF THE SPARTANS	Yolanda Celbridge	ISBN 978 0 352 34078 8
☐ SLIPPERY WHEN WET	Penny Birch	ISBN 978 0 352 34091 7
☐ THE SMARTING OF SELINA	Yolanda Celbridge	ISBN 978 0 352 33872 3
☐ STRIP GIRL	Aishling Morgan	ISBN 978 0 352 34077 1
☐ STRIPING KAYLA	Yolanda Marshall	ISBN 978 0 352 33881 5
☐ STRIPPED BARE	Angel Blake	ISBN 978 0 352 33971 3
☐ TEMPTING THE GODDESS	Aishling Morgan	ISBN 978 0 352 33972 0
☐ THAI HONEY	Kit McCann	ISBN 978 0 352 34068 9
☐ TICKLE TORTURE	Penny Birch	ISBN 978 0 352 33904 1
☐ TOKYO BOUND	Sachi	ISBN 978 0 352 34019 1
☐ TORMENT, INCORPORATED	Murilee Martin	ISBN 978 0 352 33943 0
☐ TRAIL OF SIN	Ray Gordon	ISBN 978 0 352 34182 2
☐ UNEARTHLY DESIRES	Ray Gordon	ISBN 978 0 352 34036 8
☐ UNIFORM DOLL	Penny Birch	ISBN 978 0 352 33698 9
☐ WEB OF DESIRE	Ray Gordon	ISBN 978 0 352 34167 9
☐ WHALEBONE STRICT	Lady Alice McCloud	ISBN 978 0 352 34082 5
☐ WHAT HAPPENS TO BAD GIRLS	Penny Birch	ISBN 978 0 352 34031 3

☐ WHAT SUKI WANTS	Cat Scarlett	ISBN 978 0 352 34027 6
☐ WHEN SHE WAS BAD	Penny Birch	ISBN 978 0 352 33859 4
☐ WHIP HAND	G.C. Scott	ISBN 978 0 352 33694 1
☐ WHIPPING GIRL	Aishling Morgan	ISBN 978 0 352 33789 4
☐ WHIPPING TRIANGLE	G.C. Scott	ISBN 978 0 352 34086 3
☐ THE WICKED SEX	Lance Porter	ISBN 978 0 352 34161 7
☐ ZELLIE'S WEAKNESS	Jean Aveline	ISBN 978 0 352 34160 0

NEXUS CLASSIC

☐ AMAZON SLAVE	Lisette Ashton	ISBN 978 0 352 33916 4
☐ ANGEL	Lindsay Gordon	ISBN 978 0 352 34009 2
☐ THE BLACK GARTER	Lisette Ashton	ISBN 978 0 352 33919 5
☐ THE BLACK MASQUE	Lisette Ashton	ISBN 978 0 352 33977 5
☐ THE BLACK ROOM	Lisette Ashton	ISBN 978 0 352 33914 0
☐ THE BLACK WIDOW	Lisette Ashton	ISBN 978 0 352 33973 7
☐ THE BOND	Lindsay Gordon	ISBN 978 0 352 33996 6
☐ THE DOMINO ENIGMA	Cyrian Amberlake	ISBN 978 0 352 34064 1
☐ THE DOMINO QUEEN	Cyrian Amberlake	ISBN 978 0 352 34074 0
☐ THE DOMINO TATTOO	Cyrian Amberlake	ISBN 978 0 352 34037 5
☐ EMMA ENSLAVED	Hilary James	ISBN 978 0 352 33883 9
☐ EMMA'S HUMILIATION	Hilary James	ISBN 978 0 352 33910 2
☐ EMMA'S SUBMISSION	Hilary James	ISBN 978 0 352 33906 5
☐ FAIRGROUND ATTRACTION	Lisette Ashton	ISBN 978 0 352 33927 0
☐ THE INSTITUTE	Maria Del Rey	ISBN 978 0 352 33352 0
☐ PLAYTHING	Penny Birch	ISBN 978 0 352 33967 6
☐ PLEASING THEM	William Doughty	ISBN 978 0 352 34015 3
☐ RITES OF OBEDIENCE	Lindsay Gordon	ISBN 978 0 352 34005 4
☐ SERVING TIME	Sarah Veitch	ISBN 978 0 352 33509 8
☐ THE SUBMISSION GALLERY	Lindsay Gordon	ISBN 978 0 352 34026 9
☐ TIE AND TEASE	Penny Birch	ISBN 978 0 352 33987 4
☐ TIGHT WHITE COTTON	Penny Birch	ISBN 978 0 352 33970 6

NEXUS CONFESSIONS

☐ NEXUS CONFESSIONS: VOLUME ONE	Various	ISBN 978 0 352 34093 1
☐ NEXUS CONFESSIONS: VOLUME TWO	Various	ISBN 978 0 352 34103 7
☐ NEXUS CONFESSIONS: VOLUME THREE	Various	ISBN 978 0 352 34113 6

NEXUS ENTHUSIAST

☐ BUSTY	Tom King	ISBN 978 0 352 34032 0
☐ CUCKOLD	Amber Leigh	ISBN 978 0 352 34140 2
☐ DERRIÈRE	Julius Culdrose	ISBN 978 0 352 34024 5
☐ ENTHRALLED	Lance Porter	ISBN 978 0 352 34108 2
☐ LEG LOVER	L.G. Denier	ISBN 978 0 352 34016 0
☐ OVER THE KNEE	Fiona Locke	ISBN 978 0 352 34079 5
☐ RUBBER GIRL	William Doughty	ISBN 978 0 352 34087 0
☐ THE SECRET SELF	Christina Shelly	ISBN 978 0 352 34069 6
☐ UNDER MY MASTER'S WINGS	Lauren Wissot	ISBN 978 0 352 34042 9
☐ UNIFORM DOLLS	Aishling Morgan	ISBN 978 0 352 34159 4
☐ THE UPSKIRT EXHIBITIONIST	Ray Gordon	ISBN 978 0 352 34122 8
☐ WIFE SWAP	Amber Leigh	ISBN 978 0 352 34097 9

NEXUS NON FICTION

☐ LESBIAN SEX SECRETS FOR MEN	Jamie Goddard and Kurt Brungard	ISBN 978 0 352 33724 5

- - - - - ✂ -

Please send me the books I have ticked above.

Name ....

Address ....

....

....

.... Post code ....

Send to: **Virgin Books Cash Sales, Thames Wharf Studios, Rainville Road, London W6 9HA**

US customers: for prices and details of how to order books for delivery by mail, call 888-330-8477.

Please enclose a cheque or postal order, made payable to **Nexus Books Ltd**, to the value of the books you have ordered plus postage and packing costs as follows:

UK and BFPO – £1.00 for the first book, 50p for each subsequent book.

Overseas (including Republic of Ireland) – £2.00 for the first book, £1.00 for each subsequent book.

If you would prefer to pay by VISA, ACCESS/MASTERCARD, AMEX, DINERS CLUB or SWITCH, please write your card number and expiry date here:

....

Please allow up to 28 days for delivery.

Signature ....

Our privacy policy

We will not disclose information you supply us to any other parties. We will not disclose any information which identifies you personally to any person without your express consent.

From time to time we may send out information about Nexus books and special offers. Please tick here if you do *not* wish to receive Nexus information. ☐

- - - - - - ✂ -